Philippa East grew up in Sc[...]
Psychology and Philosophy a[...]
After graduating, she moved to London to train as a Clinical Psychologist and worked in NHS mental health services for over ten years.

Her debut novel *Little White Lies* was longlisted for the Guardian's 'Not The Booker' prize and shortlisted for the CWA John Creasy New Blood Dagger. Her second psychological suspense novel *Safe and Sound* is out now, and she is currently working on her fourth. Philippa now lives in the beautiful Lincolnshire countryside with her spouse and cat. Alongside her writing, Philippa continues to work as a psychologist and therapist. You can find her on Twitter: @philippa_east.

Also By Philippa East

Little White Lies
Safe and Sound

I'll Never Tell

Philippa East

ONE PLACE. MANY STORIES

HQ
An imprint of HarperCollins*Publishers* Ltd
1 London Bridge Street
London SE1 9GF

www.harpercollins.co.uk

HarperCollins*Publishers*
Macken House, 39/40 Mayor Street Upper,
Dublin 1, D01 C9W8, Ireland

This edition 2023

1
First published in Great Britain by
HQ, an imprint of HarperCollins*Publishers* Ltd 2023

Copyright © Philippa East 2023

Philippa East asserts the moral right to be identified as the author of this work. A catalogue record for this book is available from the British Library.

ISBN: 9780008455781

This book is produced from independently certified FSC™ paper to ensure responsible forest management.

For more information visit: www.harpercollins.co.uk/green

This book is set in 10.7/15.5 pt. Sabon

Printed and Bound in the UK using 100% Renewable Electricity at CPI Group (UK) Ltd, Croydon, CR0 4YY

To the D20 Authors and to Laure Van Rensburg
who contributed mightily to the salvage operation

CHAPTER 1

Julia

NOW

The streetlights flash past: orange, black, orange, black, swinging low over the windscreen, over our faces.

It's fine.

It's not fine.

It's fine.

But it's not.

This car we're in could skid off the road. Plough into a tree or oncoming traffic. I see us ripping through a crash barrier, causing a ten-car pile-up. I can see us being arrested; I see us breaking our necks.

These thoughts are wild; these thoughts are ridiculous. I'm in a car with my husband, travelling on the well-marked A40 back to Oxford, and we know where she is now: she's at home, she's quite safe. There's nothing to go crazy about; there's nothing to fear.

Chrissie's violin case slides around on the back seat, despite the fact that we've strapped it in. She left with her rucksack and her coat, but not her instrument – the instrument she loves so much. Another small thing that doesn't add up. Something she was trying to communicate to us? But what?

Chrissie, I think. *Chrissie, Chrissie, Chrissie.*

I'm still fumbling to grasp the details of what happened. We searched all over the London concert venue for her, after the fire crew gave us the all-clear. A false alarm, they eventually declared. We had been standing outside for forty-five minutes by then, but split up into different areas: audience on one side of the concert venue, and performers and staff on the other. How were we supposed to know that Chrissie wasn't there? She timed things so well, making sure she'd been accounted for among the bodies gathered outside before she disappeared.

And she wasn't back at the hotel either, the place where we'd dropped off our overnight bags earlier and the three of us took the chance to drink a half-cup of tea before the show. There was a big white double bed in that room, with crisp, clean sheets and a deep, comfy mattress. I wanted to climb right into that bed, curl up and sleep for a long time, but Chrissie was jittery – to be honest, we all were, and why wouldn't we be? In a few hours, our teenage daughter would be standing centre stage, in front of the TV cameras and the live audience and the judges.

And then, after all that build-up, the night, her performance, ended with *this*?

The seatbelt strains like a garrotte across my neck as I lean forward, craning to see beyond the cats' eyes and white lines zipping past. Paul, my husband, is in the driver's seat. He is so reliable. So safe. How much I've depended on him over the years, rightly or wrongly. Ten years together, and who would ever have believed where we're at now?

The seatbelt slides up, pressing where the skin of my jaw is still sensitive, only recently returned to its natural hue.

'She played so well,' I say, as though seeking reassurance, fighting to keep the dumb fear from my voice. 'Didn't she?'

Paul's hands tighten on the steering wheel, as though they weren't already gripping tightly enough. 'She did, Julia. She was truly brilliant.'

So why this? I want to demand of him, as though he has any better answers than I do. As though he has secrets to reveal of his own. Why did she bolt from the venue when that fire alarm went off? Why do I suspect that she set it off herself? But it makes no sense that she would run off before the winners were announced, when she had every chance of being one of them. Why do that without telling us and without then bothering to answer her phone, but instead sending us and all the staff into such a panic, wasting everyone's time in searching the Barbican and then the hotel? We had no idea where she was, until eventually Paul turned on the tracker app – the one he had installed on her phone and his after that time at the Botanical Gardens, the one I didn't know about until tonight – and, lo and behold, turns out of all places she had gone back home. It seemed she just got herself on a train from London, Paddington to Oxford, and left.

So it's fine, I tell myself. She's fine. Those images of disaster are all of my own making: because of my own guilt, my own lies.

Black-orange. Paul's face flashes again in the streetlamps overhead. 'We're going to talk to her,' he says, 'properly this time. We cannot have her acting like this.'

'Yes. We will. Of course.' My stomach instinctively roils at the thought of such a discussion, but if it comes down to it,

3

I will. I'll listen to everything she has to say. *That's over now,* I remind myself. *That's done.*

In my lap, my phone blips and I fumble to swipe the message open. Chrissie? But it isn't her, of course, it's one of the Young Musician coordinators. *Let us know as soon as you're with her. We're so sorry about this. Please let us know absolutely anything we can do.*

I text back quickly. *Thank you. We will.*

'I'm sorry,' I tell my husband. 'I'm sorry I haven't been there.' Six words that are so incredibly loaded, and I'm saying them now – of all moments – as we speed along in the dark, our daughter having temporarily vanished. But still, I got them out.

Paul gives a nod. I choose to take it to mean, *I know.*

'Almost home,' he says, and the knowledge makes me feel weak with relief. We just have to navigate Oxford's one-way system and we'll arrive at our grand, sturdy house on Woodstock Road. For the dozenth time, I check the tracker app on Paul's phone, seeking to reassure myself yet again. The little pulsing dot hasn't moved on the map; it's still hovering exactly over our house. I wish I could zoom so close in to our street, our home, that I could tell exactly which room she's in. Is it her bedroom or her practice room, our big bright kitchen or our snug? I'd like to be able to zoom in on every square foot of whichever space, and sense exactly what she's doing right now – lying in bed or fixing herself a snack or throwing herself into yet more practice … Although she couldn't do that, because her violin is here, on the back seat of the car, with us.

In a moment though, we'll know for sure.

Paul swings the car into our wide gravel drive. I can hear our dog Jackson barking fit to bust, before either of us even gets out.

Thank God. *Thank God*. There's a light on upstairs: in Chrissie's window, with her bedroom that stretches across one whole end of our house. Leaving the suitcase and her violin in the car for now, I find myself almost shaking with relief as I point up for Paul. 'Look. She's in there.'

She really is home. The adrenaline drains from my body, leaving my limbs weak. I wonder whether she walked back from Oxford train station or took a taxi. Either way, she's probably been back for close to two hours.

Jackson's barks continue to ricochet from the indoor hallway. I grab Paul's arm as he puts his hand on the knob of our front door. 'Calmly,' I say. 'We have to go in there calmly. No panic. No shouting at her. We'll just let her know how worried we've been, that's all.'

My head feels loose on my neck as I speak. Despite my anger and my lingering fear, I know we still have to get this right.

'No panic,' Paul echoes. 'No yelling. You might want to tell that to Jackson, though.'

I give a weak smile and Paul grins back, his joke letting in further ripples of relief.

He puts an arm round me in a brief, forgiving hug as I turn the knob and give the door a shove.

It sticks.

No, it doesn't stick; this door never sticks. Jackson's barks escalate.

It's locked.

'Have you got your keys?' I say, calmly, to Paul.

Silently he fishes them from his pocket and neatly slides

the right one into the lock. When the door opens, Jackson is all over us.

'Down, Jackson!' Paul says to him. 'Hey, down, boy.'

I fumble for the hallway light switch and click it on, as Paul works to calm Jackson down.

'She could at least have fed him,' he says, and I give him an eyebrow raise that reads, *what did we just agree*? And he holds a hand up to say, *okay, I'm sorry, I got it*.

'Why don't you go up first,' I say quietly. 'And I'll … put the kettle on. I'll come up in a moment with some tea for her. That way it might feel like less of an ambush.'

We follow Jackson into the kitchen and I switch the kettle on. I listen for any sound of Chrissie moving about upstairs, but our house is so big that noise doesn't always travel and I can't hear anything. Paul leaves Jackson with me and heads upstairs. I try to stay calm as I put some fresh biscuits down for him. He doesn't seem very interested and instead sits on the tiled floor, looking up at me with his big brown eyes.

'What a nightmare,' I whisper, drolly crossing my eyes at him to make another joke, as though that might ease the tightness in my chest.

I can hear Paul's footsteps now, lumbering about upstairs. The kettle's really going for it now and I hunt in the cupboards for the box of tea, clicking my tongue because Paul's moved it again in one of his tidy-ups.

The kettle clicks off.

'Julia.'

I jump, spinning round to find Paul standing there. I didn't hear him come back down, over the rumble of the water. 'What is it?'

'She isn't here.'

'What?' I say. 'She has to be.'

'Come and see for yourself if you don't believe me.'

I feel as though gravity's pull has doubled as I follow my husband upstairs, Jackson trotting faithfully behind. The doors to all the rooms up here stand open; Paul must have looked in every single one. I follow him to the doorway of Chrissie's bedroom.

Her light is on, but she isn't in there.

I grasp Paul's arm.

'Look,' he says, as though I can't see already. Chrissie is a neat child, she always has been, so now this scene is wrong in a hundred different ways. Her bed is a state, the duvet half dragged off. Her wooden desk chair tipped over on its side. Her phone on the floor, the screen smashed.

Jackson barks again. *A nightmare. A nightmare.* My mind goes wild, a whole new ream of images cascading through it. A slap, a struggle, a scream, a fall. The crash of furniture, the crack of glass, the thud of limbs.

I stand in Chrissie's room, lost in disbelief and fear because those images are all I can see.

A nightmare. A nightmare. Playing over and over and over again.

CHAPTER 2

Paul

EIGHT WEEKS BEFORE

'Wake up.' The voice was distant. 'Wake *up*.'

Paul rolled over and pulled up the covers, but the voice was persistent.

'Wake *up*, Dad.'

His daughter, Chrissie. He opened his eyes.

She was standing above him in a crop-top and leggings, her stomach on show. He sat up and looked at his alarm clock. Six fifteen. Friday morning. It was barely light. Instinctively, he wanted to roll back up in the warmth. But they had agreed on this, and what example would he be setting for her if he didn't commit?

'Yes,' he said. 'I'm coming.' Next to him, Julia continued sleeping soundly. His wife had come to bed late last night – after one. She worked late. So often, she had to work all hours.

Chrissie lifted her hands up behind her head, sweeping

8

her dark hair up into a ponytail and snapping a bright band around it.

'Go down and make coffee,' he told her. 'I'll be right behind you.'

Her silhouette flashed in the doorway as she slipped out of the room.

They had agreed yesterday that they would do this. He couldn't entirely recall now who'd had the idea first. Perhaps him, perhaps Chrissie. At this level, the two of them had come to realize, it wasn't just about talent, because everyone had talent. That alone wasn't enough, not if she really wanted to make it. You had to *look the part* as well. Hence the early morning running, another thing that Paul would now help her with, along with the hours and hours of practice.

He glanced over again at his wife's sleeping form and thought about the argument they'd had two nights before, and again yesterday morning. He laid a hand over the curve of her waist. He could feel the warmth of her through the blanket.

'Want coffee?' he murmured.

There was silence. No answer, though her ribcage continued to rise and fall. Well then, he would let her sleep. No doubt she needed it. The current project she was working on was running her ragged, and her own alarm would be going off soon enough.

He got up and got dressed. Clean T-shirt, a pair of black running shorts. He would shower afterwards, once they got back and Chrissie was changed and ready for school. Out on the landing, his daughter had already drawn back the long curtains on their tall arched window. The weather was grey and overcast, the flagstones of their back terrace darkened by last night's rain. He thought he glimpsed something, a shadow, a flutter, dipping behind the hedges. But when he rubbed the sleep from his eyes, it was gone.

Downstairs in the kitchen, all the lights had come on. They were designed like that, set to flick on whenever anyone walked into the room. He appreciated the shining brightness that came from the spotlights; in the house he'd grown up in, he'd lost count of the times the electricity had been shut off because his father had blown the money on gambling and they'd fallen months behind on the bills. Worlds away from how he lived now. You could manually override these bright kitchen halogens – and sometimes Paul did – but this morning he felt glad of them. A clean, bright, indoor sunrise, chasing away childhood memories and fears.

'You should put a top on,' he said to Chrissie. She was leaning against the counter top, arms braced, stretching her hamstrings. He could see the muscles pulling taut in her back. 'It's a pretty rotten day.'

'I'll get warm running,' she said. She ducked her head as she shifted, switching legs.

'It's cold,' he told her as he set up their coffee maker. 'And wet. Here – let me get you one from the utility.'

The smell of fresh laundry filled the neat room that adjoined the kitchen. He found her top – a grey zip-up thing – neatly folded on top of the most recent pile. When he returned, Chrissie was putting chopped fruit into a blender and any further comment of his was lost in the racket of the blades. Fresh fruit, healthy eating. She was keen on that too; so was he. It was good to include that as part of the package. Along with looks and talent. People appreciated a wholesome young star.

Chrissie switched the blender off and gave the frothy pink contents a shake. Yesterday, Julia had brought home strawberries. Strawberries in February. Wasn't life amazing like that?

'We can have these when we get back,' said Chrissie. 'I've done enough for Mum as well. I'll leave it in the fridge.'

'Perfect.'

Paul slid the top across the counter to her then set down some food for Jackson and fetched the coffees for them both. She took hers with milk and sugar – bad for her teeth, no doubt – and he took his bitter and black. He tried to remember when she'd started drinking coffee; for so long he'd associated her with orange squash and Ribena, carefully diluted. Now she drank coffee, and in two more years she'd be old enough to buy alcohol. Normal, inevitable, and yet the thought gave him a prickle of sweat.

They sat side by side at the breakfast bar, listening to the raindrops pattering outside. She swung a leg, her trainers already on, blowing on her coffee and drumming the ends of her fingers on the counter, shaping notes, musical runs. He reached out and took her hand, stilling it momentarily. 'Your nails,' he said. 'You keep letting them grow long.' Long enough to catch in the strings and disrupt her playing.

'I'll trim them later,' she said, then added, 'I didn't mean to.' He let her pull her hand away. Under the nail tips though, the calluses that she'd built up from years of pressing down on fine metal strings were as firm as ever.

'So, we'll practise the Alwyn *Sonatina* this evening, shall we?' It was a modern piece, practically a film score, but it was also demanding, parts of it sitting right at the limit of her range.

Chrissie flexed her wrist. She had small, delicate wrists, but so strong. He knew that. 'Can't we work on the Bach? Something different? We've been doing nothing but the Alwyn for weeks.'

That wasn't true, and Chrissie knew it: they mucked around with other stuff in between. But she was right that their main focus right now was the Alwyn. She still hadn't nailed it. She knew that too.

'Come on. Don't cop out. You know you've almost got it.'

'If you say so.' She slid off her stool.

He grinned at her. 'I do.'

He drained his coffee then reached for her mug too. 'Have you finished with that?' There was a mouthful left, but she let him scoop it up anyway.

'Yep.'

'Right then. Shall we go?'

At the front door, he laced up his own trainers then waited while she pulled on the grey top. A chill wind caught them as he tugged the door open. Last chance to back out, but he wouldn't do that. Chrissie needed him; this was his responsibility.

They headed out together, into the rain.

*

She ran ahead of him almost the whole way. She was fitter than he'd expected – fitter than him, it seemed, even though she'd done no formal exercise for years. He pictured her doing secret star jumps in her room. He could feel a stitch starting up and a painful wheeze in his chest, but he didn't want to let her see that. He set himself to her pace along the wet pavements, running close on her heels. It was early enough on a Friday morning that Oxford was quiet, and they had the smooth pavements, the carefully spaced trees, the shining puddles in the gutter all to themselves. They lived on Woodstock Road, in an upscale, wealthy part of the city. Handsome Victorian and Edwardian townhouses, generous square-footage, gardens to match. Their own house was worth well over two million – closer to three. He had Julia to thank for that.

Julia – and her generous parents.

Paul followed his daughter through one street and the next: Hayfield Road, Aristotle Lane and out to Port Meadow and Burgess Fields. She had presumably worked out their route in advance. He wondered how far she was planning to take them. Three kilometres, five? Maybe she'd run them all the way to Godstow. Good God, he hoped not.

There was mist across the meadow, mimicking one of those magical Oxford mornings. He imagined the rowing crews out on the Thames, starting even earlier than them. Dew seeped through his trainers and his shins hurt from the impact of each step. Chrissie's movements were graceful, fluid. Just like the way she played, she and her violin moving as one. Ahead of him, the top he'd given her flapped loose, unzipped, giving glimpses of the navy crop-top underneath. Crop-top – was that what you called it? The wind was against them, but she ran harder, faster.

'Chrissie!' he called out to her. 'Chrissie, hang on!'

'What?' She kept running.

He pushed himself and caught up with her, catching her sharp elbow. 'Stop running a sec. Your lace is undone.'

She pulled up short, almost unbalancing him, so that he had

to steady himself against her. She looked down at her trainer. One purple lace trailed in the wet.

'Here, let me do it.' His knee crunched as he knelt down. He remembered teaching her to tie her own laces, and her delight when she finally pulled the loops tight. Paul had only come into Chrissie's life when she was six. She had been a shy, awkward child then, despite her background of privilege. She'd always stood back, as though hiding behind herself. He'd finally felt her relax that time when she'd sat next to him at the piano, listening to him play 'Chopsticks' or some other silly tune. Later, he'd shown her how to hold her violin and bow properly, actually take charge of the thing. She had begun to blossom then: he'd witnessed it. He supposed she had been blossoming ever since.

The purple lace was wet and muddy. He tugged at the loops that criss-crossed her foot arch; she'd left them so loose.

'Ow, Dad. Not so tight.'

'You don't want them coming undone again.'

'But – really. Not so tight.' She leaned down, fingers plucking at the strings. He let her, returning to his feet and stepping back. *Pick your battles*, he reminded himself. It was only shoelaces. And look – she'd grown chilly now: she was zipping the top up again. The label stuck out: size small, petite, although these were adult sizes now, not children's. She was sixteen, and yet still like a doll. She got that from Julia, of course. Julia had always been tiny too. *Like mother, like daughter.* The voice of Julia's mother, Celina, in his head.

'Right. Got your breath back?' He grinned at her, encouraging. 'Ready?'

'Mmm-hmm.'

They ran on. It wasn't long before they found themselves back on Woodstock Road, busier now as the city woke up. A two-minute cool-down walk now, they agreed. He fought with himself to regain his breath.

'Shall we do it again tomorrow?' he said as they made their way up the sweep of their gravel drive and reached the porticoed front of their house. The bottles of milk and fresh orange juice had been delivered and he scooped them up from the doorstep.

'Yes,' she said, 'let's.' She was pulling her phone out as she answered – he didn't even realize she'd brought it – and nodding as they stepped inside. This would be good for her. Good for them both. Music for the heart; running for the body. It was a good plan. A good strategy. He was always trying to steer her, coach her. Thinking what was best, trying to do his job well. And this was another winner: the exercise, the running.

In the front hallway, Chrissie steadied herself on the wall to shuck off her trainers, blue-cased phone still clutched in her hand. Paul's heart rate was easing now, after their warm-down. It was slowing, returning to normal.

Until he saw the words that pinged across her screen.

CHAPTER 3

Paul

EIGHT WEEKS BEFORE

The words disappeared again almost immediately, so fast he could convince himself they hadn't been there at all or that he had misread them.

Chrissie was holding her phone casually as she balanced herself against the wall; she didn't appear to have even seen the message. Perhaps it was nothing. In all of this, he had to be reasonable. It was the only way to ensure that Chrissie listened to him and stuck to the rules. So in that moment, he said nothing. There would be other opportunities, other chances to check this out.

She had both shoes off, and she crouched down to place them neatly in the shoe rack. He had brought her up to be neat in that way and she did these things automatically now. He lined his own shoes up beside hers, calculating the hours until he could legitimately reassure himself, and the risks of letting it go until then. He was always on alert but he had to be strategic. He had to pick his moments; he couldn't just react. Steadying his breathing, he followed her to the kitchen, his sports socks leaving large damp footprints on the tiled hallway floor.

Julia was pouring hot water from the kettle. She was up now, fully dressed, make-up on, although her short hair was still wet from her shower and sticking up in bird-like tufts. Her skirt cinched in tight at her waist, creating a perfect hourglass. A sensual body, anyone might say, though she never said that and neither did he, not any more.

He set down the milk and orange juice and went over to kiss her.

'How was the run?' she asked as Chrissie crashed the fridge door open.

'Fine,' said Paul. 'Good. You could have come with us.' Even though neither he nor Chrissie had asked.

Julia nodded and smiled, extracting her stewed teabag. 'Maybe next time.'

'Dad was slow,' Chrissie said. She set out the jug of smoothie she had made earlier. 'I had to keep stopping.'

Paul caught Julia's eye and shook his head. He held up a finger. *One time*, he mouthed. *Once*. 'Her lace came undone.'

'I'm glad you had a good time,' said Julia. 'Even in the drizzle. I slept in. I've only just got up. We were working so late last night, it'll hardly be a crime if I'm not in first thing.' The lid of the stainless-steel bin clanged as she dropped in the used teabag. 'Listen. Tomorrow night. We're to arrive at eight.'

Paul felt his heart constrict. 'Eight o'clock,' he managed to say. He grabbed a glass and ran it under the cold tap of the sink, thick water bubbles fizzing.

Julia was looking at him. 'You didn't forget, did you?'

17

He shook his head. 'No. Of course not.' Tried to push it out of his mind, maybe. But not forgotten.

Chrissie set down a glass of her own and poured out the smoothie mixture, a dribble of pink liquid slopping onto the counter.

'Chrissie,' said Paul, in admonishment.

'What? Oh. Sorry.' She fetched a cloth to wipe up the spill. 'I have to come?' It was more a statement, though, than a question.

'Well,' said Julia. 'The invite is for all three of us.'

The invite. So formal, Paul thought, as though they were being summoned. But that was the way of it, wasn't it?

'I wanted to see Reece,' said Chrissie.

Paul sensed Julia hesitate. Their eyes caught. He pressed his lips together, letting her answer this one. Anyway, it was harmless really; he had to trust her. *But that message, those words* ... Chrissie's phone was lying face down now on the counter top. He had such an urge to snatch it up. Get rid of it, break it.

Sexy girl ... the message had read.

He waited.

Julia cleared her throat. 'Could you see Reece another night? Your grandparents – your grandfather ... he hasn't seen you in quite a while. He would really like to see you, I think.' She turned to Paul. 'If we aim to leave at half seven. Can you drive there and I'll drive back?' She'd got a strawberry seed stuck in her teeth. She must have been nibbling on them earlier.

'Sure,' Paul said. 'No problem.' Smiling even as he pictured the evening unfurling in front of him: the arduous drive, the knotted conversation, the unseen eggshells hovering underfoot.

'Chrissie?' Julia prompted.

Their daughter fidgeted. 'I mean … I guess so. Probably.'

Paul could sense Julia's relief. 'Thank you, sweetheart. It'll be nice with us all there. Like I said – they're really looking forward to seeing us.'

She rested a hand on Chrissie's shoulder, and Paul nodded as though he agreed.

It didn't feel true; he'd never felt Celina or Duncan *looked forward* to these visits. But Paul did his best to swallow down her lie.

CHAPTER 4

Paul

EIGHT WEEKS BEFORE

Once Julia had left for the office and Chrissie had left for school, Paul loaded the dishwasher, set out a plate of meat for Jackson and carried two piles of clean laundry upstairs. In Chrissie's bedroom, he hung her ironed white school shirts up in her wardrobe; no chance of them getting crumpled in there. Her curtains were drawn and her bed neatly made. She was such a neat child: meticulous and precise. Unlike most teenagers, she didn't do mess or clutter. Her room was minimalist and orderly, almost bare. That discipline showed in her playing as well, the way she could dedicate herself to a passage or a technique over and over and over again. It was one of her strengths; one of so many.

Quickly, and out of habit, Paul ran his hand under the edge of her mattress, fingers tracing the smooth slats underneath. Straightening back up, he tilted his head to read the titles of the books on her bookshelf, the way he had done hundreds of times before. She was well read: *Wuthering Heights*, *Little Women*,

I Am Malala. He neatened the pile of school textbooks on her desk and tucked her chair in flush. There were no dirty clothes on the floor; she'd already put them in the laundry basket. He collected the hamper now from the landing and carried it downstairs, collecting up the grey top – still damp from the rain – from where it hung over the back of a chair in the kitchen.

While the washing machine chugged, Paul logged onto his laptop in the living room and quickly googled the institute he'd been looking into. Their website was the first result and he clicked the link. He'd read all the information on here more than once, but so far had not gone further than that. However, today he needed to get things moving. There was a form to request a prospectus. First name: *Paul*. Surname: *Goodlight*. Address, email. Newsletter? Sure. The fees were listed too, on a separate page of the site. The costs were eye-watering, substantially more than the fees they currently paid for Chrissie's local private school. Strict entry criteria too. She would have to prove herself to be good enough. But what an opportunity this could be. What a blessing. He would find a way of making this work. He completed the request form and clicked *submit*, his hand shaking only slightly once it was done.

He could relax a little now as he clicked over to the website he'd made for Chrissie last year. All her achievements were listed on here. On the homepage, there was her professional headshot, details 'about me', and links to the awards and prizes she'd won. Elsewhere, there were photographs from her trips up and down the country, performing as part of an orchestra, but also alone – a soloist even at the age of fifteen. The week before, he'd updated the blog with Chrissie's 'latest news', the few paragraphs she'd agreed for him to upload: *Yay, I'm through to the Category Auditions! Only 125 musicians perform in this round! Wish me luck – only five musicians from each category go through!*

There were comments underneath with people's good wishes. He recognized the names of her tutors – like Mr Donaldson – and school friends. A couple of comments from her friend Reece.

Paul clicked the little purple icon on her *contact* page, the one that linked you straight to her Instagram. It was a carefully curated account, mainly pictures of her violin in carefully staged places, pages of the music she was rehearsing, a book she was reading, or shots of Jackson. He scrolled through her posts; he'd missed a few that she'd shared in the last few days. A close-up of her fingers resting on the violin strings, a shot of Jackson with his tongue hanging out.

This morning, she'd posted a picture of her trainers, wet from their run.

Got to look the part! she'd written. And then: *Went for a run today with my dad.*

A stream of hashtags followed: *#lifeofamusician #runningintherain #gottagetfit*. The post had received a hundred and twenty-two 'likes'.

He clicked down to read the comments. Dozens of people with made-up names and profile pictures that he didn't recognize. How could you really tell who was who on this thing? There were spam comments (*promote this on @gigwear*), nonsensical comments (*lolo 45 #sistr*), overfamiliar comments (*please message me back*). He signed into the account to delete those. Others were nicer. Benign.

You go, girl! BTW, cute Reeboks!
What? In the rain???
OMG your dad is so sweet.

He hesitated over the 'like' icon on the last comment. He thought again of those words on Chrissie's phone.

Sexy girl …

It made his heart thump so hard it was almost painful. He loved Chrissie. Dearly. He wanted the best for her. It was right, wasn't it, what he was doing? They were necessary, these arrangements he was making for her.

So sweet.

He clicked 'like', and the little heart shape immediately bloomed red even as he scrolled down further and opened Chrissie's reply. The cryptic words there caught him right in the gut:

'Sweet'? ☹ You don't know the half.

But Chrissie was happy when she got home from school. The front door banged punctually at four forty-five and Paul was waiting for her in the kitchen as usual.

'Good day?' he asked, pushing himself up from the barstool.

She shucked off her smart pink coat and her school bag. 'Pretty good.' She smiled. 'I got ninety-eight per cent on my maths test.'

He was across the room in a flash, grappling her into a bear hug, rocking her side to side. 'Well done, sweetheart! That's honestly fantastic.'

'Second in the class. One of the boys got ninety-nine.'

'Ninety-nine?' Paul laughed. 'Well, that's just greedy.'

She grinned at his joke. 'That's what I thought.'

'Well then.' He released her, grinning too. 'Okay – a snack before we rehearse. What do you want – toast or crumpets?'

'Crumpets.'

'With jam?'

'Just butter.'

'Okay. Want them down here?'

'I'm going to dry my hair. It's really chucking it down out there.'

'All right. I'll bring them up to you in a sec.'

While the crumpets toasted, Paul let Jackson out into the back garden where – Chrissie was right – it was raining again. When the crumpets were done, he put them on a plate and headed upstairs after his daughter. In her bedroom, she had the hairdryer on full blast.

'I'm just going to wash our bed linens,' he said over the racket as he set the plate down on her desk. 'Want me to do yours too?'

'Sure.' She got up off the bed to make room for him, hairdryer still going, buttery smell in the air. He manoeuvred round her to strip the duvet, pull off the soft sheet and tug the fat pillows out of their cases.

'Five minutes,' he said.

In the master bedroom, he peeled the cover off their king-size duvet. Plush cotton, with such a high thread-count it could almost feel like silk. The sheet and pillowcases were just the same. You'd think you'd sleep like a baby in such a bed.

By the time he had both beds stripped, the noise of the hairdryer had stopped and instead he could hear his daughter tuning up, sounding the open strings, low to high: G-string; G- and D-string together, A-string, E. Testing the intervals, adjusting the pegs. Her home practice room was expensively sound-proofed but with the sliding door open, you could hear her music all over the house. Other students, he'd learned, had to practise in their bedrooms or utility rooms or the corner of a kitchen: anywhere they could find a space. But Chrissie had this: purpose-built.

He set the dirty sheets in a pile at the top of the stairs, then padded along the upstairs corridor to her practice room. She was playing scales now: G-major, G-minor, and the arpeggios that went with them. Then harder scales, harder arpeggios. Bowing faster, climbing higher. Friday night, and maybe other kids her age would be out seeing friends, but those were the sacrifices you made. Those were the necessities, the way it had to be.

Paul went to the piano, where sheaves of music were laid out on top, piles of them, all these pieces she'd practised and played. There were new layers of intensity to everything now, under the pressure of the competition. Perhaps they had both underestimated its demands at first, when Chrissie had played her first round of auditions. Her tutor Mr Donaldson had been delighted, of course. And Celina. *Just what she needs*, his mother-in-law had said. And she had been right, because look at Chrissie now. A year or so ago, she had been veering off track. Paul had sensed it in her. And then … that incident.

Sexy girl.

He swallowed. Had he imagined those words or not? Focus. He had to focus. How could he expect Chrissie to if he didn't?

'Okay,' Paul said. 'The Alwyn.' He set the pages out on his stand.

It was as he turned to check whether she was ready that he

saw the device. He felt his eyebrows rise in surprise. 'What's that?'

Chrissie kept the violin under her chin, tucked in there as though it was part of her, the way you'd rest your cheek on your palm. 'It's Mum's old iPad. She barely uses it. She's got that new MacBook now.' The device was propped on the shelf among old theory books and classical CDs. 'I'm going to film myself,' she explained. 'Mr Donaldson says I need to work on my bowing. I'm going to watch the recording to see where I'm going wrong.'

'Okay … Wait – are you recording already?'

'No … I haven't started yet.' She stood there, staring at him, over the polished body of her violin. 'I was waiting for you.'

'All right. Well, do you want to switch it on now?'

'Okay. Yep.' She went over and clicked the camera icon, pressing the red circle to begin a new video. Back in position, it was only Chrissie he could see captured on the screen. At the piano, he was out of shot.

She smoothed out the pages on her stand, pausing to flex her wrist.

'Okay then,' he said. 'The Alwyn.'

He lifted the lid on the piano and rested his fingers on the keyboard. He was an accomplished pianist; he had studied music, and piano had been his instrument of choice. He had once had aspirations of making it professionally, but that had never happened. But he still loved playing, he loved music. He always had. When he'd first started dating Julia, his friends had said that they were surprised: Julia had hardly a musical bone in her body. In church – the few times they had been – she'd mouthed the words to the hymns. It was the same whenever they were called upon to sing 'Happy Birthday'. When he met her, she had possessed a total of five CDs.

It shouldn't have worked.

But then, of course, there had been Chrissie.

'From the top?' he said now, and Chrissie nodded.

'Sure.' She had gone back to her surreptitious wrist flexing.

Paul paused. 'You okay?'

'What?'

He pointed.

She hesitated. 'It just hurts a bit.'

'It hurts?'

She shook her head. 'Only a bit.'

He let his fingers slide from the piano keys. 'That's not good.'

'I mean, I don't think it's anything.' Why then did it feel as though she was testing him?

Be reasonable. Be reasonable.

Your dad is so sweet!

Paul cleared his throat. 'If you need to ... we can skip a practice.' Why were those words so hard to say? Because it was tangled up in there, wasn't it, quickening those other motivations? There were reasons to push Chrissie, to focus her energies and attention into her playing and performances. Good reasons, reasons that had been laid out for him time and again. Reasons he had come to trust. But even on those rare occasions when he longed to allow her a little give, this other motivation pushed him forwards like a secondary shockwave: the need to see realized, through Chrissie, all that he'd never achieved.

But still, he'd asked her. He'd given her the option.

Chrissie was quiet, smoothing out the already smooth pages. 'It's okay,' she said at last. 'It doesn't hurt that much. I bumped it at school. That's really all it is.'

Not muscle strain, then. Or tendonitis. 'If you're sure.'

'Yep.'

He didn't hesitate this time. 'All right.' He placed his hands back over the keys. 'At tempo or slower?'

'At tempo. Might as well.'

'All right then. Two bars in.'

As they played, he immediately felt the pull of the music. It had never left him, even when he had left his own ambitions behind. They were beginning the high passage now, where Chrissie needed to move her left hand up the neck – third position, fifth – and with no frets to guide her the way there were on a guitar. It was breathtaking to him every time, the way she could produce that river of sound as though she was conjuring it straight from the air. She made it seem effortless, but of course it wasn't. She worked and worked to be able to play like that, because it was only when the technicalities were resolutely pinned down that you were free to add expression like that. The technicalities …

Paul stopped, lifting his hands from the piano keys and lifting the foot pedal to stop the noise. 'Hang on,' he said. 'You're flat.'

Chrissie let the violin fall from her chin, swinging precariously from her hand by the scroll. For a dread moment he pictured her letting that precious instrument drop. It had taken them years to find this violin – the one that fitted with her, that could keep up. She'd had others before this, but she had always been frustrated with them, and it wasn't until they had visited a specialist in Hoyerhagen, Germany, that she had found this one. Paul had felt himself grow pale at the price and the thought of going to Julia to discuss it. It would be Julia's money, after all. But in the end it was Chrissie who had convinced her mother, in a rare display of obstinacy that Paul had never witnessed before or since.

And now she was treating it as recklessly as that.

'No, I'm not,' Chrissie said.

He took a breath. 'Chrissie, love. You are.'

This was the other thing. Paul was one of those rarities: someone who had perfect pitch, able to identify a note from nothing – and unable to ignore it when that note was out.

'You are. I can hear it.'

She turned away from him, rechecking her basic tuning. Open string, open string, open string. He interrupted her. 'It isn't that. Your tuning is perfect. It's your finger spacing, Chrissie. You know that. Play the scale. Third position and upwards. You need to hear where you're hitting it wrong.'

Silence. Then: 'Fine.'

No piano now, just Chrissie and her violin, the scale rising up, up, up, deliberately yet agonizingly slowly, until—

'There. Hold it.' He got up from the piano stool and came to stand by her, bringing his own hand parallel to hers. Close up, he could feel the heat coming off her hand – her wrist? Perhaps it was hurting more than she'd let on. 'Here, seventh position, your third finger. It's here you're going flat.'

He reached out to adjust Chrissie's slim finger: by the tiniest amount, a fraction of a fraction of an inch. 'Try it now.' And to his relief, this time when she set her bow to the strings, immediately the note resolved itself, letting forth its sweetness and heady perfection.

'You hear it now? You hear that difference?'

She held herself still for a moment, as though inwardly fighting him, as though loath to accept that he had been right. He understood; he had to allow for this small resistance. It was so difficult, so demanding: the constant requirement to get everything right and give your all to it every single time. But it was his job to push her like this, nudging her towards perfection. She was more than capable and he always made sure she knew that, clear in his praise for her. She cared about this, Paul reminded himself. She wasn't about to throw it all away. Because it was worth it. It would always be worth it. The tension within her eased, her posture softening.

'Thanks, Dad. I can hear it, yes.'

Paul squeezed her shoulder: a relief, a reward. Breathe in, breathe out. He smiled at his daughter as he sat himself back down at the piano, hands steadier.

'All right then, chickadee, let's go on.'

*

Afterwards, he made up her bed with fresh linens and collected the empty plate from her room. When he came to put fresh sheets on the master bed – his and Julia's – Chrissie's phone was lying face up on the bare, white mattress. Paul set the king-size sheets down on the bedroom chair and picked it up.

He could hear Chrissie, downstairs this time, still practising but in the kitchen now where the acoustics were different, allowing her to hear herself afresh. Her tuning was perfect now; she had fixed that slipped intonation.

He typed in her four-digit password, bringing the screen to

life the way he had done countless times before. He checked for new apps she might have downloaded; he checked her Internet search history; he checked each one of her messaging accounts. As parents, they had been advised by her school to do this. There were so many things that children or teenagers could unwittingly stumble across online. So many channels or forums or exchanges they could get vulnerably drawn into.

He read a message conversation between his daughter and Reece.

> Don't think I can come round on Saturday after all.
> That's a shame ☹
> Yeah. But maybe Sunday?
> Okay great.

There was nothing else, but Paul scrolled through anyway, further back to other similar messages in her account.

All quiet. All clear. Maybe then … that message he had seen – had he misread it?

Sexy girl. Okay great.

If you only glimpsed a text, weren't the word-shapes similar enough? An easy mistake to make, surely. Paul let out the breath he'd not been aware of holding. He continued his due diligence, moving on to click through snippets of the YouTube videos Chrissie had watched, check the *deleted* folder of her emails, flick through her podcasts. No traces of the stuff he'd once found on there; images and words he still shuddered to think of. It was fine, wasn't it? Chrissie had learned her lesson, there would be no repeat; he was making sure of that, and if confronted, he could give the reassurances required.

Stiffly – he hadn't realized how awkwardly he had sat there – Paul got up from the bed. Back in Chrissie's room, he smoothed down the already smooth sheets and adjusted the already straight pillows.

Then he laid the innocent phone down, returned to her, on the bed.

CHAPTER 5

Julia

NOW

This time, *this* time, we call the police. We don't have a choice. Because of the disarrayed bed sheets and the chair and the phone screen. And because I've been scared for weeks and weeks.

'It's our daughter,' I tell them in a rush when an operator picks up. 'Christine Goodlight. She's missing. We're really concerned that something has happened to her.'

Paul and I are crushed together at the breakfast bar, my mobile on speaker between us. The call handler takes down all kinds of details over the phone and it's so difficult, really, trying to explain, because at first they think she's gone missing in London and they try to direct us to the police force over there. And I have to convince them that, no, we're almost certain she came back here, because her phone is here and her bedroom light was on, and now we've discovered that – while the front door of our house was for some reason locked – the French doors that lead outside from our kitchen were not.

When Paul and I would never leave them open.

'We'll send someone,' they agree when I get to that detail. 'We'll come and take a look. Don't touch anything. Try to leave everything exactly as it is.'

When Paul hangs up, I do nothing except wrap my arms around Jackson. He was here, maybe he can tell us what happened, but of course that's ridiculous, he's only a dog.

'She's fine,' Paul tells me. 'Don't be silly. She's fine, of course she is.' But how can he say that? Would he really be so sure if he knew what I know? I try to run through it – what could possibly have happened? Again and again my mind locks on one fact: my parents aren't here, they are far, far away. I know they are; I have the evidence. That singular fact lodges in my brain.

Paul tries Chrissie's phone again, which is a ridiculous move, because what did he expect to happen? It rings upstairs, the sound off-kilter with the smashed screen.

'We should call the Fairshaws,' I say, wondering why I didn't think of this before. 'Sally would have come over this evening to feed Jackson, wouldn't she? She might have seen something. We should have done that before calling the police.'

It's twenty minutes now since we rang 999, and we haven't really done anything in that time.

I let go of Jackson and make myself pick up my mobile. 'I'll call her now.'

The text from the *Young Musician* coordinator is still there on my screen. *Let us know as soon as you're with her.* And then my reply. *Thank you. We will.*

We won't. We can't yet, can we?

34

I dial Sally Fairshaw's number. Our next-door neighbour. It rings for a long while before she picks up.

'Hi!' Her voice is muffled. 'Julia? Is everything all right?'

I check the time: twenty to midnight. Well, why on earth would I be ringing her so late?

'Yes. No … Sally,' I say, 'have you seen Chrissie? When you came over here this evening, for Jackson?'

'Seen Chrissie? No … why would I? Isn't she there with you in London?'

'Did you come over, Sally?' I press on. 'Were you here, in our house?' I don't mean it to sound so accusatory.

'Danny went over,' Sally says. 'Round about nine. Fed Jackson, took him out for a walk. Julia, wait a moment, what's this about?'

Danny. Their thirteen-year-old son. Little more than a child himself.

'Is Danny there?' I say. 'Please can I speak to him?'

'Yes, well, I mean … Julia, he's in bed.'

The way she says it makes it sound like a question. She needs me to tell her what on earth is going on.

'Chrissie isn't here,' I confess. 'She left the concert hall and took off back home, but now we've come back and she isn't here either and …'

Now that the words have come pouring out, they make the whole situation hideously real.

'What?' Sally says. 'You're joking.'

'No. So please, the police are on their way. Can you *please* get Danny out of bed?'

'Yes. Of course. And Julia, listen – we'll come straight round

35

to you. Stuart's away, but I'll come over with Danny. We can talk to the police with you. Anything that might help.'

'Thank you.' I almost feel like bursting into tears. 'Sally, thank you.'

I lean into Paul as I drop the phone and hang up. For the first time in months, perhaps years, I find myself craving the solid form of him. Paul who helps me, cares for me, protects me. Who is dependable, steady, who always keeps me right. He wraps his arms around me, and in that moment I want nothing but to have him hold me.

I want so desperately to believe that giving myself over to him like this is all I need to do to bring our daughter back.

*

They send us two police constables. Sally and Danny are with us by then, Sally's hair dishevelled from sleep and Danny a mass of teenage awkwardness in jogging bottoms and a hoodie with his hair un-gelled.

As I let the officers into our house, one of them – the woman – says, 'I'm going to switch on my body cam so we can record everything.' She touches the side of a small black square attached to her body armour and then I can see myself right there on the little monitor, just like watching a real-life drama on a tiny TV. I walk stiffly ahead of her, back into the kitchen, and then Paul and I show both police officers up to Chrissie's bedroom, leaving Sally and Danny downstairs to make tea. *Tea*, as though it's the solution to any crisis in the world.

With the officers here, I shove every other thought from my

head. It's like dragging an entire stage set to one side, but I do it. Nothing else matters, nothing else is connected. I have to give my mind over to what is right in front of us, right now. Chrissie is missing, that's all we know for sure, and everything else is just a distraction right now.

'We didn't touch anything,' Paul says as we reach her bedroom doorway. 'Well, we did – I mean, I did.'

I glance across at him, caught off guard.

'I just picked up her phone,' he goes on. 'I couldn't help it, I was so shocked to see it lying there, but I put it right back down again where it was. I didn't open it. And neither of us have touched anything since.'

The floor shifts beneath me. We've already almost ended up telling a lie. It could have happened so easily, even though in a situation like this I've always assumed we'd be so honest. I'm always rolling my eyes at characters in books and on TV who hide knowledge and details and create such havoc for themselves, when all they have to do is *come clean*. But I get it now: you're trying so desperately to maintain your own innocence.

Both the male and the female police officer are lovely, calm but efficient, saying all the right things to explain their procedures and put us at ease. The female officer pulls on a pair of purple latex gloves and picks her way across the room.

She lifts back the rumpled covers from the bed so carefully. What is she looking for – blood? Semen? There's nothing there but Chrissie's pale pink bed sheets, a little creased.

My chest eases the tiniest fraction, but there's still that tipped-over chair, and although Chrissie is a teenager she would never leave a mess like this. It's surely Paul that she

37

got it from – her neatness. It was never something that ran in my blood.

'Her phone,' the male police officer says. 'The screen wasn't broken before?'

Paul shakes his head. 'Definitely not.'

The female officer crouches down and picks the smartphone up carefully. 'And she definitely had this with her when you were in London?'

The male officer is taking notes. I think back. 'She did,' I say, turning to Paul. 'You remember, don't you? She thought she'd forgotten it, but then she realized she had it in her coat.' I remember her feeling for the rectangular lump in her pocket as the three of us prepared to set off in the car. *Never mind. Got it.* Her words short and clipped.

'Okay,' the female officer says. 'Well, I'm sure there's a reasonable explanation.'

Can there be? Is there? Surely there will be – we just haven't figured it out yet. Under my heel, a floorboard creaks: that one floorboard that has always been loose and I want to prise it up, dig under it, but I'm not going to. Not here, not now.

The male officer is going through Chrissie's wastepaper bin, tipping it onto its side. He has gloves on as well and he's being so careful as he lifts something out. It's a shiny, square booklet with a typed white sheet of paper attached.

'I recognize that,' says Paul. 'It's a Royal Institute prospectus. Chrissie's tutor, Mr Donaldson, sent away for them I think. For all his pupils, not just her.'

The male officer flips through it, his colleague looking over his shoulder.

'Did you say a prospectus?'

'Yes. That's right.'

'Mmm.' The officer sets the booklet down on Chrissie's desk, along with its cover letter, and makes a note of something on his pad. Maybe he's writing down where he found it. It makes sense that she would have tossed it in the bin, a simple piece of junk mail, but something isn't sitting right and I can't articulate what.

'All right,' says the female officer, scattering my thoughts before I can catch them. 'For now let's go back downstairs, shall we?'

In the kitchen, our neighbour Sally has managed to find a teapot and make tea for everyone. She's even got Danny setting out mugs. His face is dotted with inflamed-looking pimples; his growing nose and jaw look too big for his face. Being a teenager can be so hateful, I remember, and I feel for him now.

The male officer heads into the front hallway to call someone – a supervisor maybe?

The female officer sits down and accepts a mug of tea, then sets it to one side and flips her own little notebook open.

'All right, then. Let me just confirm a few basics. First off, could you describe what Chrissie looks like? Hair colour, eyes, height, weight? Later, we'd like to get a photo of her too.'

'Brown hair,' says Paul. 'Dark brown, and long. And brown eyes. And she's small for her age.' He floats a hand vaguely in the air. 'Five foot two?'

'Five foot one,' I say. She's an inch shorter than me.

'Okay, good,' says the officer. 'And weight?'

'She's slim,' says Paul. 'Not overweight at all. Just curvy.'

Curvy? But he's right. She is. Paul looks at me, and I take a guess. 'About eight and a half,' I say. 'Stone.'

39

'All right. Good. And any notable marks? A notable scar or a birthmark or a tattoo?'

Paul shakes his head. 'No, not really. Just … a chicken-pox scar under her chin, here.' He points to his own jaw. 'And a tiny scar on her right knee from when she fell off her bike …'

I rack my brains, but I can't think of anything else. Chrissie's features are regular: perfect and sweet, but that's not a distinguishing feature, is it – being attractive?

'And clothes? When you last saw her, what was she wearing?' The female officer's body camera is still recording.

'A dress,' I tell her. 'A navy, knee-length dress. And she has a pink coat. That's gone. I think she has that with her.'

'Thank you,' says the officer. She's writing it all down. 'That's all very helpful. Now, let's just try and get a few timings worked out,' she says. 'What time did you last see her?'

I look across at Paul to check. I'm really trying to keep calm. I'm really trying not to panic. 'Around seven forty-five this evening?'

He nods. 'About that.'

'And where was that?'

'In London,' I say at the same time as Paul says, 'On stage.'

The officer glances up, confused. Paul leans forwards. 'She was playing a concert in London. Hundreds of people would have seen her there.' Maybe now she can make sense of our outfits: Paul's crisp suit, and my dress and high heels. 'But then,' Paul goes on, 'there was a fire at the venue and we had to evacuate.'

'There was a fire?'

'Yes, I mean no – not actually a fire. Just a fire alarm that went off. Accidentally. Anyway, they saw her outside – a fire marshal accounted for her – but she wasn't there when we were all ushered back in.'

The officer makes a note. 'And no one saw her again after that?'

'*Someone* must have,' I say. 'But we haven't. We didn't. We only realized she'd come back here when we used the tracker app on Paul's phone.'

Panic is rising up in me after all.

'She came back ...' The officer makes another note. 'All right, and how would she have done that?'

'By train? She could have got a train straight from Paddington.'

'She must have done that,' says Paul, 'even though to get there, we drove. She's done it before though – that route, by train. Last year, she had orchestral rehearsals in London.'

I watch the officer's pencil move. *Got train*, I imagine her writing, *from Paddington to Oxford*.

'And was she ...' the officer hesitates. 'Upset at all? Is there any reason you can think of as to why she'd take off?'

Take off, the officer has said. Not *go missing*. My breathing eases a little in my throat. I shake my head.

'No,' says Paul. 'The concert – she was brilliant.'

'Is it possible,' Sally says hesitantly, 'that she just became overwhelmed? She's so good, so talented, but I imagine she was feeling under a lot of pressure.' She turns to the officers. 'This concert, you see – it was really an audition. For a big competition. She's been working so hard ...'

Sally's words are meant to reassure me, but all I can think is, *but something happened* here, *at home, in her bedroom. The chair and the bed and the phone smashed on the floor. That speaks to anger, acting out, violence. None of that is Chrissie. If she were overwhelmed she would just have curled up on the couch.* The air in my lungs sucks in tight again.

The officer turns to Sally. 'And you were here at what time?'

'Well, actually it wasn't me,' says Sally. 'It was Danny who came over. Go on, Danny. Tell them.'

Danny's voice is squeaky, painfully breaking. 'I came over at, like, nine o'clock,' he tells her. 'I was supposed to come earlier but, like … well. Anyway, I took Jackson out.'

I can imagine it. Sally having to nag him.

'Did you use our front door?' Paul butts in. 'Or these back ones?' He gestures to the elegant French windows of our kitchen.

The female officer is very good. She doesn't chide my husband for asking his own questions, just waits with her little pen poised for Danny's answer.

'Uh-uh. The front door. That's the only key my mum gave me.'

Sally is quick to back him up. 'That's the only key we have.'

Just then, the male officer comes back into the kitchen from the hallway, and he and his colleague exchange a brief look. I have no idea what the glance means.

'And you don't have any idea where Chrissie is?' the female officer asks Danny. 'She didn't call or message you or anything?'

Danny can't help looking guilty, even as he shakes his head, but I believe him. He and Chrissie have never hung out together. There's the age-gap for a start, and well … Chrissie doesn't have time for many friends.

'All right. And where did you go on your walk with …' the female officer pauses for the dog's name.

'Jackson,' says Paul.

'With Jackson.'

Danny glances over at his mum, embarrassed. 'Like, not far.'

I'm distracted. Something is nagging me about that prospectus. The one her tutor Mr Donaldson sent away for.

The officer smiles at Danny. 'That's okay. But where?'

'Only … like … across the road.'

For a moment, I want to laugh, a bubble of hysteria rising up. Poor kid, he's so embarrassed. I can just picture it: Danny walking Jackson a mere twenty metres and then standing with him next to some lamppost, scrolling on his phone while Jackson did his business.

'It's fine,' I try to reassure him. 'It doesn't matter.'

'In fact,' the female officer smiles, 'on this occasion, it might actually be better. While you were out there, opposite the house, did you see anyone come or go?'

Danny glances at his mum again. 'I don't think so.'

'And what about when you brought Jackson back in again? Anything you noticed then? For example, did you notice whether these doors were unlocked?'

Danny's face falls. 'I don't know. I just gave Jackson his biscuits.'

Poor Danny. He's so young, far too young to be caught up in this, even though clearly he's doing his best.

But even then, my heart sinks anyway, because the timings hardly add up, do they? If we last saw Chrissie at seven forty-five, and someone clocked her on a clipboard even later than that, she could hardly have been back here by nine o'clock. Even if Danny had been paying attention, at that time of night

43

there would still have been nothing to see. But, at the same time, at least this is narrowing things down, isn't it? I squeeze Paul's hand and I'm glad when the female officer asks us the exact right next question.

'And what time did the two of you arrive home?'

Paul speaks confidently. 'Eleven fifteen. All the way home, I kept checking the clock.'

'So that's good, isn't it?' My turn to lean forward. 'That's helpful. Whatever happened here must have happened between, say, nine fifteen and eleven fifteen. That's a pretty small window. Someone must have seen something. We can ask the neighbours, up and down the street.'

'Yes.' The officer nods. 'We can certainly do that. Although ...' She glances down at her notes.

'Although?' I say.

The female officer half frowns, half winces. 'Well, unless she's still in London after all.'

CHAPTER 6

Paul

EIGHT WEEKS BEFORE

As Saturday evening approached, Paul couldn't help but grow tenser by the hour. He had never got used to it, even though he and Julia had been together for a decade now. It was fine, he told himself. Nothing to be afraid of. He would be able to give a perfectly good account of himself. But he had grown up with acute senses, an uncanny awareness of dynamics, an acute attunement to the shifts that preceded his father's gambling binges; tracking his mother's fits of crying that had no rational explanation for their beginning or their end. In certain situations, that made it impossible to relax.

His fingers slipped as he did up the buttons on his expensive, freshly ironed shirt, and his head swam as he pushed his feet into handmade leather shoes that pinched his Achilles tendon. As they drove to the outskirts of Guildford, he felt the heat and sweat on him. Chrissie was silent as a ghost in the back, small and pale against the dark seats, headphones in and attached to her phone, listening to music or a podcast. Looking out the window, though, not scrolling or texting. Quiet. And Julia … well, at one point Julia looked over at him and – for a moment – took his hand.

He was almost relieved when they finally came into view of their destination – just to get out of the oppressive space of the car. As they rounded the last curve of the driveway, piece by piece the house revealed itself. It was a huge place, unapologetic in its grandeur, with its pale stonework and tall, generous windows. The main section faced them, stately and imposing, extending into two cornered wings that enclosed a tended courtyard. Unnecessarily large for just two people, it wasn't even a house but an ancestral home: *Bute Hall*. It still took Paul aback – shrank him – to think that this had been Julia's childhood home.

'Put your phone away now, Chrissie,' Julia said as they unfolded themselves from the car. It was accepted as one of the rules here: no texting, no browsing, no screens. Along with no touching of the oil paintings in the hallways, no glasses set down on the mahogany-wood surfaces, and no shouting, no shrieking, no running indoors.

In the reflection of the car window, Paul checked his tie and jacket. Did he look the part? He always tried to, but in all likelihood he never would, not properly. Because there was always more to it than the clothes you wore or the car you drove. There was a certain ineffable *something* engrained in people who came from generations of money. He'd sensed it when he first met Julia. Something he knew he'd never had and could never fake. There were other reasons why he'd been granted admission.

Julia stepped up to the huge front door and rang the bell.

Paul could hear it clanging inside. Whenever they came here, he always half expected a maid to answer the door, or a house-keeper, some kind of Mrs Danvers.

But it was Celina herself who swung the door open to welcome them. Lady of the house.

She hugged Chrissie first, her granddaughter, and then her daughter. As she drew Julia into a stiff embrace, Paul was sure he saw Celina flinch. In pain? Yes – he remembered now: Julia had said she'd had a fall recently and badly bruised her shoulder. Julia's parents were elderly now, inevitably growing frailer with each passing year, and yet still Paul could never imagine them vulnerable. After the fall, Julia hadn't even considered taking her mother to hospital. Celina, she'd said, would have refused point-blank. The Montroses were like that. Seemingly impervious. Around them, it was always Paul who felt brittle, weak.

'Come in! Come in,' Celina was saying, and she led them through the dark-panelled hallways to the sitting room where Julia's father was levering himself up from an armchair. The whole house smelled rich: leather and wood polish, silver and fine dust.

'Paul,' said Duncan. 'And my girls.'

His skin was papery as he shook Paul's hand and his eyes slid away, the way they usually did. Just as there was always a stiffness to the smiles he offered his son-in-law. Ten years, and Paul still felt he barely knew the man.

'Duncan,' he said, returning the handshake, trying to grasp some sense of affinity. *Duncan*. It still felt presumptuous call-ing him that. Even after his father-in-law's gracious insistence, it had taken several meetings before Paul could get past *Judge Montrose*.

'And here's my Chrissie,' said Duncan, releasing Paul and stepping forward to appraise his granddaughter. 'Pretty as ever.'

Julia cleared her throat.

'And Julia,' said Duncan. 'You look tired, my dear. Late nights?'

Julia hugged him in turn, then sat herself down on the couch, brushing an invisible piece of lint from her knee. 'Long hours.'

Duncan settled himself back in his armchair. 'With work?'

'Of course, with work.' An edge to her tone.

Now Duncan's eyes met Paul's, as though searching for corroboration, confirmation, and at once it was there: the undertow, the eggshells. Something hinted at and never said. Easy to think it was a simple criticism of him, the kind Julia used to rush to reassure him about: *They don't mean it like that. Of course they like you. Of course they respect the arrangement we have.* But of course, the eggshells in this family had layers. Paul knew there was more to it than that.

'Drinks?' said Celina.

'I'm driving later,' said Julia. 'But I'll have a G&T.'

'Just one,' said Duncan.

'Yes, Daddy. Just the one.'

Duncan was already drinking what looked like sherry. He tipped the glass towards Paul, eyebrows raised. Paul held up a hand. 'I'll wait until dinner, thanks.'

He knew he was going against the grain here, but he had learned through bitter experience the importance of keeping his wits about him during visits like this. There were so many ways to capsize the ship.

Chrissie had perched herself, cat-like, on one of the wide, dark couches in the room. Hands in her lap, legs in black tights neatly aligned.

'Chrissie?' said Celina. 'Something for you?'

Chrissie glanced up. 'An orange juice?'

Celina nodded. 'Of course.'

'So,' said Duncan, easing back in his armchair. 'What's new with you? How's life in Oxford?'

Paul lowered himself gingerly beside Julia on the suede couch, conscious of not letting his trousers crease.

Julia flexed a hand. 'Good. We're all well.'

Paul cleared his throat. 'Did you know Chrissie's through to the Category Auditions of *Young Musician*?'

Duncan fixed his eyes on Julia for a moment, then turned to Chrissie. 'Indeed I did know. We're certainly proud of you. Are you proud, Chrissie?'

Chrissie let out a half-laugh. 'Of course.'

'Well, that's good, isn't it.' Duncan sipped his sherry.

'It's very good, Daddy,' said Julia. 'She's been doing incredibly well.'

A movement in the doorway. Paul was careful to add: 'She's been working very hard.'

Celina was back now, bringing in the other drinks: a gin and tonic for Julia and pulpy orange juice for Chrissie. She kissed the top of Duncan's head, cheek brushing against his thick white hair as she set down the empty tray. He caught her hand in return and tenderly kissed the back of it, a move of such chivalrous intimacy that Paul had to look away.

'Sure you don't want something, Paul?' said Celina. 'We won't be eating for a little while yet.'

He did want something, really. What he wanted was a cold, dark beer, one he could drink with his eyes closed straight from the bottle. One that would wash all this tension away.

But he shook his head and repeated, 'No, thank you.' And yet he felt his stomach rumble. Duncan and Celina – they ate so *late*. Eight o'clock, nine o'clock. Growing up, he would have his tea at a quarter past five. Beans on toast. A baked potato. Buttered bread.

Celina settled herself on the couch beside Chrissie. She had poured herself her own measure of wine, and it shivered in the glass with each of her sharp movements as she leaned in to fuss with the collar of her granddaughter's blouse. Paul pulled his eyes away, chest tightening. Duncan was talking now about one of his old cases. An artist who had been a pawn in some kind of vast fraud. Paul listened, nodding. This part was easy enough. Duncan was a natural raconteur, an entertainer, and he could fill up the space with his bonhomie, his jovial charm. Paul could easily sit and listen all night, not having to contribute a word himself.

He let himself relax as Duncan moved on to other anecdotes. From time to time, he mentioned names that Julia nodded at, in recognition. And why shouldn't she know them? After all, at a certain level, Julia's natural level, the social circles were very small. Practically a single social set.

He was brought back to himself by Julia rising lightly from the couch and Chrissie – cat-like – uncurling herself too. Eventually, finally, dinner was ready. Following their cue, Paul stood up stiffly, his knees clicking. Celina led them through to the dining room where they took their seats in the large, chilly space, a weighty chandelier hanging over their heads.

Duncan sat at one end of the big wide table, Celina at the other. Julia and Chrissie were placed together on one side, Paul by himself on the other. There was already wine in his glass.

Now there *was* somebody to serve them, like something out of *Downton Abbey*. He tried to catch the young woman's eye, to show his appreciation and his solidarity – to communicate somehow, *I'm not really one of them*. But she passed him by with barely a glance as she set down the plates with their complicated little starters. He was eating with these people, wasn't he? He was married to Julia. *You chose this life*, said the voice in his head, *and you've done what you can to cling on to it ever since*.

'And how is work going?' Celina asked Julia, seated on her left.

'It's good. It's fine. I've been assigned a big case. You know – the one I mentioned before. The father whose son was facing manslaughter charges.'

Paul thought he saw Celina shudder. 'Horrible situation. Yes.'

'We have a good case. There were so many errors. Clear prejudice. The father is quite right to sue.'

'Of course he is,' said Celina. 'And quite right that you're representing him.'

Paul watched as, across the table, Chrissie's pale hands broke up her bread. Valuable hands. Perhaps one day they would need to have them insured. Even now, he always tried to make her take care of them. Chrissie was talking to her grandfather about school, her recent maths test. That would please Duncan.

'We're pushing for a settlement,' Julia continued, her eyes flicking over to Chrissie too as though constantly checking on her. 'One that will leave both sides happy. I'm hoping, in time, we'll be able to talk them round. If they're smart, they'll see we're presenting good points. Currently, though, this may still end up in court.'

Celina shook her head, picking at her plate. 'More legal fees that way,' she said. 'More expense.'

Julia gave a wry smile. 'From the firm's point of view, that's not necessarily a problem.'

Paul bit into the vinegary, sharp little salad and thought of the money that his mother had left to him when she died last year. It wasn't a lot, not by these standards, but it would have been all she had. His father had died years before, smokers' lungs finally undoing him. How his mother must have scrimped and saved to put away an amount like that, close to eight thousand pounds – a fortune in her eyes. Compared to the amounts he and Julia spent on holidays, Chrissie's academy fees, a new sofa, it was ridiculous, and yet that was all the money he had to his name. He didn't work; he hadn't done in years. Being a house-husband wasn't a paid job. The house itself – the house he lived in – had been bought with a deposit gifted by Duncan and Celina, and it was Julia's salary that paid the small remaining mortgage. They lived in it together, but the deeds were in Julia's sole name.

He felt a hand on his arm. Celina was leaning along the table towards him. 'Paul,' she said, 'tell me more about this *Young Musician* competition. It sounds as though Chrissie's doing marvellously well.'

His heart thumped, though on the surface it was an innocent question. He swallowed his mouthful and wiped his lips. The napkins here were stiff and heavy. 'She's practising so hard,' he told Celina. 'Every day after school, and at the weekends, sometimes for three or four hours.'

'Goodness. And you practise with her?'

'Of course.'

'Quite a commitment from you.'

'You know I want the best for Chrissie,' Paul said.

At the far end of the table, Duncan laughed and Julia's fingers tensed on her wine glass. Celina tilted her head. 'Yes. Don't we all.'

Paul glanced across at Julia, but she was distracted, too busy listening in to the conversation between Duncan and Chrissie to be aware of her mother's subtle codes.

'Well … Maybe if she wins you should up her allowance.'

At the other end of the table, Chrissie's head turned. Celina had spoken loudly enough for her to hear.

Paul smiled across at his daughter and replied, softly, to Celina. 'Maybe.'

Everything sounded so innocuous; Celina had expressed nothing but support of Chrissie's music. But Paul's heart was still racing; he couldn't seem to make it stop.

*

In the gap between main course and dessert, he excused himself from the table. He needed the bathroom and he needed a break, to gather himself for the last hour or so. Julia's eyes tracked him as he got up from the table and he gave her what he trusted was a reassuring smile. He hoped that they were already through the hardest part now and that no one would dig any deeper tonight. He could make it from here. Dessert, more wine, a liqueur if he had to, and then they could be in the car, safely on their way home.

He climbed the main staircase, unexpectedly steep and the steps awkwardly curved, the banister slippery-smooth under his hand. He tried not to think of what he knew about this staircase. Julia had had a fall here during the final month of her pregnancy. It had been so bad that she'd ended up in hospital, and Chrissie had been born early, urgently, as a result. The fall had been the result of dizziness, light-headedness due to the pregnancy. It was only later that another narrative had emerged via Celina: *dizziness* was a far kinder story, she had implied, than the one suggested by Julia's later blood tests. Drugs in her system, Paul came to understand. But no one ever talked about that. Pieces of information like this were imparted to him quietly, gradually. It was a while before he came to understand the full extent of the difficulties Julia had had. What was being asked of him – what was required – only became apparent many months into the relationship. And given how he felt towards Julia by then, it had been far too late for Paul to disentangle himself.

On the upstairs landing, he couldn't help himself. The door to Julia's old bedroom stood open.

Even after twenty years of her absence, the space still smelled of her. He couldn't have described how, but it did. Her bedroom was kept the same as when she'd last lived here, in the holidays between her intensive terms at Oxford University. Her college scarf was still draped over her wardrobe, and if he opened the doors, he knew he'd find her subfusc and gown. Her old law textbooks were stacked on her bedroom shelves. Naturally, she'd come out with a first.

These things in here, they belonged to his wife. Symbols of who she was, parts of her that he couldn't ignore. It was a room that housed her contradictions. Almost unconsciously, he opened one of the small drawers in her vanity and found a few old hairbands and notebooks nestled inside. And a pack of photos. He had seen these before, though she'd never shown them to him herself. He knew he shouldn't look at them again, and yet he couldn't seem to help himself. After all, she was the one who had kept them. He lifted the flap and let the shiny prints slide out. These photos were from the days before smartphones. Real photos that you got printed and didn't put up online. They were in black and white, a classy printing choice, and one that could make this other, younger Julia seem somewhat distant and unreal. He sat down on Julia's old bed to let himself look.

Even within the hallowed halls of Oxford, there were still places only a few could access. Invite-only to those with the right names and the correct pedigree and connections. Only the chosen, the bright young things. Everyone in these pictures was beautiful and the clothes they wore were lavish in the extreme. Headdresses, tail feathers, animal fur, silk. Make-up that was exotic, extravagant, almost violent: *A Midsummer Night's Dream* meets *Eyes Wide Shut*.

Paul stared at Julia, there in the centre. Dress slipping off one shoulder, one perfect breast exposed and lying in the lap of a man he'd never met. He wore a crown of laurel leaves and his eyes were blackened with kohl. All the pictures were like this. Young women and men in wild, abandoned poses. Drunken, giddy, reckless, high. Just looking at them made Paul's skin burn.

He jumped at a movement in the doorway. Celina, wine glass cradled in her hand.

'... Thought I'd find you in here.'

Hastily, Paul pushed the photographs back into their packet, but not before she saw them.

'You must wonder,' she said, stepping up to where he still sat on Julia's bed – he should have got up – 'why I haven't thrown them away. Why Julia hasn't. After all, who wants to look at them now?'

But Paul understood. 'Better to remember though, isn't it? Safer that way. If you're not careful, it can be dangerous to forget.'

Celina set her wineglass down, unsteadily, on the desk. She was dressed in her usual style: a dark blouse fastened up high on her neck, long sleeves shaping down to narrow bands at the wrists. Buttoned up, covered up as always.

'You're clever,' she said. 'I spotted that in you, right from the start. You're perceptive. Your own background, I suppose, taught you that.'

He felt like a wriggling insect, pinned open. He had learned to read her, and she had learned to read him. She held out a hand and he passed her the photographs.

'I still see it in her,' she said.

Paul went still. He swallowed, his throat dry from this dusty, muffled house. Celina set the photographs back in the drawer, but he knew the conversation wasn't over.

'These pictures,' she said now. 'You're right. I remember. I can always remember.' She swayed, smiling, and tapped one finger to her nose. 'And I *know*,' she said. 'You haven't said anything, but I sat next to her tonight.'

Celina picked up her wineglass again, her hip bumping against the still-open drawer. She was drunk, Paul realized. How had he never seen it in her before? Even after her G&Ts

or so many glasses of wine, he had never perceived her as anything but poised and self-assured. Her upbringing, her breeding could clearly conceal a lot. That fall, he thought now, when she had bruised her shoulder. Maybe it wasn't age-related after all. *Like mother, like daughter.* Celina's own mantra came unbidden to his mind.

Her next words were muffled; Paul was sure he'd misheard. 'What?'

Celina leaned down close to him, swaying, one hand pressing on his knee to steady herself. Her breath next to his cheek was sour with wine. This time, her words made their way straight into his ear.

The words were so vulgar, so offensive, and yet Paul's stomach plunged.

Celina was drunk, but her eyes were fixed unwaveringly on him. There was no hiding. He had seen what he'd seen, though he'd tried to dismiss it, and he hadn't told Celina, and yet, sickeningly, they had both come to the same conclusion.

'I said, *you can practically smell it on her.* Paul,' she continued, her whisper slurred, 'you know we're so grateful. You were so good for Julia, back then. You know if she weren't like this – the same – we would hardly even *need* you.' There it was: the fist in the glove; the threat. 'But things being as they are, sweetie – *what are you going to do?*'

CHAPTER 7

Paul

SEVEN WEEKS BEFORE

On Monday, like every weekday, Paul was left alone in the house. He spent the morning paying bills, doing a food shop and cleaning the upstairs bathrooms. Come the afternoon, he whistled Jackson in from the garden, the dog's tail whipping his legs as Paul grappled to clip on the lead.

Outside it wasn't yet raining, but the sky was solidly overcast. Paul tucked the collar of his anorak up to his chin and pushed his hands into his pockets, Jackson's lead hooked tightly round his wrist. He let the dog tug him along, unconcerned with what direction they were headed. Jackson was simply happy to be outside, pushing his nose into walls and bushes. After a while, he stopped short, bringing Paul to a halt too. He watched as their pet shuffled his hind legs and squatted. Cars slashed by on Woodstock Road while Paul waited. Then he fished a plastic bag from his trouser pocket. Stoop, scoop, and he threw the whole mess in a nearby bin.

In another fifteen minutes or so, they had reached the far

edge of their long, narrow loop and here they were, in front of Julia's office block, the inevitable destination to the route he and Jackson had followed.

'Look, Jackson,' he said, pointing, and Jackson barked. There was her car in the car park, just as expected. No reason for it to be anywhere else.

If he waved up at the building right now, perhaps she would glance out of a window and see him.

Hi Paul! she might call down, delighted.

Hi Julia! he'd reply, with a wave.

He imagined that. How cute.

He knew that in reality it wouldn't happen. He'd been to her office only once before. It was in the centre of the building and didn't have any windows to look out of. Just a big desk with her sleek laptop perfectly centred, and a sofa that almost swallowed him when he'd sat down. He thought about the other morning in bed when he had slipped an arm around her. These days, Julia spent more time at that desk than ever. Throwing herself into her work – a different world. She didn't have to work; people from her kind of wealth often didn't. But it was good for her – necessary, even. Over the years, Paul had come to understand that. He'd only had a glimpse of the dangers when they'd first met; he hadn't witnessed the worst of it, all those weeks and months when Celina and Duncan had had to step in to care for Chrissie, because Julia had been in no fit state. Even now, it shocked him to think about that; it was hard for him to imagine. She had sorted herself out so quickly once he arrived on the scene. With Paul there to help her with Chrissie, Julia had quickly secured a well-paying, demanding job. She had a first-class law degree after all, plus naturally it helped that her father was a judge. She grew to be someone responsible and well-adjusted, those photos in the drawer mere relics of a past life. It had fallen to his mother-in-law, Celina, to apprise Paul, over time, of the other side of Julia, those traits that could easily run in the blood. And over the years, Paul had come to understand the fine balance that Julia had struck and that he was now being asked to maintain: immersing herself in the world of work, she kept herself on the straight and narrow, while leaving it to him to stay at home with Chrissie, stepping up into the role of parent. So that had become his role in their clan: a dependable presence for both mother and daughter, a plain, steady man to look after them both.

He tried never to let Chrissie feel her mother's absence, always ensuring he was there in Julia's stead. He tried never to question the arrangement they'd agreed on: Julia as the breadwinner, Paul the stay-at-home dad. Yet every so often, he felt it. When Julia was at work, she felt far away, centred in a world that held her apart from him.

Even when he was standing right outside.

Paul was damp and chilly now: time to head home. Jackson looked tired out as well, his seemingly boundless energy drained. 'Come on then, Jacks.' Paul tugged gently on the lead, ready to turn back.

Jackson turned to follow him – and yelped.

Admittedly, Paul was startled too; the man had appeared out of nowhere.

'I'm sorry,' he said. He tugged Jackson sideways, trying to give the man room to pass. Instead, the dog strained at the leash, letting out an uncharacteristic volley of barks.

The man held up a hand and smiled – so charming. 'Don't

worry. It's fine.' He was taller than Paul, and expensively yet effortlessly dressed. Paul caught the scent of his cologne – woody, peppery, intense.

'He isn't usually like this with strangers. I don't know why ...' Jackson continued to bark, up on his hind legs, and Paul could imagine the picture they made, glad that Julia couldn't see them now. 'He's not dangerous. He's only trying to be ... friendly.' The comment was stupid, but what was setting Jackson off? Paul hated himself in that moment, conscious of his faded jeans, muddy trainers, and his flailing, yapping dog. 'Sorry,' he repeated. He almost added, *sir*.

The man skirted round them, glancing from dog to owner to dog again. Paul dragged again at Jackson's lead, his dog's claws skittering over the pavement. 'Jackson!'

The man gave another charming wave of his hand. 'Don't worry. It's nothing. You have a good day now.' So easily dismissing them.

Paul watched the man carry on lightly up the shiny pavements of the street, disappearing after a moment or two into Julia's building. Jackson let out a final salvo of barks, dropped back on to four feet, and stood there, panting, his wordless eyes explaining nothing at all.

It was late now, and Paul was colder than ever: he hadn't intended to come all this way. The flash of shock and shame had left him shaky.

'Come on, Jackson,' he repeated. He would feel better once he got the two of them home.

*

When he got back, there was a letter waiting for him on the doormat. Paul tore open the thick white envelope and pulled out the glossy brochure right there in the hallway. He flipped through the pages, the paper slippery against his fingers, taking in the pictures of the grounds, the students, the dormitories, the practice rooms. He skim-read the neat text, heaped with glowing claims. *Focus … encouragement … opportunities … dedication …* In a place like this, music would be your life. It was the kind of place he would have given anything to have attended, but growing up there'd barely been enough money for food, never mind for studying in a place like this. And music – what was that when the wolf was at the door? A luxury, an indulgence, a daydream, a waste.

He turned to the last section where the fees were listed, and his heart hollowed as he took in the numbers. He thought of his mother's inheritance: that shameful, pitiful amount. He was trying; he was doing his best for Chrissie, but he was always so constrained, lacking in agency and resources and influence. There was always such a sense of dependence, stark limits to the choices he could make.

He wasn't going to speak to Julia about this. He knew already how that conversation would go: at this stage, she would never easily agree. Upstairs, he set the prospectus in a drawer for safe-keeping, resigned to the knowledge of what he needed to do. He needed to make the possibility a reality first if he was ever going to persuade her it was a good idea. Same with Chrissie.

A *fait accompli* would be so much better. It was up to him, then, to get it done.

CHAPTER 8

Paul

SIX WEEKS BEFORE

The following week the email came through with final details of Chrissie's Category Audition. Place, time slot and confirmation of the pieces she would play. Paul forwarded the details to Julia on the off-chance, not expecting her to be free. Lately, it had seemed almost impossible to pin her down.

But she surprised him.

'I'm due time off,' she told him. 'I can take the day. Come to Cardiff with the two of you.'

He wanted to embrace her then, he really did. And the next day, Chrissie shrugged and squirmed about it, but he could tell that she was delighted too.

*

On the morning of the Category Auditions, Paul was up at the crack of dawn, checking the oil and coolant in the car, putting coffee on, waiting for Julia and Chrissie to get dressed and come down. The drive would take them close to two hours, and heaven forbid if they were late. They were going to be picking Reece up on the way as well. Chrissie had insisted that he come. *For moral support*, she had said, even though her mum was supposed to be coming to provide that. But all right.

While he waited for his wife and daughter, his conversation with Celina replayed in his head. Now more than ever, he couldn't stop thinking about that comment he'd seen on Chrissie's phone – that message that he realized now had arrived on Chrissie's phone *before* that conversation with Julia in the kitchen – the conversation *after* their run, the one that would have led Chrissie to cancel her plans with Reece.

Sexy girl … Not *Okay great*.

When Chrissie had given him her phone to check, he'd found nothing, but still every time he recalled those words, that same sharp panic arrived in his chest, along with a replay of Celina's weighted words. *Tell me, sweetie, what are you going to do?* Well, he would do something. He had a plan.

Julia appeared now in the kitchen, grey shadows under her eyes.

'Morning,' he greeted her, getting up from the breakfast bar. 'Coffee?'

She nodded. 'Lovely. Thank you.' She was dressed in jeans for a change, not her usual tailored trousers, and a jumper he remembered her buying last year: green, with little fancy sequins dotted across the chest.

'Here.' He handed her the steaming mug.

'Thanks.' She sat down on one of the breakfast stools, swivelling round to look out into the garden. Paul topped up his own mug of coffee, and for a minute or two they just sat there.

'The grass out there is getting long,' Paul commented presently. 'Probably all the rain we've had lately.'

'What?' said Julia. 'Oh yes. Maybe a little bit. It looks nice, though. The garden. You really do a good job with it.'

She smiled at him and he smiled back.

'I'm really glad you're coming with us today,' he said. 'And obviously, Chrissie is delighted.'

'Well. Me too.' Julia rubbed at the corner of one eye. The skin there looked dry and red. 'And like I said, I was due some time off.'

Was due? thought Paul. *Or needed?* These days she seemed worn out, worried. Edgy and exhausted. *Are you working too hard?* Duncan had been right. Paul should talk to her about it. He *would* talk to her. In fact, he would do it right now.

But already he could hear Chrissie's footsteps coming down the stairs, and then she appeared, outlined in the doorway of the kitchen.

Julia's phone bleeped. Work – always work. It was necessary, but lately it was just too much. If there was one thing he had learned with Chrissie, it was that you needed balance. You had to push hard, but never more than she could take.

'Leave it,' Paul said quietly.

But Julia was already swiping at the screen, her jaw tensing even before she opened the text. She pushed her stool back and Paul saw it immediately – the way Chrissie's face fell.

'Julia—'

Julia slipped off the barstool. 'One second,' she said. 'I just need to reply to this.' She gave their daughter's shoulder a squeeze as she slipped past her in the doorway. 'One second,' she repeated, over her shoulder, 'and then I'm all yours.'

Paul kept his smile in place as Julia disappeared back upstairs, the study door clunking shut behind her a moment later.

Chrissie stood there by herself in their shiny, bright, expensive kitchen. Seeing her properly now, instinctively Paul got to his feet. 'Goodness,' he said. 'Don't you look smart?'

She was dressed in tapered navy trousers that hugged her ankles and a fine cream blouse with silk panels on the sides. Little low heels with a neat blue strap. The blouse sat high on her neck, low on her wrists, reminding him of Celina and the way she always dressed. No jewellery though, no dangling earrings or necklaces. Chrissie couldn't hold her violin while wearing anything like that.

Paul swallowed. 'You look lovely,' he made himself say.

Duncan's voice: *Pretty as ever.*

It was true. But it did little to ease the clench of anticipation in his chest.

*

They set off for the audition venue, Paul driving. Behind him, Chrissie slipped off her heels and rested her bare feet up on the rear heating vent. She had small, neat feet, the toes from big to pinkie all descending in a smooth line. Not ballet dancers' feet, Chrissie had once said. You had to have a big middle toe for that.

Gently, Paul reached behind him and pressed on her ankles. 'Put your shoes back on, please.'

Outside of Reece's house, they had to wait a few minutes while, for some reason, he and Chrissie texted back and forth.

'What's wrong?' asked Paul. 'Isn't he ready or something?' He checked the clock.

'He's just coming,' Chrissie told him. 'In, like, thirty seconds.' And a moment later he was coming down the steps from his ordinary-looking house. His brown hair was parted on one side and longish, and he was wearing pale jeans and a neat blue jersey. Paul wondered if he'd dressed up for the event.

He got in the back seat and closed the door after him. 'Hello, Mrs Goodlight. Mr Goodlight.'

'Hello, Reece.'

The space filled up with the smell of his deodorant. *Lynx Africa*. Classic.

'Thanks for letting me come.'

'Sure,' said Paul, smiling at the boy in the rear-view mirror. 'It's what Chrissie wanted.'

Chrissie turned in her seat; she had her shoes back on now. 'Here.' She held out one of her ear buds to Reece. He took it from her and tucked it into his ear, easily, as though they'd done this dozens of times. Paul tried to catch Julia's eye, but his wife was busy answering a text. It was okay though. Chrissie had told them years back that Reece was gay. He didn't pose any danger, no threat. All of *that stuff* neutralized. No different to Chrissie being best friends with a girl, he'd told himself.

'All right,' he said, before putting the car in gear. 'All got your seatbelts on?'

Chrissie rested her head against the window, the little white ear bud nestled in her ear. 'Of course, Dad,' she said, as though *he'd* been delaying them. 'We're all strapped in fine. Let's go.'

*

It was a fair way to drive, but they made good time. The sat nav and event signs led them reliably to the venue, and as they turned into the car park, the sun was out, a little bit dazzling, glinting off the windscreens of the other cars. In the passenger seat, Julia looked up from her work phone, sending a quick message, then sliding it into her bag.

Inside the venue there were bright yellow posters and big, clear arrows, and staff on hand to help them find their way. A group of girls and boys in the foyer shrieked and waved their arms to welcome Chrissie over. Paul vaguely recognized some of the faces from the regional heats. So these were the talented ones who had got through. The ones Chrissie would be competing against now.

'Go on then,' said Paul. 'Go and talk to them.'

Chrissie stepped away, leaving Paul holding her violin, her coat and her folder of music. Reece followed her, close behind, and Paul watched as Chrissie introduced him to her friends. He looked nervous; Chrissie had once told him that kids at school hadn't always been that kind to her friend.

Paul double-checked the details and checked his watch, then he felt a tap on his shoulder. A man was standing there – a parent; someone Paul recognized from regionals too, though he couldn't for the life of him remember the man's name, only that he'd had a wife who had been dumpy and exuberant, and who had touched his arm incessantly.

'Hello, Paul. Great to see you here again.'

Paul fumbled the folder of music under his armpit to release a hand to return the handshake. Chrissie's coat was still draped over his arm. 'Oh hello, congratulations. Your son got through then?' He was glad to have remembered that much at least.

Julia smiled and held out her hand as well.

'Oh yes,' said the man. 'Elaine and I – we're very pleased.' He shook Julia's hand. 'And it's wonderful to see the lovely Chrissie here too, though it doesn't surprise me in the slightest. She really is a talent, your daughter.'

Paul watched the way the man's eyes slid over Chrissie as she listened to what one of the group was saying, tilting her head in that way she had. Such a long neck, like a swan – it had been a nightmare finding chin rests that would fit her, spanning the tall distance between shoulder and jaw. *Pretty as ever.* He felt his discomfort at the man's words rush through him.

'Yes. Well, thank you. She works very hard.'

The man nodded approvingly. 'I'm sure.'

'Paul?' Beside him, Julia cleared her throat. 'We should make our way along to the audition room, shouldn't we?'

'Sure.' He checked his watch again. 'Right. Yes.' He waved an arm and called out, 'Chrissie! Reece!'

'Well,' said the man. *Greg*, was that his name? 'Break a leg – isn't that what we say?'

'So lovely to meet you,' said Julia. She shook his hand again to say goodbye, but Paul couldn't bring himself to repeat the handshake. Instead he put an arm around their daughter as he hurried her away.

*

The four of them made their way down the narrow, signposted corridors to the small waiting area outside the main audition room. There were other rooms open along this corridor, places where you could tune and warm up. Two doors along, they found an empty one. Paul handed Chrissie her violin case to unpack and sat down with Julia in one of the grey plastic chairs by the wall, Reece loitering awkwardly by the door. Paul hoped the boy's nerves wouldn't put Chrissie off. But they were friends, he had to remind himself, and Chrissie had chosen to have him here. Clearly she appreciated his act of support.

Paul did some finger stretches of his own to prepare. Only a few minutes of this – there would be other musicians waiting to warm up too. He checked again that he had the correct music. He'd brought the wrong pages once before. He had almost died from the mortification of it and he had never made that mistake again. No, here they were: the Bach and the Alwyn.

Julia was making small talk with Reece, asking him about his plans for the summer. Travelling, by the sounds of it. And how would Chrissie spend the summer? Playing, practising – and what else? The competition would be over by then. He thought of the glossy pages tucked in his dresser drawer. He needed to speak to Julia. He *should* speak to her. But there was such a risk that she wouldn't understand.

After another moment, he checked his watch yet again. Five minutes now, if the schedule was running smoothly and none of the players had gone over time. A twelve-minute performance: that was all they were allowed. He and Chrissie had timed it, setting their tempos carefully. Their two pieces, back to back, came in at eleven minutes and three seconds. So plenty of time, if she needed it, to breathe in between.

A young woman with a clipboard popped her head round the door. 'Christine Goodlight? Paul Goodlight?'

By now Chrissie had her violin out and was tuned and ready, rubbing last-minute rosin on her bow. 'Yep?'

The woman smiled. 'You're next. Would the two of you like to come with me?'

Paul felt a thin sheen of sweat build up, the way it always did in the moments just before he had to perform. *It's not about you or me, Dad. It's about the music.* So often, Chrissie would say that, and she was right; but it was about so much more than that too. Paul knew his daughter could go the whole way in this competition. She was good enough, absolutely. But even if she got through to the Finals and won it, the competition would still come to an end – and what then? She was still only sixteen. The next step, then. He needed to secure the next step. But his thoughts looped back round to the money. It was too much of a risk to come straight out and ask Julia. He had to work round that. He had to find a way.

Right now, though, it was hugs and kisses from Julia and *good luck*. Not *break a leg*, for heaven's sake.

'See you on the other side,' said Julia. 'There's a little window, Reece and I can watch through the door.'

The four of them stepped back as the previous performer – a cellist – came out. He looked furious. His accompanist gave a thin smile as he exited too, a tiny shake of the head. A mistake? A memory slip? It hadn't gone well, that was clear enough. Paul shivered; it could happen to anyone. He glanced across at Chrissie to reassure her, but she wasn't even looking at him, busy snapping off a loose bow hair instead.

He leaned back against the wall for a moment, closing his eyes and readying himself.

'*Dad.*'

'What?' He snapped his eyes open.

She pointed. 'Mind the fire alarm.'

He checked over his shoulder. 'Whoops!' He'd been leaning against the little red box.

The woman with the clipboard ducked inside the audition room, then reappeared a few seconds later. She held the door open for them. 'All right. The judges are ready. Best of luck!'

'Good luck, Chrissie,' Reece echoed as they passed through the door.

Inside, the room was smarter than the space they'd had in the last round. This one had polished wood floorboards and thick purple drapes to cover the walls. Three judges ready and smiling, and the piano and the music stand that Chrissie wouldn't need. She had memorized her pieces.

Paul glanced back over his shoulder, glimpsing Julia and Reece as the heavy door swung shut. Then he settled himself at the piano: a Steinway, very nice. He set his music out carefully on the stand, then turned to look at Chrissie. Her dark brown eyes met his and held his gaze steady.

'When you're ready ...' said a judge.

Ready? Chrissie lifted her violin up under her chin in one assured, fluid movement. Paul turned to his music.

Yes. Of course they were.

CHAPTER 9

Paul

FIVE WEEKS BEFORE

She played wonderfully. Paul was so proud of her; he had seen the admiration in the judges' faces and had no doubt that she would get through. For the next round he would have to push her further still, but she would do it. And he was lifted as well, ever closer to the prize.

The following morning, on his way to the gym, kit bag slung over his shoulder, he pulled his mobile out of his pocket. The walk to the gym would give him time; the exercise at the end would burn off the adrenaline that was already building. He tried not to think of what it said about him, the sense of reaching out, cap in hand. This was necessary, securing the next step. It took him a beat, two beats, three before he could steel himself to do it, but eventually he made the call.

He listened to the ringing of the familiar landline number, then Celina answered. It was almost always Celina.

'Paul ...' Her voice was crystal clear now, no hint of the slurring from the other night.

'Celina. I wanted to say thank you again for the wonderful dinner the other weekend. It was a lovely evening.'

'Well, I'm glad. Duncan and I enjoyed ourselves very much too.'

'The food was delicious ...'

'Mmm.'

'That monkfish. Julia was saying, we should ask you for the recipe.' He made no reference to the whispered conversation they'd held in her old room. It wasn't done. It had been the same in his own family. There was the surface layer, and the layer underneath. And that was how you learned to read between the lines. Suddenly, a memory flashed across his mind: an evening last week when an exhausted Chrissie was watching television downstairs. He'd come upstairs slowly and quietly, not with his usual thumping steps, and spotted Julia through the crack in Chrissie's bedroom door. She was kneeling on the floor, fiddling with something. He shoved the door open wide.

What are you doing?

She got to her feet, brushing down her trousers. *Nothing. There's a floorboard here that seemed a bit loose.* She'd repeated herself again, with a smile. *It's nothing though. I fixed it.* She'd poked it with her foot to show him.

Why was Paul suddenly thinking of that now?

'Of course,' said Celina. 'I can write it out for you.'

Paul had lost the thread. 'I'm sorry – what was that?'

'The recipe.'

'Oh – yes. That would be wonderful.' Paul sidestepped a woman with a buggy on the pavement. 'Chrissie said she had a lovely time too.'

'Oh good.'

Paul was at the junction, waiting for the pedestrian lights. As the conversation foundered, he cleared his throat. There was never an easy way to do it – open up the topic of money. You had to tread so carefully in that field.

'Speaking of Chrissie ... She and I ... we've been talking about boarding school. There's the Royal Institute where she could study. It would be invaluable in furthering her career.'

The green man flashed on and the crossing beeped with a harsh, strident tone.

'Is that so? You know boarding school was good for Julia,' Celina mused. 'And ... well – like mother, like daughter, as I've always said.'

'Yes,' said Paul. 'Exactly. However ...' The pavement on the other side of the junction was cracked and uneven. Paul slowed, taking care with his footing. 'The fees are high. And Julia ...'

He didn't need to finish the sentence: Celina understood him. 'Julia. Yes.'

He hadn't talked to her at all about the application. Julia had always been vehemently against sending Chrissie away, despite the fact she had boarded herself in her school years. *But it wasn't good for me to be away from home like that*, she'd told him. *Away from my parents.*

But it's you who's always away from your daughter these days, he'd wanted to retort.

'So that's difficult ...' He was a little out of breath now, walking and talking and carrying a kit bag. Never ask outright, he'd learned. Only hint. 'I hope you don't mind my mentioning it.'

It took a moment before Celina answered. 'Paul, you know, ordinarily we wouldn't hesitate to contribute. But lately ...

75

Duncan …' Her voice grew faint and Paul found himself straining to hear. The traffic was loud: the roar of a taxi and the racket of a cyclist ringing her bell.

'Yes? You said – Duncan …?' Paul stopped walking and pressed the phone to his jaw, blocking his other ear so he could hear. He missed a bit, caught the rest.

'… Spending money we don't really have. His mind … Such a fine mind, but he doesn't always think straight.' Celina's voice was brittle. 'He's become terribly impulsive these days.'

Paul's voice died in his throat; what was he supposed to say to that? The statement was the closest Celina would ever come to admitting anything was wrong. But was it even true, what Celina was telling him, or was this just another way to hold him at arm's length – by refusing his rare request for a favour? But he wasn't asking for himself; he was asking for Chrissie, and they'd always said they'd do anything for their granddaughter. Perhaps then they really didn't have the money to spare. If so, he had really stamped his foot in it. He shouldn't have asked. He had embarrassed her; he had embarrassed them both, putting her in a position where she was forced to reveal that. *Spending money … doesn't always think straight …*

Paul cleared his throat, with a desperate urge to get off the phone. 'Of course. Not to worry. I'm sure when I look into things, I'll find a suitable way.'

'I'm sure you will. You're a clever man, Paul. And – as I've often said – we are *very* grateful.' Her voice was stronger now, picking up its familiar authority, and Paul could almost hear the unspoken message down the line: *it's your responsibility now, I'm asking you to step up for this. You should know by now what's expected of you.*

'Understood. Well, I won't keep you. Really, I just wanted to thank you.'

'Of course. You're most welcome. As I've said, I've always known I can count on you.'

*

That evening, Paul readied a favourite meal for Julia. He needed to speak to her. He wanted to assure himself that she was okay. He told Chrissie she could go round to Reece's; it was a reward, he said, for doing so well in the Category Auditions. Though he made her promise to be home by eight thirty.

At seven, he set the formal table in the dining room, not the white kitchen table where they typically ate in a rush. He took a clean linen napkin out of the drawer in the sideboard, folded it, and laid it next to the silver cutlery. He set a candle on the table and lit it. All these things to soften her up.

Julia came through the front door half an hour later than she'd promised. The food was past its best by now, faintly congealed, but he served it to her anyway, on one of the best plates.

'What's all this?' she said, shrugging off her blazer.

'I wanted to say thank you. For coming to the audition. For being there for Chrissie.' He led her through to the dining room.

'You don't have to thank me for that.'

'A treat then. Just something nice.' He pulled out a chair for her and re-lit the candle he'd had to blow out earlier.

'It *is* nice.' She took her seat and smoothed the crisp napkin onto her lap. 'This is lovely, Paul. Delicious. Aren't you having any?'

He sat alongside her. 'I ate earlier. You know I'm not good at eating so late.'

'Oh. Well, thank you even more. I didn't get lunch today. This is great.'

Silence a moment while she took a mouthful, then a second. She was eating quickly, hungrily.

'Where's Chrissie?' she asked. 'Upstairs?'

'Round at Reece's.'

'On a school night?'

Paul cocked his head. 'Well, she insisted.' He leaned his elbows on the table, then lifted them off again, recalling how Julia had once told him it was *uncouth*. He looked across at her. 'And how have you been?'

Julia glanced up at him, distracted for a moment by a faint buzzing of her phone through in the kitchen. 'What about me?'

'How are you? How is everything going at work?'

She pushed a wisp of hair back from her forehead. 'You know.'

Not really, thought Paul, *I don't*.

'This case,' she said, bending her head to her food again. She had already cleared half her plate. 'It's intense. There are so many challenges.'

'Hence the long hours,' Paul said, like a prompt.

'Hence the long hours,' she confirmed.

The clock on the mantelpiece ticked loudly in the gaps between their words. 'If there's anything else,' he said. '... Any other ways I can support you, while work is so busy.'

Talk to me, he wanted to say to her. *Warn me now if something is starting to go wrong.*

'That's kind of you,' Julia said, her fork squeaking against the china plate.

Of course it is, Paul thought. *I'm meant to be kind. I'm your husband. You're supposed to come to me for support.*

'It's just very full-on right now.'

'Yes.' Paul watched a thread of molten wax slip down the candlestick, thinking, *you said that already.* 'I'm aware …' He hesitated, then pushed on. 'You've seemed distant lately. I mean, not just physically with the long hours.'

'Distant?'

'I think,' he said carefully, 'we should try to spend more time together.'

'O-kay …' Julia set down her knife and fork. 'Right. Well, I'm here now.'

'Yes, of course, but—'

'But what?'

Paul retreated, stung by her abruptness. The candle flame on the table flickered. He thought of their therapist: *don't do it. Don't let yourselves play accuser and accused.* Julia dropped her linen napkin on her plate and pushed both away, the way she did whenever they dined in a restaurant, a strange show of disregard that Paul had never understood, as if she never thought of the person who had to launder those cloths.

'Thank you for supper. It really was delicious.'

'Julia …' From the hallway came the sound of Chrissie's key, scratching in the door lock.

Paul pulled his chair towards Julia and placed one hand on top of hers.

'Julia,' he repeated. 'I'm here for you. You know that, don't you?'

He and Julia were holding hands – it would look that way from a distance anyway. The front door banged open, shuddered, banged shut. Paul held his wife tight, his thumb printing itself on her wrist as he tried to steady himself.

'I do,' Julia murmured.

Chrissie's footsteps in the hallway; her outline in the far doorway.

'Then please, Julia,' Paul whispered. 'Please don't throw my kindness back in my face.'

CHAPTER 10

Julia

NOW

The constables offer to drive round the city to see if they can spot her. It seems as good an idea as any.

They've asked us for a photo, and now we dig one out for them: the professional headshot that's on Chrissie's website as well. Along with the photo, they ask for her toothbrush. For DNA. The thought makes me shudder as I hand it over: the little pink Oral-B one from her bathroom. I want to put that brush in my own mouth, like kissing it. Instead, I just let the officers slip it into an evidence bag.

For the drive round, we tell them to try the Botanical Gardens, the academy and her school. The male officer studiously jots these locations down, and then heads out to the car, while the female officer stays in the house with us. Sally and Danny are still here too, and Sally has made us another round of tea. But once the front door closes again and I hear the police car rev in the street, I have to leave them in the kitchen and escape upstairs. I just need a break. I tell them I need to call my parents, who are on the other side of the world, in Kenya. Instead, I go into the bathroom and lock the door.

Once inside, I lower myself to my knees, forehead to the bathmat: 'child's pose' in yoga terms. I close my eyes and, like a good lawyer, try to compile some reasonable explanations. Maybe Chrissie's phone screen *was* smashed before and she just didn't say anything because she didn't want a telling-off and that was why she only pretended to bring it to London. Maybe she *did* leave her bed in such a state this morning, and maybe it was Jackson who tipped over the chair.

But why leave her phone just lying on the floor like that?

And where has she gone if she didn't come back here?

My phone bleeps yet again in my pocket and I drag myself upright, forcing myself to sift through the texts that are already cluttering the screen. By now, we've sent out messages to everyone we can think of, but no one seems to know anything. Just friends desperately trying to be good friends. I try to answer a few – *thank you, we'll let you know as soon as we hear anything, we'll keep you posted, we appreciate the support*. Among the deluge, though, there are messages that are missing – ones I've got so used to expecting but which now, for some reason, aren't there.

A moment later I hear Paul calling upstairs for me. *'Julia?'*

And then Sally's voice in the hallway downstairs. 'It's okay, let her be, I'm just on the end of the phone. Or tell Julia to just come round, it doesn't matter what time.'

Sally and Danny are leaving. As silently as I can, I get up and unlock the bathroom door, but I pause on the staircase, holding the banister tight, unable to face anyone yet.

The front door slams shut. Paul returns to the kitchen.

When I'm sure he isn't coming upstairs, I go into Chrissie's bedroom and crouch down. I lift up the loose floorboard – the place I know Chrissie keeps her diary, the place I easily discovered because it's so similar to where I used to keep mine when I was a child, under a loose floor panel in the corner of my room. I've read Chrissie's diary so many times; it's the way I feel close to her and it's the way I can protect her, too, and I'm always so careful to put it back in the same position, so she'll never have to know. I'm not sure exactly what I'm expecting to find when I lift the floorboard this time, but in the end it feels inevitable when I see that there's nothing there. She has got rid of it, and I find myself wondering now whether she knew all along that I had been reading it.

I sit back on my heels. There is nothing here that can help us or explain where she has gone. We have to keep going, look elsewhere, carry on. I go back to the top of the staircase, finally ready to go back down. I pause and listen out. Now there's silence below me, and I'm about to head down when there's the sound of thick paper rustling, and the female officer speaks: 'May I ask a little more about … this?'

'Oh … yes,' says Paul. 'The prospectus.'

'It's for a residential school. Did Chrissie talk to you about it?'

I feel dizzy. My heart catches in my throat.

'We had some conversations.'

'Mutual conversations? You saw eye-to-eye on this?'

'Of course. Chrissie's always clear with me about what she wants.'

I still can't see them, only hear their voices, but I feel as though my heart is unravelling. That isn't what Paul said before, when the officer found the brochure – the prospectus – in Chrissie's room, in the bin. Then, Paul said that Mr Donaldson ordered the prospectus for her – along with all his other students. Now Paul is saying that he and Chrissie talked about it. How can the police officer realize the significance of that? But I saw the cover letter and the prospectus was clearly addressed to *Mr Goodlight* and not *Mr Donaldson* – and my husband never said one word about it to me.

I drag myself to my feet and descend to where they are, holding tight to the banister the whole time.

'As we mentioned,' the female officer is saying, 'if my colleague has no luck, we'll contact CID, although they may not respond until later this morning. But your daughter may well have reappeared by then. Chrissie's a sensible girl, isn't she?'

Paul replies: 'Of course she is.'

'And listen, would she have some ID on her? In case – you know – she's been involved in an accident of some sort. Hurt herself somehow. Has she got a bus pass, maybe, or a citizen card?'

An accident? My mind races off again. Hit by a car, tripped and hit her head, attacked by someone …

'Not a bus pass,' Paul says, and I'm almost at the kitchen now. 'But, yes, she'll have ID. Her passport. She had to take it for the competition.'

He's so composed, so cooperative.

'Excellent,' the officer says. 'So that's good. Listen, like your friend Sally said, sometimes teenagers just need to get away for a while, especially if they've been under a bit of stress lately. Which I take it she has? As I say, almost always, they just show up. *Especially* if this sort of thing has happened before …'

The female officer glances up, catching sight of me in the doorway. Paul hasn't seen me yet; he still has his back to me. The officer directs a tight smile at me before glancing back over at Paul.

'... *Has* this happened before, did you say?'

We didn't say. As far as I know, no one has yet asked us that question.

Well, now she is asking.

And Paul says *no* just as I say *yes*.

CHAPTER 11

Paul

FOUR WEEKS BEFORE

The following weekend, the Goodlights held a party.

It was something they did every so often. Julia insisted on it. 'We get invitations to all our friends' houses. We have to reciprocate. That's just the way it works.'

And with Julia's schedule and long evenings at work, the easiest way, they'd found, was to invite a whole group of people over all at once. More of a drinks party, not a sit-down meal. Alcohol, canapés, music and – if their guests got drunk – sometimes a little dancing. But nothing outrageous. It was all very civilized. For years, Julia had never slipped up on that.

It was usually Julia's friends and associates who attended. They had never invited Julia's parents to these gatherings. In fact, Celina and Duncan rarely came to their house at all. Celina on occasion, over the years; mothers and daughters, after all … But Duncan? He never visited. It was as though there was something about their lives – his and Julia's – that she instinctively shielded him from. It was an unspoken arrangement, one of many among the Montroses that Paul had never questioned. So, at this party, there weren't many people who were directly Paul's guests, although there was the head of Chrissie's academy and his wife. Paul always invited them and they usually came. This evening, they had twenty-five, maybe thirty people coming. Most of them Paul knew, but there were a couple of Julia's work colleagues that he'd never met.

He rarely enjoyed these evenings. He drank little; usually he busied himself with playing host, ensuring their guests were fed and watered, while Julia mingled between groups. Chrissie usually stayed in her room.

In the master bedroom, Julia was dressing for the evening in a long, dark gown. Paul loved this dress; she always looked stunning in it. He watched as she slid in her earrings in front of the mirror. 'You look amazing,' he told her. 'New earrings?'

'Yes.' Julia hesitated. 'I treated myself.'

Paul smiled. *Saint Laurent*. He recognized the brand. She'd trained him to know such names and carefully taught him how to pronounce them. Julia returned his smile in the mirror, her new earrings in place. 'You're not looking bad yourself.'

He was wearing an outfit he'd purchased a few years ago, one of the many he'd accumulated over the years, under Julia's guidance. The first time Julia had picked out such clothes for him, his eyes had – quite literally – watered. *Yes*, she had said. *But they're excellent quality.*

She'd been right, of course. His skin had never felt material like it. And yet, even now, he couldn't always suppress a shudder at the extravagance. One jacket at a price that would have fed him for a year as a child.

Now though, as he stood at Julia's shoulder and looked in the mirror, he was glad of these clothes. They allowed him to keep up with her. Match her. It helped him keep his head up when welcoming each guest – guests who were beginning to arrive. He heard the doorbell ringing. For a change it wasn't accompanied by Jackson barking, since Danny from next door was looking after their dog for the night. Paul went down and opened the door. It was the Fairshaws, Sally and Stuart, and Paul felt a little tug of relief. He knew these people, their long-term neighbours.

'Lovely to see you,' said Sally, kissing his cheek, and Stuart's grip was familiar as the two of them shook hands.

The house filled up quickly after that, a mass of bodies and names and faces. The caterers they'd hired had done a great job. All the platters were laid out in the kitchen. All Paul had to do was carry them round the guests and keep their wineglasses topped up as well. Fine wine. Expensive wine. In the kitchen were cases and cases of it.

He forced himself to circle the room. It was easier when you were carrying a tray or a wine bottle. Then he didn't really have to join in or talk, just keep a welcoming smile on his face. *You're as good as all these people*, he told himself as he wove his way round the little sparkling clusters, catching the trails of their conversations.

Nathan will be sitting his GCSEs this year, of course. Well, yes, A and A-stars, we've been assured …

You really should try this place in Tuscany … yes, do it – just hop on a flight!

We're looking to buy a property somewhere on the south coast, for holidays, maybe, or just to rent out.

How did people talk like that about such privilege? As though it was nothing, something as simple as putting out the bins. He always had to remind himself: a fish doesn't recognize the water it glides in. You're the outsider. For you, it's sink or swim.

'Paul!' Someone caught him by the arm, and he turned. Roger Wesley, head of the academy, and his pretty wife, Emilia.

Paul set down the open wine bottles he was carrying – one red, one white – and held out a hand to greet them. 'Lovely to see you both. Thank you for coming.'

'Of course. It's a pleasure.'

Emilia leaned in to place a kiss on his cheek. 'I've been hearing so many great things about your daughter. Star pupil!'

Paul nodded. 'She's doing very well.'

Roger looked around. 'Is she here tonight?'

'Well, she's upstairs.' Paul forced a smile as he released Emilia's hand. 'Staying out of the limelight.'

Emilia nodded, kindly. 'I imagine it's a lot. Such a big competition. And she's still so young.'

Roger nodded. 'We're just delighted to have her as a member of our academy.'

Paul didn't mean to say it; the words just came out. He hadn't drunk that much wine but what he had imbibed felt thick and cloying. 'We're actually looking into other options for next year. A residential arrangement.'

Roger's brow furrowed. 'You are?'

'Not that we're not grateful. We are – hugely. We just feel she might benefit from … a more focused environment. Where she can really dedicate herself.'

'Really? But she already seems so committed.'

Paul could feel the red heat climbing his neck. It was as though he was confessing something or trying to convince himself. He wasn't sure why he was saying it to these people;

the words just ran on, falling out of him. 'We think it's for the best. We had some trouble with her last year ...'

'How do you mean?' Emilia was frowning too now. '"Trouble"?'

What was he saying? What had he said? 'Nothing. I'm sorry, I shouldn't have said anything. Please don't mention anything to Chrissie. We don't even know whether it will be possible yet. The fees, we aren't ... I'm sorry, please – will you excuse me?'

He took a step backwards, half stumbling as his shoe caught on the upturned edge of a rug. He picked up the bottles again, repeating, 'Excuse me,' as he pushed himself away into the crowd.

'Paul!' Another voice calling him, another hand on his arm. Kay, was it? Kate? 'This is lovely wine, Paul. Where did you get it?'

He steadied himself, reminding himself who he was, where he was. Host of a delightful party in their own charming home, along with Julia, his beautiful wife. All these fine clothes, rich voices, thick perfumes.

Kate was beaming at him, head cocked to one side, her lips shiny under the lights.

'The wine?' Just for a moment, Paul wanted to say *Aldi*, and see what she said. Instead he said, 'a friend of ours' – he pointed across the room to Julia's work colleague, Peter – 'brought some back from a vineyard in France.'

'Really?' said Kate. 'I'll go talk to him later. For now, a top-up, please, darling.' She held her empty glass out towards him, and automatically he tilted the open bottle. The red wine streamed too quickly, slopping over the sides, dripping onto her hand.

'Sorry. Damn. Here, let me get that.' Paul fumbled in his

top pocket for a handkerchief: ironed, white. The wine stained it through. 'Clumsy of me,' he said.

'And so wasteful!' Kate laughed.

'Never mind. There's plenty more. Here. Why don't you just keep the bottle?' He thrust it into her hand, along with the handkerchief.

'How lovely of you. You really are the best.'

Paul kept on smiling, jaw muscles aching now as he turned back towards the kitchen, his sanctuary, where he could pull out a new bottle of red wine to replace the one he'd just jettisoned, and get away from this crowd and catch his breath for a minute. He made to squeeze past another group, three men and a woman; Julia's work associates, if he wasn't mistaken. They'd arrived late, while he was sorting more wine in the kitchen, and he'd somehow missed proper introductions. The woman laughed and swayed sideways, blocking his path again, almost treading on his toes. God, the room was crammed.

'Excuse me,' he said, though nowhere near loud enough to cut through the group's conversation. A tall man was talking, with his back to Paul. Grey-silver hair was swept back on his head.

'... An uncle of mine, a gem of a business. You should see their figures. A niche company, but they're expanding into all the right places: Scotland, Norway, northeast US. More to the point, they've landed a significant government contract, something they've been pushing for since day one. Trust me, the whole thing is about to go ...' The man snapped his fingers to show what he meant.

Paul stood still, the single white wine bottle clutched in his hand. The man continued, his voice low and confident. 'My advice would be to invest fast and deep in this. You must see that everything is going that way. Clean energy, renewables. It's the future.'

Slowly, carefully, Paul set the bottle down to listen in to what this silver-haired man was saying.

'In six months to a year, you want to double, triple that? Take it from me. This is your one.'

'What about you?' one of the men in the group asked. 'Will you be investing?'

The silver-haired man laughed, and this time Paul caught his face in profile. It was strangely familiar. 'Trust me, I've got a close eye on this one. As I say, the CEO is my uncle and the founder a good friend.'

'The name again?' said the woman in the group, leaning forward.

The man kept his voice low, but Paul still heard him. He made sure to lock the company name tight in his brain.

'Anyway,' the silver-haired man concluded. 'That's my tip, for what it's worth. You can wait and see for yourself when the share value rises, but naturally, they'll be pricey by then. As I'm sure you know, it's always best to have got in at the start ...'

'Paul? Paul, darling?' Julia was calling him. There she was – his beautiful wife, her ears, her neckline bare, he noticed – she must have taken those earrings off. She was smiling at him and beckoning him over. The guests gathered around her were smiling at him too, welcoming, expectant. 'Where have you been? We've missed you!'

He left the half-empty wine bottle where it was and stepped over to them, letting his wife enfold him into her charming, sparkling group.

Come eleven p.m., he needed a breather. He'd served so much food, poured so much wine, done his best to talk to so many people and now his head was swimming. Julia was a natural at this, brought up with a social confidence that was practically engrained. For years she'd politely stuck to her limits. The perfect hostess. And Paul a perfect host.

Paul let himself out into the garden, half lit up by the bright lights from inside. The cool air at his throat was welcome. Sometimes he understood what smokers liked about this.

He closed the French windows behind him and stood in the cool night air, the chatter and music muffled behind him. Above he could see faint constellations of stars, smudged by the lights of the city. He breathed in deeply, one, two, three. He found evenings like this so difficult. Sometimes he had dreams that left him drenched in shame and sweat, a sea of assembled guests turning on him. *You don't belong, you've never belonged, what are you doing here, how dare you?* And then there would be the sickening sense of falling, plummeting, with nothing to catch him and nowhere to land …

Something moved at the end of the garden. He started. A fox? A person? He stood still, eyes fixed on the shadows. Were his eyes playing tricks? No – something moved there again.

Hardly thinking, he stepped off the patio and walked towards it – this shape, whatever it was. He pulled out his mobile and lit up the torch.

A figure emerged. Paul came to a halt.

'Sorry. Sorry, Mr Goodlight.'

The torch function lit up the teenager's guilty face.

'What are you doing out here?'

'I just – came to visit Chrissie.'

'Then you should have come round the front, Reece,' Paul said, 'and knocked on the door.'

'I know. Sorry. Just – you were having a party. I texted Chrissie a … little while ago. She said she'd come down.' Paul turned and they both looked up now at Chrissie's bedroom window. The curtains were closed, the lamp low. A shiver ran through Paul. How had the kid even got in? They kept the gate locked – had he crawled right over their eight-foot back fence? 'She never told me you were coming.'

'She was angry with me. We had an argument after her audition. But I needed to see her. I've come to … explain. Like I said, I thought she was coming down.'

'Oh. Right. To meet you out in the dark, at the back of our garden?'

The kid muttered something.

'What?' said Paul.

The kid was only wearing a T-shirt, a bright, printed thing. What did it say on it? Paul peered through the dark. *Save the Whales.*

'It's nothing. We're friends. Chrissie isn't like that. You know she isn't.'

'I don't know anything. What I see is a boy sneaking around my garden in the middle of the night under my daughter's window.' Paul fought to regain his breath. 'I think you'd better leave,' he said, trying to keep his voice steady.

'Yes, of course. Sorry, Mr Goodlight. I didn't mean to disturb you or your party.'

Paul found himself taking the boy by the arm. Holding

him harder, maybe, than he'd intended as he led him across the damp grass.

'Ow! It's all right, Mr Goodlight, I'm going.'

But there was more fear than he'd realized crowded in Paul's chest. 'You can't just turn up,' he said. 'When Chrissie sees friends, she needs to make arrangements.'

'I know. Of course. I know that.'

They were at the back wall now. Paul tugged open the tall gate and pushed the boy outside, into the alleyway that ran behind the house. His chest felt funny, as if he'd pulled a muscle somewhere. It was now that he realized the back gate hadn't been locked at all.

He held himself up on the side of the gate, snatching at breaths. 'My daughter will say if she wants to see you. For now, Reece, please go home.'

Reece was breathing hard as well, lifting his hand to straighten the neck of his T-shirt where Paul had rumpled it. 'But for the record, Mr Goodlight, I wasn't sneaking. She *asked* me.'

'Enough. *Enough.*' Paul yanked at the gate, shoving it closed again, shutting the boy out. Just as he shot the bolt back into place, he could hear the boy call out one last thing from the other side, words that were ridiculous, stupid:

'I *know* your daughter. I know all about her! *And*, Mr Goodlight, I know about you!'

CHAPTER 12

Paul

FOUR WEEKS BEFORE

On Sunday, once the debris from the party was cleaned up and all the regular Sunday chores were done, Paul took his laptop upstairs into the master bathroom and locked the door. He wanted to trust his daughter, he longed to trust her, but if anything went wrong, if he ever let Chrissie get herself in trouble again, he would be the one to blame. He would be the scapegoat they would all point to, abdicating responsibility themselves. Conditional. It was *all* conditional. He had a place in this family only if he earned it, and if he delivered on what was asked. Celina had always been able to read him. She had clocked his intentions right from the start and she held that knowledge like a weapon, close to her chest.

He had to have a plan. If there really was something, a problem, he needed to show he had everything in hand. Six months to a year, the man had said. No time to wait then. He had to act now.

Paul's hands were shaky as he worked through the steps. *Choose your platform, choose your investments …*

And yet it was so easy. The touch of a button. There the company was, listed on the London Stock Exchange. Last night, once Julia was finally in bed, Paul had done his best at his own due diligence. He'd checked updates online, scoured the *FT*, searched for every press release he could find. There wasn't much. In fact, there was very little compared to coverage of some of the giants in the game, but what he read fitted with what the man at their party had said: a small but niche business, poised to explode. Paul had downloaded the company's annual report and read through it, cover to cover. The government contract was confirmed in there. It checked out. He'd wanted that, hadn't he? Someone to point him in the right direction, and his prayers had been answered. For a moment, he was pulled back to the night before: Reece in the garden, Paul pushing him out through the gate. Afterwards, he had gone to check on Chrissie, to make sure there was no need to worry. To ask for her phone, because he had the right to do that too: to check it spontaneously as well as once a week. As he'd headed upstairs, he had passed a man coming down; no doubt this guest had been using the upstairs bathroom. Tall, silver-haired: it was the man who had been talking about investments – Julia's colleague. So strangely familiar. A moment later, down below in the kitchen, Paul had heard voices. *Ah, Francis, there you are!*

Now, sitting here in front of his computer, it hit him: Paul realized where he'd seen the man before. That afternoon with Jackson. It was the same man they had run into in the street. These little coincidences all added up, like a trail of breadcrumbs leading the way. It made him feel as though this was meant to be, that the decision he was making was perfectly correct. The universe was guiding him, encouraging him even. He sat back on the cool tiles of the bathroom floor, leaning against the soft wooden side of the bath, the tension easing in his chest, a sense of rightness and certainty replacing it. Even setting superstition aside, one thing had become absolutely clear to Paul, through his research. Every week in the last two months, the company's share price had steadily gone up.

He set his fingers once more to the keyboard. A moment later he had done it.

He'd exchanged his mother's money for company shares, all eight thousand pounds of it.

*

On Tuesday morning, Paul came downstairs at first light. Julia was already in the kitchen in her dressing gown. She was on a phone call, hunched over the breakfast bar, mobile pressed to her cheek, fingers pinching the bridge of her nose. She hadn't seen him; he was shadowed at the foot of the stairs. With no make-up on, Paul was shocked at how pale and thin she looked. Had she lost weight lately? Under the ceiling spotlights, she looked almost … gaunt.

'She doesn't mean to,' Julia was saying.

In the silence of the morning, Paul made out a word on the other end of the line … *drinking* …

He slowly felt the hairs on his neck rise up.

'Listen, I'll come over … No. Don't come here. Daddy, stay where you are … She doesn't *mean* it.'

The voice on the other end was loud, agitated.

'Please, Daddy. Don't do anything. Listen to me ... Fine. *Fine*. I'm coming. Just leave the door closed.'

Paul stepped forwards. 'Is everything all right?'

Julia jumped, startled, the phone dropping from her ear. 'You startled me.'

He pulled out a stool next to her. 'What's going on?'

'It's nothing. Mummy's not feeling well. And Daddy ...' Julia shook her head. 'I'm going to drive over.'

'You're going over there? Now? Should I come?'

'No. No, of course not.'

Of course not.

'Everything's fine. I'm just going to check up on them. Drop off some medicine, then I'll head in to work straight after.' She leaned over to kiss him. 'Everything's fine. I'll see you tonight.'

*

They had a TV screen in the kitchen, fitted straight into the kitchen wall – touch screen, iPhone compatible, all mod-cons. Paul often left it on with the sound down low for some company while he was home alone. That afternoon it was tuned to their local BBC channel, with relentless coverage of the latest investigation into the government's awarding of private contracts. Paul was loading the dishwasher when he glanced at the ticker-tape scrolling across the bottom of the screen. He immediately set down the dirty bowl he was holding and grabbed the remote control to rewind.

The images flickered backwards, then the words appeared again.

Students from another school – not Chrissie's – had been lured into sharing compromising pictures of themselves online.

On the breakfast bar, his mobile buzzed. Julia was calling. Julia never called during the working day. He picked it up.

'Paul? Have you seen this?'

'You mean the story on the news?'

'It's on the news? I just got an email. From the school. Haven't you?'

'Wait, maybe, yes – let me check.'

He flicked to his email. Here it was, just arrived. He clicked it open.

Concerns have been raised … speaking to our students … advising parents …

'We'll need to talk with her,' said Julia.

'Yes, of course.' He felt sick. 'She's a smart girl, Julia. She wouldn't do anything. Not after …'

Not after that time when he had discovered the WhatsApp group, the one she'd set up with classmates from a partner school, both girls and boys. The group on which they had shared pictures of themselves. Selfies that Chrissie had taken in her own bathroom en suite. Paul had found it all on her phone, seen the pictures and the messages in response. He had been sickened, sick. *She has tendencies.* Celina's words, which over time had become his. Now he felt the same way again. *Tell me you haven't, Chrissie. Tell me you wouldn't do this again. Tell me you've learned to control yourself by now.*

'But she's okay, isn't she?' said Julia. 'I mean, I'm sure nothing's happened. This isn't even in our area. But listen, let me come home early and talk to her.'

'You don't need to do that. I'll be here when Chrissie gets home. I can handle it.' He *had* to handle it.

'No, I want to. Something like this, it isn't for a father … I mean, she's a girl. I think it would be best.'

'What are you saying?'

'I mean I'm her mother. It's sensitive. She's sensitive.'

Sensitive? You think so? He had never told Julia about the WhatsApp group. He had been too scared that he might come right out and blame her. *Like mother, like daughter.* He had taken it to Celina instead. It was Celina who had given Chrissie a talking-to. Was it then that things had changed with the allowance? Was it then that it had been made clear to Chrissie – carefully, subtly, words between the lines – that the money was conditional? Wasn't it then that Chrissie had seemed to fall more in line?

'Paul?'

He shook himself.

'Will you let me do that? Please, Paul. I swear – I'll come home early. Let me speak to Chrissie tonight.'

*

For once, Julia was as good as her word. She was back at five to five – earlier than he had ever known – and just ten minutes after Chrissie had got home. Chrissie was having her snack in the kitchen, the one Paul had prepared for her, as he did every day. Paul had been as good as his word too and had said nothing. He'd clamped his teeth down on his tongue. Now he let Julia lead their daughter into the sitting room, softly closing the door behind them.

Paul eavesdropped. Of course he did, although he could barely make out any words, just the low murmur of Julia's voice and Chrissie's monosyllabic replies.

One phrase made it through the thick wood to his ear, though, sending the blood thumping in his veins.

I know, Chrissie, sweetheart. You're just like me.

CHAPTER 13

Julia

NOW

When daylight comes, they send a detective.

Our daughter Chrissie is still not home.

I've hardly slept. Paul has somehow, lying in bed next to me, letting out little snores while I stared at the ceiling. All night my phone has been awash with messages of shock and concern, and offers to pitch in.

We'll help put the missing posters up, one message said; words I wasn't ready for at all and which immediately made me want to be sick.

The school and the academy say they will canvas all their pupils – all her friends, her classmates, anyone who might know. A whole network is moving into action. The messages of concern and support are all very well, but no one can say what might have happened to Chrissie.

So I just delete them.

In fact, I turn my phone to silent, because these days its beep and buzz has become like a trigger, sending shoots of anxiety-pain through my chest. It never used to be like that; it used to be completely the opposite. *Completely* the opposite. Delight, excitement, but now all it generates is guilt. I think about the emails I send my father every fortnight, the ones to which I always receive a dutiful reply: *I appreciate that, Julia. Very good.* He knows I'd never lie when I send him these updates and, in all these years, I have never, ever had to. I've worked so hard to keep everything steady, balanced, harmless. But now ... Anxiety spreads to my jaw, my legs.

Sally comes round again on her way to work, knocking on the door at half past eight to check whether we're both okay and whether there is any news.

No to both, really. I tell her about the detective who will be coming, how the officers who first visited have contacted CID because there was no sign of her on their drive around the city. Sally says it good that they're escalating, it's positive that they are taking it seriously, but I feel as though it's getting ever harder to breathe because they are going to keep searching and in the end who knows what they might find?

At half past nine, the detective, DS Brayford, arrives. She is much older than I expected. 'DS' is – I think – quite a low rank for detectives, so what's happened in her life or career that means she isn't higher up by now? Questions like that swim about in my head.

Also, she's got a proper Oxfordshire accent; not the tones of dreaming spires and colleges, but the original county accent with its dropped t's and stretched a's and common-sounding edge. Her hand, when I shake it, is dry and rough, in need of proper hand cream, and for a moment I think about offering her a tube and then kick away such a horrible, patronizing thought. I married Paul and yet I can still be such a snob, and that's the last impression I want the police to get of me.

Like the female police officer did before her, DS Brayford picks her way across Chrissie's bedroom. Is it officially a crime scene now? It's not as though they've strung police tape across the door or anything; there are no people in white boiler suits setting down their little evidence triangles, nothing like that.

It's just our house and Chrissie's bedroom, tilted and torn up.

All of it feels like a puzzle that, as her mother, I should be more than capable of figuring out. But without her diary – or even with it – none of this is making any sense, and with that gap that whole stage-set of knowledge that I set aside earlier threatens to come slithering back in again. For a moment I have to sit down on the upstairs landing outside Chrissie's door, because it all feels too much.

'Why don't you go downstairs?' DS Brayford says in that unintentionally abrasive accent, pulling on latex gloves over her chapped hands. 'I'll just go through things up here again. Why don't you go down and have a cup of tea?'

Oh my God, bloody *tea*!

I ignore her; I don't go downstairs. I go into my study instead and try to check my work emails, but for once I can't focus – it's all just a blur. I've called in sick today, for the first time in eleven years, and I'm not even poorly. I had to tell my boss that my daughter was missing, unleashing yet another deluge of shock and concern.

But I haven't told my parents yet, even though I should have told them right away. Word will be circulating by now: we have had to tell so many friends and acquaintances, it's only a matter of time before the news makes its way to them, even on the other side of the globe. I've been putting it off and off, but it will be so much worse if they hear it from someone else, I know that. This way, maybe I can effect a little damage control, edit out the worst of it for them. They are in Kenya, I remind myself. *In Kenya.* They are meant to be there another week at least. I force myself to dig out the details of where exactly they are staying; I know they might not be using Dad's mobile, but I'm sure they'll call us from a hotel landline as soon as they've got my message, logging on to the Internet from some air-conditioned room. Still, I know there will be so little they can do from a safari lodge halfway across Maasai Mara National Reserve.

I riffle through the files on my desk, looking for the Post-it I'd scribbled the details on. Here it is: the hotel number. Do I send my parents an email or do I call the lodge direct? In the end, I decide to do both, and I'm lifting a stack of paper to clear space around my laptop when I freeze. What is that?

What *is* that?

It looks like a decapitated hand on my desk.

It isn't, of course, it's just a grey leather glove, but I'm frozen, staring down at it. I know exactly who this belongs to, but what is it doing here, how did it get here? I drop the pile of papers I'm holding and they hit the edge of the desk and scatter across the office floor. Did Jackson get hold of it from somewhere and drag it in here? He likes to carry things about in his mouth. So maybe, maybe … But stuffed under a pile of papers like that? I rack my brains, trying to remember back to the night of our party, whether that could explain … But that night was mild, wasn't it? Our guests barely needed coats, never mind leather gloves. So was there another occasion then? Another time that I don't know about when this made its way into my house?

I grab it by its grey leather finger, unnerved even to touch it. I just want to get rid of it; to hide it at least.

Shakily I pull open a drawer in the desk. If Paul saw this, if he asked me about it and I told him, I couldn't bear how he'd react. It was bad enough when he discovered the cocaine. I know the narrative he carries around in his head, the one I was never able to disabuse him of: that in my blood, I'm irresponsible and reckless and wild, and that I do things decent people would be ashamed of. He doesn't know the half of what I really am. Because I was never allowed to talk about it, because we would never expose ourselves like that as a family, especially not to an outsider like *Paul*. I couldn't even tell him, *my own husband*. And yet without knowing the context of the history, how can he begin to understand why I am the way I am?

But I don't think this glove could have got here by accident – and my mind leaps to the thought that someone planted it deliberately, left it there for me to find. It makes me feel as though there's someone looking in on our family, observing us, and taunting me with what they know. The thought sends a shiver up the back of my neck, and suddenly I'm questioning whether *all* of this is planned, deliberate. Is there someone out there staging all this? The disarray of Chrissie's room that was neither one thing nor another. Nothing so overt as to worry us unduly, but enough to unnerve us sufficiently so that we would call the police. Who would come and ask all kinds of questions to uncover all kinds of secrets …

I stuff the glove into the drawer, instinctively disgusted with myself as well, and I've only just managed to get the drawer shut again when Paul appears in the doorway.

I don't say anything; it's as though I'm frozen again. The papers I dropped are still scattered all over the floor at my feet. I don't crouch down to scoop them up, but Paul doesn't seem to have noticed anyway.

He takes a step towards me, then another. *He isn't like that*, I tell myself. *He isn't*. Empty-handed, I step back until I'm pressed up against my desk. Is this it? Is this the moment when everything spills out? All I can do is watch as he comes towards me. Normally I can read him so well, but suddenly, I have no idea what my husband is about to do.

'Paul …' I choke out.

'Julia.' His voice breaks. 'Come here.'

He opens his arms and takes me into them, and I find myself collapsing against his chest. He holds me, more tightly than I can ever remember. We cling to each other, helpless and horrified. I know; I can feel it. We're both desperately praying for this nightmare to end.

But I have a terrible feeling this is only the start.

CHAPTER 14

Paul

THREE WEEKS BEFORE

The email with the results of Chrissie's audition arrived a few days later, on Saturday afternoon. She came thundering down the stairs, so fast that Paul was afraid she would trip. He straightened up from unpacking the dishwasher to see her pull up short in the kitchen doorway, as though all her excitement had suddenly been sucked dry.

'What is it?' he asked.

She held her phone out to show him. He only glimpsed the first line of the email but it was enough.

'You're through,' he exclaimed. He shouted to Julia, outside in the garden. 'Julia! Come in here!'

'Chrissie!' Julia said when Chrissie again shared the news. 'That's wonderful! Through to the Category Finals.' She hugged her.

'When is it?' Paul asked, pulling out his own phone. They would have sent a copy of the confirmation to him too. As usual, his screen was open on the app where he checked his shares, day-by-day, even hour-by-hour. In the last couple of days, they had plateaued a little, jumped up, plateaued again. But even if he sold now, after a mere matter of days, his investment would already have gone up by almost a fifth. A *fifth*. It was amazing to Paul. Was this how they did it then, so easily – how the rich got richer? It made him think of those words from the Bible: *to those who have shall be given, and in abundance; to those who have not shall be taken away.* The very idea of it made him feel dizzy. Dizzy, but at the same time certain of his plan.

Paul flipped over to his email inbox and spotted it. Subject line: *The Category Finals*. He opened the message and showed it to Julia. *Delighted. Congratulations. Such an achievement.* What date? Maybe Julia could come with them again.

'Three weeks,' said Chrissie. '*Three weeks*.' Her face was pinched. 'I've got to practise.' *This* was the Chrissie he knew. *This* was the Chrissie he strove to encourage. Focused, dedicated, unwavering, determined.

'Give me five minutes and I'll come and join you,' said Paul. 'I just need to finish clearing up.' He checked his watch as Julia looked at him over her coffee mug. He didn't catch Chrissie's reply. She was already running away back upstairs.

He looked down at the email again. 'It's great, isn't it?' he said to Julia.

'Yes, of course it is.'

'Well … shall we have a fresh cup of coffee before we both have to go? You don't have to rush off right away, do you?' She was headed in to the office, but maybe they could sit in the garden for a while first.

Julia's turn now to check her slim gold wristwatch. She tucked a tiny strand of hair behind her ear – too short really to stay put.

'Why don't we sit in the sun for five minutes?' he pressed

her. 'I'm sure Chrissie can wait.' He could picture her, setting up Julia's iPad to record.

His wife looked at him but didn't reply. Such a simple question, and yet she had suddenly become so indecisive, as though his question had put her into shock. He suddenly felt something cold shudder right through him. *Won't you sit for five minutes in the sun with your husband? Don't you want to do that? Why are you so thin and tired and distracted? For God's sake, Julia – what's wrong?*

'Julia?' was all that he managed.

His question hung in the air between them. For a moment, he really thought she was going to say yes. It looked as if she was willing to humour him at least.

But instead, Julia stood up, smiling at him apologetically, charmingly. 'I won't stay long. Probably only an hour or so. And I could pick up some takeout for us all on the way home.'

Her breeziness was disconcerting, throwing him off balance.

'Sure,' he told her. 'That would be lovely.'

But he felt the dread the moment she was gone.

*

The practice session with Chrissie that morning was one of the best they'd ever had. Now she was through to the next round she seemed more focused than ever. Something had taken her over, driving her harder than she could drive herself alone. This competition. It drew you in; that was what contestants from years past had said, in their TV and radio and newspaper interviews. The best training for a future music career ... Well, Chrissie was showing that now already. She played perfectly;

she played brilliantly; he knew every run, every rhythm, every note and he barely had to correct her. Instead, he allowed her playing to sweep everything else from his head. What could go wrong when she played this well? What could be impossible when she was this good? He was on the right track. They would make it. This was their path; no more risk of veering off it; he'd set everything in motion.

There was no turning back now.

*

Later, Julia was home, upstairs in her study, but still working on her nightmarish case. She'd come back from the office after only two hours, but walked through the door weighed down with files – and with no sign of the takeaway she'd promised. Paul picked up after her, straightening the boots she'd tugged off in the hallway and hanging her scarf on the peg so that its two ends hung down equally. Her coat too … it was due a trip to the dry cleaner's. She would be switching to her spring jacket soon. He felt through the pockets, checking for loose change, used tissues. He pictured that scene in the movie when a wife finds a telltale receipt in her husband's work jacket, the one with a dinner tab that's clearly for two. But Julia's pockets were empty. He folded the coat over his arm and carried it through to the kitchen, ready to mention to her later.

In the privacy of the den, he opened up his investment account on his laptop. The share price was rising, but after the initial adrenaline thrill had worn off, Paul had done the cold, hard calculations and realized: it wasn't going to be enough for what he needed. Seven thousand pounds a term, twenty-one thousand pounds per year, and Chrissie would be there for two years, maybe even three. *You have to focus her until she's past the danger point,* he heard Celina's voice in his mind. *Until twenty-five, let's say. She'll be well out of her adolescence by then.*

Well, there was no way he could amass the full amount so quickly, but he'd calculated that if he could make enough for the first two terms at least, then Julia would see how good it was for Chrissie, and together they could discuss the funding beyond that. But time was short. Chrissie was compliant now, focused on her next round of auditions, but the competition would end in another two months at most. He needed to secure her a place now, for the autumn term.

He had already sent off a completed application form in Chrissie's name and received an email offering Chrissie a date to sit the Royal Institute's entrance exam. She would get in, that went without saying, but if he didn't have the money ready to go, what would that matter? There were no scholarships for this place, and with Julia's wealth, Chrissie would never qualify for an assisted place.

He needed to get more from his investment, and faster. Even at the rate the shares were rising, the return on eight thousand pounds could only be so much.

He had an answer, though. It only took a few clicks of the mouse. It was so strange, when you thought about it: the way so much of your money these days was purely electronic, just numbers on a computer screen, data in a bank. He thought of that scene at the end of *Fight Club*, when the computer servers of all the credit card companies exploded. It was as easy as that for the debt of the world to be wiped out.

The flip side was how easily you could do what you needed.

In a few simple moves, Paul had transported numbers from one place into another. It was a lot. This time, it was really a lot, but he was doing it for Chrissie. It was exactly what she needed. In the long run she would be grateful to him. When she was older, she would understand.

He was tired now. It had been a long day. He wanted to crawl into bed, but there was still the dishwasher to empty and the cast-iron casserole dish to scrub. He closed down the laptop and flicked on the TV. *The Apprentice*. He thought about calling Chrissie down from her room to watch it with him. She liked the show; they'd watched the whole of the last season together.

In the end, he watched it on his own. He let himself sink onto his side, tugging out a cushion to use as a pillow. Sometimes he would find Chrissie lying in here like this, in the brief spaces between school, their practice sessions, homework, dinner and bed. He'd watch her sometimes, her hair a dark wave against the cream fabric.

The dishwasher beeped next door, announcing the end of its cycle. Paul knew the sound so well. He could just close his eyes here for three minutes, five. He slipped his hand beneath the cushion, adjusting it against his check.

His fingers scraped along the edge of something. Small, soft, though it crinkled under his touch. He sat up and pulled it out. He stared at it.

It was a little white plastic packet. No – not that. It was a little plastic packet of *something white*.

It was just lying there. It must have slipped out of someone's pocket then. An accident. An oversight. He swallowed, his gums watery.

Oh, there was such an obvious explanation. After all, there

was his teenage daughter upstairs. Teenagers did drugs. Of course they did. Why should his family be any different? Why should he and Julia be spared that?

If he confronted her, it was possible she would explain that she was only keeping it for a friend. He could imagine her blaming young Danny from next door, or Reece, or any one of her fellow musicians or school friends. Then he would just have to convince himself she really was telling the truth.

But Paul didn't need to call Chrissie down. He already knew she didn't use drugs. He already knew that neither she nor her friends had anything to do with this, but it didn't help a bit because the real explanation was much worse. He felt as though the flooring was shifting out from under him. He'd been so focused on watching Chrissie, doing everything he could to keep her on track. He'd never imagined that *this* was the direction the slip-up would come from – the wrecking ball crashing through their elegantly papered wall.

He dropped his head to his knees. *I've had enough with Chrissie to deal with. And now* you *are doing this to me?* But Celina had always warned him. She'd told him from the start about the other side. It had been years since there'd been any hint of it, though, so he'd thought it was over. Instead, the shadow had been hovering, waiting. Now here it was, stealing into their lives again, with this tiny plastic packet of cocaine.

Paul thought of his wife's thinness, her exhaustion, her distraction. He pressed a fist to his mouth to keep the sounds in.

Oh Julia, he silently begged her, *what are you doing? What have you done?*

CHAPTER 15

Paul

THREE WEEKS BEFORE

He was brave though. He went upstairs and knocked on the door of her study. A second later she replied. 'Come in.'

He opened the door. 'Julia?'

'... Yes?'

It was always so hard to get her attention. 'I wondered if you'd like to have dinner? I thought maybe the two of us could go out.'

He had to talk to her. He had to steady the ship, and if they were in public, she couldn't easily walk off or shout at him or make a scene. Neither of them could.

'I have to finish this.' Julia craned forward to peer at her screen. He took in the back of her neck, the closely trimmed hair. The cut was stylish, but almost boyish. She had styled her hair shorter and shorter over the years – from mid-length to shoulder-length to a pretty layered bob – but he hadn't seen the next step coming. It had been disturbing and dislocating when she had cut it all off.

'Well ...' he said. 'How long might that take?'

'I don't know, Paul. About another hour?'

'Okay ... Well, let's go after that?' He smiled at her from the doorway, ignoring the banging of his heart in his chest.

'And leave Chrissie on her own?'

'She's sixteen.' Plenty old enough to stay home alone.

Julia swivelled her black office chair round to face him. Those dark circles under her eyes – they were a permanent feature now. How on earth had he missed all these signs?

'Listen,' he said. 'Why don't I book us a taxi and reserve us a table? All you'll need to do is pick out some clothes. It will be nice, don't you think? I reckon Lynn would approve.'

He wished right away he could take back the last part. It was unfair of him, throwing down a challenge like that and using their therapist to hold her to account. But to his relief, Julia pushed the loose strands of hair back from her face and leaned back in her chair. 'All right. Give me half an hour. Book the taxi and the restaurant – you choose.'

*

The place he initially tried to book was fully reserved, so he had to go for his second option, a classic French restaurant where the portions always seemed too small. He got changed, then waited for Julia in the kitchen. When she finally came down, she was wearing a halter-neck dress, all long ombré shading, and a bright red lipstick shade he'd never seen on her before.

'Well!' he said, the words slipping out of him. 'Aren't you dolled up!' Then he shook his head and said, 'Ignore me. Just kidding.' He held his arm out for her. 'Julia, you look lovely.'

But when they climbed out of the gloom of the taxi at the restaurant, Paul noticed that she'd wiped the lipstick off.

Inside though, things felt better. He'd forgotten how much Julia liked this place; how she'd told him that – for her – the portions were just right. He ordered drinks for both of them at the bar: a lager for him and a vodka martini for her. It was the drink she'd been holding – spilling – the first time he'd talked to her, and the drink she'd ordered the first time he'd taken her out.

'Two olives,' he told the bartender now, 'and make it a double.' He really wanted Julia to relax. He pulled out his wallet to pay for the drinks. 'Here,' he said, handing over his debit card. 'Wait – sorry, not that one. Here. Use this.' He switched the debit card for a credit.

'We've a table booked as well,' he said to the bartender. 'Is it ready?'

'One second … Yes. Are you all right with those drinks?'

'Of course. I can carry them.'

'No problem, sir. Do follow me.'

Paul spilled a little of Julia's drink carrying them to the table, slopping it over the side of the wide, shallow glass. And just like that, the memories came spooling, all the way back to when they'd first met. She and her friends had come bursting into the bar where he was playing piano: drunk, even high, a gang of beautiful people. They'd ordered champagne and cocktails, disappeared to the toilets sometimes, emerged with reddened nostrils, and he could tell at once the class they were. These people came from wealth, the kind where money was no object; the kind of wealth that came close to obscene. He'd watched them from the corner of his eye while he played.

He'd presumably looked smart, cute, in the rented tails he was wearing for the gig, red carnation in his buttonhole, as though he'd just finished a set of university exams, even though he'd never set foot inside those hallowed halls.

Towards the end of the night, he'd been playing a jazz piece, a complicated number that he didn't usually include in his set. She had come up to him, shining dark hair, bright white smile, and slopped her martini over the bar's piano. Julia Montrose. She had been twenty-seven then and he'd been twenty-nine. They'd stayed late at the bar together after his set was finished and her other friends had left for some club. He'd been exhausted by that point, desperate for his bed, but he had forced himself to stay up talking with her, letting her talk to him. She had a first-class law degree, she said, but now she was a single mum. She had a daughter, Chrissie, six years old, and no, Chrissie's father wasn't in the picture. There had been a car crash. He had died.

Paul spent what tiny amount of money he had on buying her drinks; she claimed to find him charming. They'd left the bar at two a.m. and, standing out on the frosty street, she had kissed him. They'd ended up going home together that night; Chrissie had still been with her grandparents then.

Now he reached his hand across the table and took hers. 'Julia Goodlight,' he said. 'It's really good to see you.'

It seemed like the strangest thing for him to say. After all, they saw each other all the time. They shared a bed, for heaven's sake. But she looked up at him and said, 'You too.'

'How are your parents? Is your mother better?' Natural, innocent questions, carefully leading up to what he really needed to ask.

'They're fine. It was all a misunderstanding. Cleared up now.' She let out a breath. 'You know they're going to Kenya shortly?' She pronounced it *Keen-yah*.

'To Kenya?'

'Yes. I'm glad. I hope … it will be good for them. A little time away.'

Good for us all, Paul found himself thinking. Wasn't that somehow also the subtext of her words? He was still holding Julia's hand. He took a deep breath.

'Julia,' he said. 'I found it.'

'Hmm? Found what?'

'You know. The cocaine.' Her hand went rigid in his but he refused to let her pull away. 'The packet. It was on the couch in the den.'

For second after second, she didn't say anything. Was she going to deny it then, to his face? Her hand in his was limp, unmoving. Paul felt that coldness again on his neck. A sudden premonition – or recognition?

'Julia?' he prompted.

'Please don't tell Daddy.'

'What? I'm not going—'

'It was only once. Twice maybe, that's all. It's been part of the culture at work. All these hours we do, this case. Paul …'

Not a denial, then. A minimization.

A waiter appeared and set down their menus. 'Thanks,' Paul managed, making himself smile up at the man. 'This looks lovely.'

Julia didn't let go of his hand; instead, when the waiter withdrew again, her fingernails were digging into his palm, and Paul caught her lifting her napkin to her cheek. Was she *crying*? It would be so unlike her. But her white napkin was darkened now with tears. This wasn't right. It wasn't what he'd expected. Where was her anger, her defensiveness, her carefully constructed, lawyerly defence?

'Julia?' he said. 'Julia, what is it?'

A wave of panic crashed over him, the way it always did when his footing in this relationship slipped. *Please God, don't tell me you're leaving me. I will have nothing. I'll have nowhere to go.*

'It was just a mistake, a slip-up. It was just one time and I've stopped.'

Paul clenched his teeth. 'Please just promise you won't do it again.'

'I'm sorry.'

'You don't have to apologize. Just promise.'

Julia shook her head, pressing the napkin to her eyes. 'But I'm *sorry*. I don't know why I did it, Paul.'

'Listen,' he said. 'It doesn't matter. You're working on it. *We're* working on it, aren't we? Look, we're here now.'

He squeezed her hand back, steering her away from the cliff edge. 'Let's just enjoy this meal and have a nice evening. We'll keep working. We can even book another session with Lynn if you want to. It doesn't matter what's happened before now. Julia, I love you,' he said, to convince her. 'You know that, right? Just the same as when we first met.'

In the ten years of their relationship, eight years of their marriage, he had done so much for her, given her so much, and look at all he'd been awarded in return. A beautiful daughter, a beautiful life. What was that if it wasn't love?

'… And I know you love us, me and Chrissie. I know you're trying your best, and I appreciate everything.'

For a moment, Julia only pressed her napkin harder to her eyes, the muscles in her jawline so tightly clenched. 'I do. Of course I do.'

'Then stop crying.' He gave her hand a shake. 'Come on now, Miss Montrose. Buck up.'

*

It was what her old housemistress used to say, and it worked. In the taxi home, they held hands; they did more than that. Something had been rekindled and was breaking over the two of them. At home, Chrissie's light was on upstairs; she was safely in her room. They had hardly stepped inside the front door before Julia was kissing him.

Paul kicked off his shoes in the kitchen, lifting his hands to the ties of her dress. They couldn't go upstairs – not with Chrissie there – but they couldn't wait either. 'In here,' Julia whispered. 'In here.'

The utility room, amidst the smell of fabric softener. He lifted her onto the counter top, almost blind with desire. She murmured, clutching at him.

It was over quickly, the intensity of it leaving him breathless. Afterwards, he leaned against her, forehead to her chest. He wanted to stay with her like this for ever, in the after-glow, in this tiny, secret, domestic space. He and Julia; how long was it since they'd connected like this?

'Thank you. Thank you.'

She was shivering now, her muscles trembling. She gave a low laugh. 'I need to take a shower.'

He let her slip away upstairs, leaving him alone in the cool of the kitchen. He ran himself a glass of water from the tap, trying to calm the swimming in his head and the pounding in his chest.

He tidied the kitchen, the snug and the sitting room, settling back into himself all the time. Then he set his used glass in the dishwasher and made his way upstairs to Chrissie's room.

He knocked on her door.

'Yes?'

'Can I come in?'

A hesitation. 'Yes.'

He opened her door wide. Chrissie was sitting at her desk, even though there was nothing in front of her.

'What are you doing?' he asked. Her bare feet were bluish. She looked as though she had been sitting there for hours.

'Nothing. I'm getting ready for bed. Did you and Mum have a nice time?'

'We really did.'

'That's good.'

'Chrissie?'

'What?' Her voice was flat.

He thought of Reece, skulking in the garden, and all sorts of arrangements Chrissie might have made behind his back. 'Has anyone been here?'

'What are you on about?'

'Well, have they?'

Chrissie pushed her chair back from the desk. She was wearing thick pink tartan pyjamas, and her skin looked red, freshly scrubbed.

'No, Dad. I didn't invite anyone round. I know the rules. I wouldn't do that.'

She stood there for a moment, waiting for him to say something else, but there wasn't anything.

'All right, then. Good night.'

'Night.' She was already turning away from him, towards bed.

'I love you,' he said. 'You know that, don't you?'

'Yes, Dad. I love you too.'

*

Later, once he was sure Julia was asleep, he got up in the darkness and went to the deep bottom drawer of his dresser where he kept old jumpers and shoes. He lifted the clothes and felt in the space for where he'd put it, keen to touch those pale gold glossy pages again.

But his fingers only scrabbled at the rough wooden base of the drawer. There was nothing there. The prospectus he had taken such care to hide was gone.

CHAPTER 16

Paul

TWO WEEKS BEFORE

On Monday, Chrissie was late coming home. Five o'clock came and went, then five thirty. Then half past six.

Paul called Julia but got no reply, just her voicemail. He texted, but how many times had she ignored his messages at work? He called Chrissie's phone again and again – no answer. His texts to her went unanswered too.

He paced the kitchen in an attempt to tamp down his rising panic. She was sixteen, sensible, she wasn't a kid. He called her school and then the academy, but the administrators had clearly all gone home by then. He left messages on the answerphones anyway.

He sent another text to Julia. She'd be winding up for the day now, surely. He sat with Jackson in the kitchen, feeling sick, giving it ten more minutes, then another ten.

Finally, at half past seven, the front door banged. *Chrissie.* Paul jumped up from his seat, hushing Jackson who had started barking. He caught his shin on the leg of the table, a brutal crack, but he steadied himself, ignoring the pain.

He heard the click of heels in the hallway. Julia, not Chrissie.

She came into the kitchen. 'I got your texts so I got a taxi. Where is she, Paul? Is she still not home?'

Wordlessly, Paul shook his head. It was a punch in the stomach that it was Julia and not Chrissie who had walked through that door.

'Let me try calling her myself.' Julia pulled out her own phone and clicked the number. She hadn't even taken off her shoes and coat and still had a thin scarf wrapped around her neck. They stared at each other, both listening as, yet again, Chrissie's phone went straight to voicemail. Julia hung up without even bothering with a message.

'I thought maybe I saw her,' she said now, breathless. 'Earlier on today. At work.'

'At work? At your office?'

'Yes. Well, walking past. You know her pink coat. I wondered if it was her.'

'What would she be doing there?'

'I don't know. I couldn't leave the meeting. I couldn't just say, *oh, I think that's my daughter* and rush out.'

I would have, thought Paul.

'I honestly wasn't even sure if it was her. And anyway, when I finally did get out of there, she was gone.'

'What time was this?'

'Just after four.'

Hours ago. How did that help them now?

'Jesus,' said Julia, dialling Chrissie's number again. 'Where *is* she?'

'Who else can we try?' said Paul. 'I've already contacted the school and the academy.'

Julia hung up and looked at him. 'Reece? Have you tried Reece?'

'I was about to.' He dialled the number he'd made Chrissie give him. The phone rang and rang but there was no answer.

'Send a text,' Julia said. 'Kids never take calls.'

Paul clumsily typed it out. *Chrissie is late coming home and we are trying to establish where she is. Please get in touch as soon as you receive this message.*

Send.

'What about your parents?' he asked.

'She can't have gone there.'

'Why not?' It was possible. Reassuring, even. Celina would set her straight. 'Let's ring them.'

'No. *No.* I don't want to upset them. If she was there, they would already have called. What about her other friends?' Julia was scrolling through her phone. 'We can try their parents. Chantal Lawson. Nina Tosca. Does she still hang out with them?'

Chrissie didn't. Not really. She only had time for practising these days. 'I'm not sure,' he said. 'Try the numbers you've got, anyway,' he said. 'But wait – let's do it from the car.'

'The car?'

'Yes. Let's drive around. Past the school and your work and wherever else we can think of.'

'Okay. Yes. Okay. Jesus, Paul, I'm going to shake her so hard when she gets home.'

It was nearly eight now and getting dark. He backed out of the drive with the headlights on. On the dashboard, his mobile buzzed and he glimpsed the text from Reece. Four words: *She's not with me.* Paul grabbed the phone and shoved it into his pocket.

'Oh, hello, yes …' Julia said into her phone beside him. 'Is that Ms Lawson? It's Ms Goodlight, Chrissie Goodlight's mum.'

Paul accelerated along Woodstock Road.

'We're just wondering if Chantal is with Chrissie this evening?' said Julia. 'She isn't home yet – we're assuming she's headed off to a friend's … No? Okay … well … of course, yes, thank you. I'm sure she is. And to you, all right then, bye-bye.'

She hung up and shook her head. 'Not since this morning.'

Paul signalled sharply, took a left turn. 'This fucking one-way system. You can't get anywhere. Nina Tosca's mum, then. Try her.'

The first time Julia tried, it went through to voicemail. She was dialling again when Paul's phone rang. Crammed in his pocket, under the seatbelt, there was no way he could get to it in time.

'Pull over,' said Julia, cutting her own call. 'Here.'

'Double yellow,' said Paul.

'It doesn't matter! Just stop.'

He jammed the car into the side of the road and yanked the slippery mobile out of his pocket. By the time he managed to pull it out, there was a missed call and a message from an unknown number.

With a shaky finger, he put the voicemail on speaker.

'*Uh, hello, my name is Alan Baxter. I have your daughter with me. Chrissie. She's here. At the Oxford Botanical Gardens. We're closing up now. If you get this message, could you come? I'm not sure about letting her walk home on her own.'*

Paul stared at Julia as, out on the road, cars went zipping past. Julia stared back at him, both thinking the same thing: *what the hell?*

*

They found her at the main gates of the gardens, an elderly man with her – Alan, Paul presumed. His whole body felt suffused with embarrassment as they climbed out of the car, seeing Chrissie in her school uniform and pink coat – she *was* wearing a pink coat – with her school bag dangling off one shoulder.

'I found her,' explained Alan, 'in one of the glasshouses. She seemed a bit upset. I got a number off her, eventually. She agreed I could call.'

They had found her, and this Alan had taken good care of her, but what on earth was she doing here at all?

'Thank you,' he said to Alan. He felt as though he should tip the man some money. 'Thank you,' he repeated. 'We can take it from here.' He opened the back door of their shiny car.

Silently, Chrissie climbed in.

'What's going on?' Julia asked as soon as the three of them were inside, doors closed. 'What happened?' She twisted in her seat to face their daughter. 'Why did you just disappear like that?'

'Nothing. I was tired.'

'You ran away because you were tired?'

'I didn't *run away*. I needed to breathe. I just needed to *think*.'

'About what?'

Silence.

'Chrissie, *about what?*'

'You want to—'

But Paul needed her to stop. It was too much; Julia was pushing too hard. 'Leave it,' he said to Julia, turning on the engine. *Be reasonable. Be reasonable.* They were walking a tightrope. Grip too hard and you would lose all control. 'She's exhausted right now. We'll talk tomorrow. Not now. Let's just all get back home.'

Paul was shivery. He hadn't eaten since noon. He had to return them all to the warmth and familiarity of home, and tomorrow they would smooth everything over. It was dark now, the city full of red taillights. Twenty minutes and they'd be back home. Chrissie was a good girl; let her be a good girl.

In the passenger seat, Julia was texting Ms Lawson. *False alarm*, she'd be writing. *Sorry to disturb!*

The tyres crunched on the gravel as he turned into their drive. The clever security light snapped on. He switched off the engine and got out, heading to the house to unlock the front door. Julia followed with Chrissie, carrying her heavy school bag for her. He shoved the door open and Jackson jumped up to greet them, barking, paws on Paul's stomach, happy tongue hanging out. The strength suddenly gone from him, Paul crouched down and wrapped his arm around his friend's shaggy neck. 'Good boy,' he whispered, burying his face in Jackson's bushy fur. 'It'll be all right, Jackson. Good boy.'

CHAPTER 17

Paul

TWO WEEKS BEFORE

He meant to talk to her once she got home from school the next day. In the morning, she had got up late, bolted her breakfast and escaped from the house before he'd had a chance to say a word.

He gave it half an hour, until five fifteen, holding himself back while she went upstairs to get changed. He had to tread carefully, walking that tightrope. He had to re-set the boundaries without pushing her away.

Counting down the minutes, heart quickening, he texted Julia:

She's home. I'm going to talk to her now.

Thank you, she replied. *I'm trying to get away, but I can't yet.*

Paul clicked his phone off and went upstairs. He found Chrissie in her bedroom, a black bin-liner clutched in her hand.

'What are you doing?' he said.

She glanced at him, but then half turned away again. 'Having a clear out.'

'Really?'

She opened a drawer in her desk and rummaged through it. 'Yes.'

He stepped into her room without asking. Sometimes it was better to simply take charge.

'Chrissie? Listen. About last night. Really, you can't do that. You cannot just go off in that way.'

She had picked up a can of hairspray and was reading the text on the back. 'I'm sorry.'

'So what happened? What was it about?'

'I needed space.'

'Well, yes. You said that.' Paul could almost see the words, like a cast-iron edict, floating in the space between them. *We have one goal; we have one focus. Everything else we push out of the way. That's the way it works and it always has done. How else do you think we got this far? How else do you think we're going to keep going? You can't capsize this ship when we're so close to succeeding. You cannot break our agreement now.*

'If you need a break, some respite, then you should communicate that,' he spelled out to her. 'To me or your mother. You don't go off without telling anyone where you are. You have a lot people supporting you who have put a lot of time and money into getting you to where you are now.'

'You mean, like you. You mean like *Grandma*.'

'Certainly, your grandmother.'

She went on throwing things into the black bag. 'Yes, but sometimes there are things that aren't *music*. Not everything is auditions and practice and *Bach*.'

Next to her, on the desk, her mobile phone buzzed. It was face down, but Paul still made out the lock screen lighting up.

'Chrissie.'

'What?'

'I should check that.'

'Uh-huh.' But she didn't hand it to him.

'*Chrissie?*'

This time, he saw her flinch. 'Okay, listen. Last night? It was about Reece. That's why I took off, what I needed to think about. That's all. He's gone travelling, and I miss him. After my audition, we argued – then he left.'

Her words made sense – and hadn't Reece said something similar? And yet ...

The phone buzzed again on her desk. She scooped it up without even checking it.

'Chrissie? Let me see that.'

'Why? It's nothing.'

'*Because*, Chrissie, we have rules about this.'

Still she didn't hand it over, and Paul's stomach plunged. 'Chrissie,' he said quietly, softly, firmly, 'give it to me.'

In the end, he had to pull it out of her hand.

He took it through into the master bedroom, where she should have left it for him on Friday night. It seemed, somehow, they had both forgotten. He didn't even need to unlock the screen before a whole cascade of messages flooded in.

He dropped the phone onto the bed as though it had scorched his hand, wiping his palm again and again on his jeans. He wanted to throw up. He wanted to vomit.

He yanked open the door. 'Chrissie!' he yelled across the landing. 'Chrissie, get in here.'

He went back to stand in the middle of the room, arms folded, heart pounding against his ribs. She was already crying when she came through the door.

'Don't do that, Chrissie. Don't *cry*.'

'It's not what you think,' she was saying, through her tears.

'These messages?!' He read them out to her.

Hey there, slutbitch.

I'll stick it in you.

I'll give you what you've asked for.

Little whore.

She covered her face with her hands, shaking her head.

'Jesus Christ, Chrissie, what have you been doing?'

'Nothing! It's not what you think. It's not my fault, I can't stop them!'

'Oh my God. Just get out. Get out of here for a moment. I need a minute. Go down to the kitchen and wait for me there.' He had to calm down. He had to compose himself. What was this in him – the hideous desire to shake her, hit her? Why was his shock twisting into such rage? She was his daughter, he was there to protect her, but instead he wanted to throw her across the room.

He could hear her still crying as she made her way downstairs. He paced the bedroom, bashing the heel of his hand against the walls. He hated it. He hated having to stand up to her – *for* her – like this, shortening the reins on her time and again. Why couldn't he let go of everything and throw the doors wide open, leave her free to do whatever she might want? But you couldn't, could you? Look at the mess his father had made when given free rein, draining the bank accounts because he just couldn't help himself. Paul had learned first hand: some people can't control themselves. Some people need someone else to step in. Look how Julia had been. Now look at *Chrissie*, involving herself again in something so disgraceful, despite all his efforts to keep her on track. Why was she like this? Why couldn't he stop her? Why did she keep putting herself in situations like this and making such hideous, horrible mistakes?

Eventually, he picked up the phone again and unlocked the screen. This time he made himself sit down on the bed the way he normally did, and go through the messages properly, one by one.

This time, as he read, it started to make sense, and the anger in his chest changed to something else – pity? He shook his head, his muscles growing weak. How could he have missed this, after all the care he took to supervise everything she did? Why had she not told him? What kind of father was he, to have no idea this was going on?

He managed to take himself downstairs, where Chrissie was sitting at the kitchen table, her arms clasped around Jackson's neck. The dog panted happily up at Paul as he set the phone down on the table.

Slowly, she looked up at him.

'Why are they doing this?' he said.

Chrissie wiped the tears from her eyes. 'Because I tried to stick up for him.'

'For Reece?'

'Yes.'

'These boys were bullying him.'

'Yes. I tried to get them to stop.'

'And now this.'

The messages were disgusting. They were *designed* to disgust – and silence and shame.

'Yes.'

He picked up the phone again. 'We can report this, you know. To your teachers. Probably even the police.'

'I don't want to do that. It'll only make things worse.'

Paul was silent for a moment, taking it all in. 'Is that why Reece left, even before the summer? Because of the bullying?'

'I think so. Partly.'

'And you miss him. Plus – all of this.' He was an idiot for getting it so wrong.

Chrissie hesitated then shrugged, burying her face back in the fur of Jackson's neck. He stared at her, trying to see past his fear and instincts. He tried to see her as just *Chrissie*, his daughter. Just a girl, and – right now – a target for bullies. *Talk to her like that. Listen to her.*

He drew a breath. She was so tiny, his daughter. 'Listen, Chrissie. I'm sorry I shouted. I'm sorry I got completely the wrong end of the stick.'

'It's all right. I forgive you.'

Well, wasn't that right – that he needed forgiving? Yet her words landed strangely; the casual magnanimity seemed to disguise a sharp edge. She went on hugging Jackson, but she was no longer meeting Paul's eye.

'You know that we can block these numbers,' he continued. 'And if you want me to come into school about this, then I will.'

Silence, except for Jackson's happy breathing. 'Like I said. It's okay. I guess if you just block them ...'

She seemed calm now, all her tearful protestations gone. Was that why something still didn't feel right ... or was he just so used to scouting between the lines? Had he become incapable of trusting someone, incapable of taking what his daughter said at face value?

Rounding the table to crouch down beside her, he took in the scent of her strawberry shampoo and gum.

'All right then. Let's make sure to block all of them.' He set the phone on the table between them. 'Here. Look at me. Let me show you how.'

*

That evening, when Julia got in, it was a kinder story Paul chose to tell her: their daughter was upset about missing her best friend.

'Oh gosh … I remember,' his wife said as she tugged off her tight shoes. 'Reece was talking about it at the Category Auditions, wasn't he? I didn't think. Poor Chrissie. I didn't know how she was feeling.'

'It's not your fault. I didn't know either. She should have told us instead of running off.'

'Well, thank you for talking with her. I'll go up and see her, shall I?'

'No. Not now.' He didn't want to worry her. 'She's finally doing her homework, I think.'

'Are you sure?'

'Yes. She's fine. We had a good talk, and then a good rehearsal. She knows she shouldn't have worried us like that.'

'I'll just put my head round the door.'

'Honestly, Julia.' *Please just leave it.* 'I really think it's best right now if you don't disturb her.'

'Okay. Okay.' She was too tired to fight him. 'I feel so bad, Paul. I try. I know I'm not always here and I just – I wish I'd known.' She dropped her head into her hands. 'All day at work I've been so worried. And now ... I'm just exhausted, Paul.'

He let his hands come to rest on her shoulders. 'It's all okay. Honestly. She's fine, don't worry. Look, stay there and I'll draw you a bath.'

As he ran the taps in their clean, elegant bathroom, the swirl of the water and the lavender bubbles calmed him. It was fine. No harm had come from this incident. He had got to the bottom of things, finally dragged the nasty facts into the light. No need to worry Julia, and definitely no need to involve Celina in this.

When the bath was ready, he called down to his wife. Chrissie's door was still closed; when he pressed his ear to the wood, he could make out the sound of her laptop keys tapping. Homework. She would leave her assignment on the bed for him to check later.

He brought his wife's towel and bathrobe through from the bedroom and let her check that the temperature of the water was right.

'Enjoy,' he said as she stepped out of her work clothes. 'Take your time.'

'Thank you, Paul.'

'You're welcome.'

Everything was fine now. He blew a kiss as he closed the door behind him, hearing the little *click* as Julia slid the tiny gold bolt into place.

CHAPTER 18

Paul

TWO WEEKS BEFORE

In the confusion of it all, Paul had forgotten about the planned visit from the competition film crew. A recorded interview had been mentioned in the email that Chrissie had received after her audition, but all the other things had knocked it clean from his mind. It was a complete fluke that all three of them were home that Saturday when the cheery producer called and said they'd be arriving within just half an hour.

The producer's name was Upsana and she had one of those bright, friendly faces that Paul had come to associate with all the people connected with *Young Musician of the Year*. Encouraging, enthusiastic, pastoral.

It was a breezy but clear, sunny day, making it perfect for filming outside. However, first they wanted shots of Chrissie in her practice room. After all, it was an impressive space, Upsana declared once they made it upstairs. They crowded in with their cameras and mics and cables and stands. They seemed to have so much equipment, all of it being dragged through their house, leaving score lines in the carpets and scuffs on the tiles. Such an intrusion. An invasion of sorts.

'Do you want to play us something?' said Upsana to Chrissie once everything was finally set up. 'You don't have to, of course, only if you want.'

Chrissie nodded. 'Yes, of course, no problem.'

Despite the last-minute rush, she was dressed smartly, stylishly – in a long skirt this time, but with the same cream blouse she'd worn for her last audition. Her hair was caught up in a high, neat bun, with not a single strand out of place.

'Lovely,' said Upsana. 'Whenever you're ready.'

To Paul's surprise, she picked one of her hardest pieces: a score they'd considered for the competition, but then set aside. The music curled as she propped it on the stand, needing clipping into place, and he wanted to tell her to choose something easier: something she could enjoy and play just for fun. Under the scrutiny of the film crew, she was supposed to display how much she loved all this – how it was her passion, her life's dream. Instead, she was preparing to play a passage she'd only recently – barely – mastered, as though she was trying to prove something to herself – or to him? *See? Look, Dad, I can do this. Honestly, I'm good enough.* As she set her bow to the strings, Paul clenched his jaw, expecting and dreading the mistakes – but in the end there were none. Just a sheen of sweat on her forehead and a stiffness to her movements as she lowered her violin, muscles contracted from concentrating so hard.

Upsana clapped her hands. 'Lovely! All right then.' She hadn't noticed – or was ignoring? – the strain on Chrissie's face. 'Some shots of you now, Paul, at the piano? It's such a nice touch. The father–daughter team!'

Paul did as she directed, pulling out the accompaniment for an old piece in Chrissie's repertoire. It was an easy one for both of them these days, something they usually only bothered with to warm up, and yet his fingers were clumsy, tangling with the keys. He embarrassed himself with how badly he played.

'Perfect,' declared Upsana, regardless, checking back through the footage.

'Do you want a bit of us both playing together?' said Paul. Father and daughter. That was how it should be; that was their whole 'story'. That way, he was sure he'd play better.

'Sure!' said Upsana. But Chrissie was already packing her violin away.

'Never mind,' said Upsana. 'Shall we do the interview now instead? Out in the garden? We'll have your mum join us too, shall we? And' – she laughed as Jackson came bounding up the stairs – 'your dog?'

Paul closed the piano lid and they headed back downstairs.

They set the camera up on the patio and the three of them sat together on the garden bench, Paul, Chrissie and Julia. Jackson sat on the ground beside them, panting, Paul surreptitiously restraining him on the lead.

Upsana had her own little fold-out stool. 'I take it everywhere with me,' she laughed. 'You never know when you'll need to sit down!' She crossed her legs while the cameraman dangled a fuzzy microphone above them. Paul found himself glancing over to check whether the garden gate latch was bolted shut.

'So,' Upsana began. 'Chrissie, have you always wanted to be a musician?'

Chrissie had always been good at interviews and speaking in public, her natural poise tending to shine through. He had every faith in her this time too. When the notice of the filming had first arrived, with details of the interview questions in advance, Paul had written out notes for her. A sort of loose script. Thankfully the camera wouldn't be able to pick up the tang of sweat from her exertions earlier, exacerbated now by the warmth of the day. Paul noticed though. And surely Julia did too.

'I suppose so,' Chrissie was saying. 'I began playing when I was six. It was my grandmother's idea.'

'*Very* young!' exclaimed Upsana. 'And what about your parents?' She smiled at each of them. 'Are they musical too?'

'Well, my mum loves Abba.'

That was well played, thought Paul, that little joke he'd suggested. She'd delivered it just the way they'd rehearsed.

'... But my dad is a musician, like me. We practise together. He plays the piano.'

Upsana knew all of this already, of course; Chrissie understood that. She knew she needed to say it all to camera.

'And who are your biggest musical inspirations?'

Paul had made a list of names for her too. He knew her so well; they talked about her inspirations all the time.

'There's so many,' Chrissie said now, twisting her hands together as though struggling to think when, really, all she had to do was remember. 'Nicola Benedetti is an inspiration, of course. I'm also inspired by other performers, like the stage presence of Taylor Swift.'

He couldn't fault the content of what she was saying, and yet she was so stiff. What was it – was she just trying too hard? But when Chrissie tried hard, she was usually brilliant. This was something different, something he'd rarely seen: she seemed agitated and distracted, as though there was something else clawing at her thoughts, some other pressure she was fighting against. Something he'd missed, something he didn't know about …

'And in five years' time?' said Upsana.

Chrissie coughed. 'Sorry.'

Upsana smiled. 'Not at all. We'll edit.' She checked with the cameraman, who nodded to confirm. 'So, Chrissie, in five years' time …'

Chrissie coughed again, but this time it was different: more like a gasp.

'Chrissie?' said Julia. 'Are you okay?'

Chrissie shook her head. Her breath wheezed, caught, wheezed again. She didn't speak. It seemed she *couldn't* speak.

'Oh my goodness.' Julia jumped up.

'What is it?' said Paul. 'What's happening – did you swallow something?' He was on his feet now as well.

Upsana was off her stool and squatting down beside their daughter, as Chrissie bent forwards over her knees.

'Get it out,' Paul exclaimed. 'Get it out!' Jackson barked frantically. Paul had to use all his strength just to keep him still. 'Julia – hit her on the back. Hard. You need to dislodge it.'

'Breathe out,' Upsana was saying. 'It's okay, breathe *out*.'

'How can she breathe?' said Paul. 'She's choking!'

'She isn't …' said Upsana. 'It's anxiety.'

Paul stepped back. He could hear Chrissie's breath again

now, wheezing out, wheezing in. Julia sat back down beside Chrissie on the bench.

'It's a panic attack,' Upsana said. 'That's it, just keep breathing. In for four, out for six.'

Julia put an arm around their daughter. 'It's all right,' she was saying. 'It isn't dangerous. You're fine.'

Chrissie was coming back to herself now, her shoulders relaxing, her breathing easing.

'Have you had a panic attack before, Chrissie?' Upsana asked Chrissie.

Paul answered for her. 'No,' he said. 'You haven't, have you, Chrissie? Never.'

'It can be stress-related,' said Upsana. 'My sister used to get them. She said it felt like her whole throat closed up. I'm so sorry' – she rested a hand on Chrissie's knee – 'if today's been a bit much.'

Chrissie shook her head. 'No. It's fine.' Her voice was raspy. 'It wasn't the interview. I'm fine, honestly. I guess it just happens.'

Upsana shot a nervous smile at Paul. 'Well, we've got plenty of lovely footage. So don't worry at all about that. We can call it a day. You've done great, Chrissie. Honestly, we've got everything we need.'

*

'What was it, do you think?' Julia asked Paul later, once the film crew had packed up and left them in the bright cool of their kitchen. Chrissie was upstairs having a lie-down. 'Do you think we should take her to see the GP?'

'I don't know. I mean, maybe – if it happens again. It will probably just be a one-off though. Like Upsana said, just anxiety with the TV crew and all that attention. It probably surprised Chrissie to feel like that because she's never nervous on stage.'

He was trying to reassure her and reassure himself: unexpected anxiety. A brief moment of panic. Surely that was all it was. But still his heart pounded. Something else kept flickering through his mind too: something he couldn't make sense of or place. The other day, he'd returned home from his early evening walk with Jackson to find a scent in the air of the kitchen: woody, intense, familiar, but he couldn't give it a name. He'd just had the sense that someone had been here: across the tiles, he'd spotted tiny flecks of dried mud.

The smell was gone now; the mud flecks too. But as he brushed invisible crumbs from the worktops in the afternoon light and straightened the tea towels that were already straight, the sight of his daughter, suffocating, fists clenched, knuckles white, went on playing and playing through his head.

*

It was later that he saw the bruises.

On the underside of her jaw, plus something just to the side of her chin. Bluish-green, perhaps not quite a week old.

She was in the bathroom, removing her make-up with sweeps of a cotton pad.

'What's that?' he said, stepping up close.

'What's what?' Julia said.

He turned her sideways so she could see for herself. 'There.' He pointed. 'Right there, on your jaw.'

She was surely able to see them now in the mirror, under the unforgiving lights of their en suite: a cluster of bluish-green blotches. She tilted her head, peering closer, then lifted a hand up to cover the skin.

'Oh!' she laughed. 'The other day we were moving a – what do you call it? – flip-chart in the office. You know, the one on those stupid stands, and it slipped and caught me …' She gestured. 'Gave me a bit of a whack.' She rubbed at the marks. 'I'm surprised you can see anything though. It doesn't actually hurt now.'

But as she snapped off the light above the sink and turned away from him, in the sudden gloom he found himself dizzy, as the thought flitted up the staves of his mind: *those looked like finger marks on her neck.*

CHAPTER 19

Julia

NOW

An hour later, DS Brayford tells us she needs to head back to the station. She or one of her colleagues will come back later today to update us, but for now she needs to see how the officers have got on with contacting the transport police and to chase up the CCTV from the concert venue that they've requested too. They've got Chrissie's phone and laptop to review as well.

Paul and I are back downstairs in the kitchen now, trying to do the right thing: making ourselves available while keeping out of the way. I try to slow my breathing. I had forgotten about that. Chrissie's phone. There will be so much on there. Phone records, text messages. Teenagers do so much on their phones these days. Her phone could reveal all kinds of information but I'm no longer sure I want the police to go digging. I don't think I want them involved any more. I wish now that we had ignored official instructions and just looked at her phone by ourselves, never mind the smashed screen. We might have found her already. There could be a text on there, literally from last night, that would tell us everything we need to know. But it's too late: DS Brayford has them packed up. All of this is out of my hands.

As she leaves, the detective closes the front door carefully behind her, not letting it bang, the way Chrissie would.

Now Paul and I are left alone with each other.

As though on autopilot, Paul starts getting on with the usual tasks of the home – the things I'm never normally around to see him do. Sometimes I forget how much it involves to keep this house running as smoothly as it does, and it's a stark reminder for me to see him do it now.

He puts a load of laundry on. Some of Chrissie's clothes are in there. Those clothes will smell of her now, but if they're cleaned, they won't any more. I almost want to tell Paul not to wash them, because what if Chrissie doesn't come back …? I open my mouth to tell him to stop, but it's already too late as water floods the drum.

Now Paul is lugging out the vacuum cleaner to clean downstairs.

'Should you do that?' I ask him. 'What if we aren't supposed to? What if we might be disturbing evidence?'

He looks at me then looks at the parquet floors. 'Should I call and ask her?' he said. 'DS Brayford?'

'Yes. No. I don't know.'

Paul drags the Dyson back into its cupboard. 'I'll leave it for now. Better safe than sorry, and the floors are clean enough.' He's always done such a good job of the housework. 'I'll make us some more tea,' he says instead.

'Here.' I jump up. 'Let me clear these.' For something

148

– anything – to do, I gather up last night's used mugs from the table, pouring the cold, half-drunk tea down the sink. While Paul switches the kettle on and digs out yet more teabags, I carry the dirty cups through into the utility room, memories flickering of what happened in there – what we did only a few weeks ago. I tug open the door of the dishwasher; of course Paul has emptied it, he never lets crockery remain stacked up in there for long. I pull out the upper tray, ready to arrange the tea mugs, a simple task that even I should be able to manage. Instead, the tray sticks, the mechanism jammed.

Still holding my clutch of heavy porcelain mugs, I bend to see what's making it stick. There's something tangled in the plastic slats, and I reach my free hand in to unhook it, fingers closing on a cool, thin string of metal. It scrapes as I drag it out, pulling the tray with it, then comes loose with a jerk.

I stare down at what I'm holding in my hand. I recognize it. It's hers.

*

I drag Paul outside; I hardly know why. I'm acting as though our house is bugged and we can only speak in the garden in case we incriminate ourselves. Outside, it's sunny and breezy, not unlike that day when the TV crew came. That feels like years ago now, but it was only a matter of weeks. Jackson barks, demanding to come out to join us too. If only our dog could talk. I need to know what the hell happened here.

The sun and the space outside calms me a little, although I've still got the necklace clutched in my fist. Now I open my hand to show him.

'What's that?' he says. The breeze whips his hair in wild strands about his face.

'You don't know it?'

Paul shakes his head.

'It's my mother's.'

'Okay. Well, what are you doing with it?'

'I found it. Does she come here? Does Celina visit our house, Paul, when I'm not around?'

I'm watching like a hawk to see his reaction. I expect him to frown and look confused. Instead, the colour washes from his face, only to be replaced a second later with a bright red flush.

'Is that how it works, Paul? Does she come here and help you? Does she come with Duncan? How long have the two of you been meeting behind my back?'

'It isn't like that—'

'Then what is it? How else would my mother's necklace find its way into our dishwasher?'

'The *dishwasher*? Are you kidding me?'

'That's where I found it ...'

'Jesus, Julia. You know your mother. I'm not sure she's ever stacked a dishwasher in her life.'

I flinch at his words, the sharp reverse snobbery, digging a blade into one of our painful fault lines. 'Really, Paul?'

'Well – you're standing here accusing me of what?'

It feels as though I'm accusing him of everything, except I am slowly joining the dots. The necklace didn't fall in there by accident, did it? It's evident to me now that things *all through* our house were staged. I suspected it before, but now I'm almost certain. Just like Chrissie's bed and the glove and her phone, this necklace was placed where someone would find it;

it was left in the dishwasher, of all places, presumably so that *Paul* would find it. Because Paul is the one who deals with all of that: dirty dishes, laundry, cooking, cleaning. It was only chance that – for once – I took over the task.

I should push him on all of this – my mother's necklace, the prospectus, what it all means. But now I'm wondering whether I can trust him. I'm asking myself whether he should trust me. In that moment, I want to tell him everything. Everything that has happened and everything that I have done. I've been longing to for weeks; I almost did, that night when he took me out for dinner and held my hand, and I cried. But how can I? It would be so much, too much, when we're facing such a crisis right now.

I can sense Paul fighting with himself as well, torn between yelling at me or forgiving. In the end, he draws back, and it makes me wonder again what secrets of his own he is keeping. 'For God's sake, Julia. We're supposed to be *finding Chrissie*.'

'I know, but—'

'No! I can't. I *can't*.' He spins away from me and back towards the house, slamming the French doors shut with a bang.

I press a fist to my mouth. He's completely right. Chrissie is missing. Our daughter could be lost or harmed and terrified. She has always been the glue that binds our marriage, the lynchpin keeping everything in place.

After all, look what's happening to us now that our beloved daughter is gone.

CHAPTER 20

Paul

ONE WEEK BEFORE

Two days later, after walking Jackson, Paul came home to find his mother-in-law at the breakfast bar. He did a complete double-take, while grappling to prevent the dog jumping up.

'Paul,' Celina said. 'How nice to see you.'

'Here, wait. Let me put him out in the garden. I'm sorry. He's got mud all over his paws.'

Celina sat, watching him all the while.

Once Jackson was safely outside, Paul closed the French windows. 'What brings you here?'

'Oh!' She raised her eyebrows wryly. 'Am I not allowed to pop round?'

'Yes, of course you're always welcome. But I wasn't expecting you.' He pulled out his phone. 'Did you call?'

'No, Paul. I just came to visit.'

But it would have been a half-hour drive, and he'd been out. She had a key, clearly, but she could have found herself alone here for hours.

'Do you want tea? Fruit juice, a snack of some sort?'

'No, thank you. I made myself a coffee earlier.' She showed him her empty mug. 'You have a rather … niche taste in beans.'

He let it slide. What was the point anyway? 'Do you mind if I get myself a glass of water?'

Celina waved her hand, ironically. 'Be my guest.'

He drank it quickly, feeling her eyes on him. He was flushed, dishevelled, hungry, off guard. He set the glass down.

'Well, it's good to see you too. Was there something particular you came for?'

'Not really.' Her eyes slid away, strangely. 'I just decided to get out of the house. I suppose I wanted to check up on things. After all' – and there was the sting in it – 'it isn't all that often you call.'

She was fiddling with the gold chain of her necklace, sliding the little attached pendant back and forth. If she weren't careful, she would end up breaking the clasp. Paul allowed himself now to pull out his own stool and sit down at the breakfast bar too.

'Things are fine,' he said. 'We're all doing fine. Julia's working, of course, and Chrissie's at school.'

Never mind that there were all kinds of things he wasn't telling her: Chrissie going AWOL, the drugs, the bullying, the panic attack. He really didn't need Celina knowing all that. He could really do without her censure and inevitable wrath. There'd been so many messes he'd found himself dealing with lately, but he'd been managing it, hadn't he? A good captain, in control of his ship. He tried to push the fear out of the way. He had something useful and good to share with her. She would be pleased and reassured. No need to trouble her with anything else that had been going on. For a moment, he felt like a child or a dog, presenting a gift for approval and praise.

'In fact, Celina, it's good that you're here. Honestly, I was about to call you.'

'Mmm?'

'I've managed to arrange something. For Chrissie, like we said.'

Celina went on toying with her necklace. 'Oh yes?'

Sometimes he felt so entangled with his in-laws, with Celina especially, and yet at the same time he always felt one step behind, blind to her play and the moves she might make. He thought of the message he'd once sent to a friend – a throwaway comment he'd written on Facebook the very morning after he'd met Julia. A message his mother-in-law had found years later – just the thought of it now brought him out in a cold sweat.

'It's a residential music school. If you want, I can show you the prospectus. Chrissie could be there for two years or more.'

'So you found a way, then.'

'To cover the fees? Yes. An associate of Julia's helped me out.' What he wouldn't give to take that old message back, or prevent Celina from ever finding it. He'd only been joking around, lads' talk, he would swear it, but Celina had sensed a tiny kernel of truth even though he'd come to feel so differently later.

I met this girl, fucking gorgeous, and – guess what – she likes me. Best of all though, mate, she's filthy rich.

Celina still had a screenshot of that message. How far back through his timeline must she have trawled, digging back through every nook and cranny of his life, until she found a shard of something to incriminate him. One she'd been silently dangling over him ever since. Paul wasn't naïve. He knew the influence Celina had over his wife. It was Celina who had persuaded her to study law at Oxford instead of languages. And at Oxford, not Cambridge – that went without saying. It was Celina who'd talked her out of ever studying abroad, and Julia had given up plenty of boyfriends, too, on Celina's say-so. So now, even eight years into their marriage, should Celina ever choose to unleash the ammunition that was his old message, it wouldn't be hard for her to convince Julia to drop Paul.

'An associate of Julia's?' Celina queried.

'No – well, I mean, only indirectly. Anyway, what I wanted to tell you is, this place – it's near you and Duncan. When Chrissie goes there, you'll be able see each other all the time.'

'Me and Duncan?'

Paul wasn't expecting that reaction at all. He'd thought she'd be glad, pleased with the elegant serendipity of the arrangement. Instead, Celina's face turned white as a sheet.

Paul jumped up from his stool. 'Are you all right? What happened?'

She shook her head. She leaned forwards, necklace dangling loose from her neck. 'Just a bit dizzy. It's nothing.'

'Here. Let me get you some water.' He filled a fresh glass from the filter.

'It's fine, really. I'll be fine in a minute.'

Was it just coffee she'd had, Paul wondered? Or had she drunk something else? He steadied her, holding lightly on to her elbow as he handed her the glass, trying to remember which was her bad side – the one she had hurt in her fall.

She took a tiny sip then set the glass down again. 'Thank you,' she said. 'I feel better now.'

'Are you sure? We can step outside, get some fresh air.'

'No. No, that won't be necessary.' She tugged at the sleeves of her blouse, the ones that were already pulled down low on her wrists. 'What were we talking about? Yes – this place. So you've got her a place, have you? It's all guaranteed?'

'Well, no. It isn't. She'd have to sit an exam. But you've heard her play. You know how capable she is.'

'Yes. Right. And I'm assuming that you've done your research on this place – this institute. Looked into its reputation. Its results. Are you really sure this place is suitable?'

'Yes. Absolutely. I mean, I thought …' He trailed off. 'I thought this would be what you wanted.'

He saw suddenly how small and frail she really was. He'd never imagined he would ever see that.

'It's fine, Paul. You're trying. I can't fault you for that.' She was gathering her things up: her bag, her jacket. Their conversation was over, she'd called it, and he knew better than to challenge her on that. He didn't understand, but she wouldn't deign to explain herself. One step behind, as always, he readied himself to walk her to the door. 'It really was good to see you, Celina.'

'Likewise, Paul. I just wasn't expecting … You weren't to know. Anyway – keep me posted this time, won't you? I shouldn't have to drive all this way again.'

*

For the Category Finals, Julia wasn't with them. Paul drove Chrissie to London by himself.

It was spotting with rain all the way there, the windscreen

wipers screeching across the windshield. It wasn't dry enough to turn them off, and not wet enough for the wipers to run smooth.

'Fuck's sake,' said Chrissie.

'Hey! Language.'

She was tetchy. She always said that performance nerves didn't get to her, but of course they did. How could they not, when the stakes were so high?

'Here,' he said, 'why don't we just turn up the music?'

He flicked to her favourite radio station, but she said, 'I don't want to listen to any more of that.'

She turned away from him, head against the window, yanking at the seatbelt that wrapped across her neck. Paul kept his eyes on the road. He'd checked the route a half-dozen times before setting off. No way would he let them get lost, or – heaven forbid – be late. As they waited in yet another line of London traffic, he resisted the urge to flick open his phone and check the share prices yet another time. Last week, the share price rose another fifteen per cent. A snowball effect: the better the shares did, the more people wanted to invest. They've passed the flurry of early investment now. Yesterday, at 2.05 p.m., for the first time, the weekly graph on his screen had shown a dip; earlier today, the line on the graph had stuttered: dip – plateau – rise – dip. But Paul had read that could happen and he had more than enough now to replace what he owed. It was almost better this way, alleviating the sense of *too good to be true*.

The traffic lurched forwards again, and Paul released the clutch with a jolt. As he accelerated again, he glanced across at his daughter, still turned away from him: this investment was all for her. It made him feel generous, determined, proud. The adrenaline of it though; that, he hadn't expected. It both enlivened and concerned him. Hadn't his father also been driven – addicted by this kind of thrill? Paul didn't like to think about what might be lodged irrevocably in his genes. *Like mother, like daughter; like father, like son*. Bad blood that could follow you anywhere. He pushed the thoughts away, focusing instead on the sweeping road ahead. If he didn't, there was the risk of that adrenaline tipping into fear – flickering terror at how much he had gambled on this. How much there was to lose.

*

In the auditorium, Paul felt better, back in a world that he felt at home in. He sat in the audience this time: at this point in the competition, an assigned person accompanied each of the contestants, so that none of them would have an advantage over anyone else. This might be their trajectory from now on – Paul offering his support from further and further away. It would be like that if – when – Chrissie went to the institute; he would have to accept that. But in that place, he could be sure she would be in the safest of hands.

It was another violinist who took to the stage first: a boy. He looked young – about fifteen – with hair that flopped down over his forehead. Paul did his best to concentrate, be present, connect himself to the here and now. He tried only to focus on the music. The pieces the boy played sounded impressive, and he played them with a certain vigour, but Paul knew – and the judges would know too – that it was style over substance.

Safe pieces, made more for showing off really. He had a certain talent, though, Paul could admit that. Maybe next year, he thought. Or the year after that.

A viola player next, a tall girl in a blue dress. Even from here, he could see the cameras placed around the hall – at the sides and in the small gallery that floated at the back. The TV crew were recording proceedings even at this stage. Material they could use later, clips of whoever might become the ultimate winner. Soon Chrissie would be lodged on that tape.

He oughtn't to do it, but he couldn't help himself. It really was like an addiction, though Paul couldn't recall being addicted to anything ever before. He pulled out his phone and checked the share price again, ready to ride any tiny fluctuation. The last dip had corrected itself, and all last week the shares had risen up again, as though happy to prove Paul's superstitious mind right. He had almost enough now to replace what he'd borrowed, and the relief that came with that was piercing. So much was at stake; he had jumped in deep and fast. In his hurry to secure the money they would need, it hadn't been just his mother's money he had gambled.

He had invested thirty thousand pounds of Julia's money as well.

The viola player's bow moved faster than ever now, building up to the climax of the piece. A final flourish, enthusiastic applause, and then the competition announcer, her face almost clownish with TV make-up, took to the stage with her microphone to announce Chrissie's name.

The announcer turned towards the side of the stage. Another pause. Waiting. Paul pictured his daughter backstage, flexing her wrist. She had never mentioned it hurting her again, but he'd often caught her rubbing at it, feeling it, as if testing the bones. At the piano, the accompanist shifted in his seat. A gap. The audience murmured, waiting as well. The empty moment stretched, almost beyond bearable then, finally, Chrissie stepped out. Applause swelled around him. *Jesus Christ*, he wanted to say. *Where were you?*

She played beautifully though, all those painful hours paying off. She had it all: technical brilliance and perfect expression. You couldn't fault her. There wasn't a single fault. When she finished, the applause was long and loud.

Paul staggered to his feet to clap as well. Chrissie didn't look for him, though. She bowed, thanked her accompanist – and disappeared from the stage. He stood, still clapping, continuing the automatic motion of palm on palm. She had done incredibly well. His ear hadn't detected a single mistake. For the first time in weeks, he felt relief wash through him. Everything would be okay. Chrissie was triumphing in this competition. Surely she would get through to the next round, and he almost had all the money he needed for the next stage. The next arrangement to keep Chrissie out of harm's way. It was all coming together.

Before he knew it, the judges were ready to announce who had won. Paul wanted to run through the auditorium and find his daughter, tell her how amazing she was, but already they were bringing the musicians back on stage for the prize-giving – all of the categories, not just hers. He could hardly see Chrissie among all the rest of the contestants; she was so small, even next to her peers. All he could see were the rigid, fixed smiles. He imagined these children would have rehearsed this part too. *Be a good loser. Be a good sport.*

But he and Chrissie – they weren't going to lose.

Brass, Woodwind; they announced these winners first. And now, at last – the String Category winner. Paul pressed his knuckles into his cheeks. When they announced Chrissie's name, it just confirmed everything that Paul already knew.

This was the most prestigious prize she'd won so far. Paul found himself on his feet again, clapping, his body going through the motions on its own. It was too dark in the auditorium for Chrissie to see him – no doubt she would be dazzled by the bright lights of the stage. But afterwards he would hug her, kiss her, and tell her how exceptionally proud of her he was.

On the stage, Chrissie lifted the trophy above her head, finally smiling, her arms thin against the heavy weight.

He clapped harder, riding the high and ignoring the images that forced themselves into his mind, a vision that played over and over:

A slow-motion dive of this beautiful trophy. Tilting, falling, shattering at her feet.

CHAPTER 21

Paul

THE DAY OF

They were poised for the semi-finals. The round took place just over a week after the Category Finals, and Paul was taking her, along with Julia. The car in the driveway was running, door hanging open, waiting. Paul had already loaded their overnight suitcase into the boot and Chrissie's violin was strapped in the back seat. Julia was in the passenger seat, fixing her hair in the pull-down mirror. Chrissie was still in the house.

Paul went to the open front door. 'Chrissie!' he called into the cool shade of inside. 'What are you doing in there? We need to go.' In the hallway, Jackson echoed him with a volley of barks.

Last-minute nerves, he told himself. He did his best to keep normality in his voice. Two nights ago she'd been late getting home from school. Not long – only ten minutes – but it was enough to make Paul panic all over again. He wanted to shake her when she finally walked through the door, saying she'd met a school friend's parent on the towpath, an admiring mother who'd heard about her competition success and who had forced her to stop for a chat.

'Chrissie, come on!' Paul called again.

Finally she appeared in the hallway, out of breath. She bent down to hug Jackson, pulling him to her as he barked and licked her, his claws scrabbling against the floor. 'Goodbye Jackson,' she whispered. The neighbours were going to be coming round to look after him, but she looked as though she didn't ever want to let him go.

'All right then, come on.'

Finally she stood up and stepped outside. Paul locked the front door carefully behind her, giving it a shove afterwards to check.

Chrissie had her night bag – a little rucksack – slung over her shoulders, pink coat folded over her arm, and she was wearing her Jericho Music Academy sweatshirt. Paul took the bag from her and added it to the boot. 'Got your ID? Got all your music?'

She nodded.

'All right then, get in.'

'Wait,' Chrissie said, halfway into the car. 'My phone.'

Julia twisted round in her seat. 'Haven't you got it?'

'No, it's okay.' Chrissie felt the pocket of her folded coat before clambering in. 'Never mind. It's here.'

'Right then,' Paul said, getting in himself. 'Let's go.'

But he had a strange feeling as they drove away from the house. In the rear-view mirror he could see Chrissie craning to look backwards, watching the house and the gravel drive and then their street disappear. She stayed like that until they were well out of town. In the passenger seat beside him, Julia leaned her head against the window. The bruises on her jaw had faded, but he couldn't recall ever seeing her look so worn out. She hadn't got home until after midnight the other night, and when she did she'd been physically trembling with exhaustion when she had crawled into bed.

She had gone on trembling even as he held her. 'You can't keep doing this,' he'd whispered to her in the dark. 'I can go back to work, take up tutoring jobs – anything. Anything that means you don't have to keep doing this to yourself.' Perhaps for the first time in their marriage, he meant it.

Her short hair scratched against the pillow as she shook her head. 'It's fine. This thing ...'

'The case you've been working on?'

'... Yes. We settled. It's finally over.'

Sunlight flickered through the trees that lined the road, patterning like a strobe light on Julia's forehead and cheek. He reached over and took her hand. 'I'm really glad you could make this,' he told her.

A new vision flashed across his eyes: of himself, running in the dark, running, running, running. Fight or flight. Fight or flight. These two women in his life: how well did he really know them? How far could he really trust them?

Julia squeezed his hand, and he let her do it. Here they were: mother, husband, their precious daughter in the back. Driving to their destination. Driving to what felt like destiny, for sure.

CHAPTER 22

Paul

THREE HOURS BEFORE

He drove them to the hotel first, to check into their rooms and drop off their luggage. They were early and they could walk straight to the Barbican from here.

In Paul and Julia's double room, Chrissie threw herself into a chair. She had her headphones on – big chunky things clapped over her ears. Paul couldn't tell what she was listening to. They let nothing in and let nothing out.

There was a TV, armchairs, a sparkling en suite and refreshments. He filled the kettle and cleared his throat. 'Tea?'

Julia nodded. She had prised her heels off and was sitting on the edge of the bed, running her hands over the crisp white sheets. 'Yes. Thank you.'

He switched on the kettle and yet again checked his watch – out of habit and nervousness. Five fifteen. They still had plenty of time.

'Do you want to get food before?' he asked them. 'Or after?'
Chrissie turned her eyes to look at him with a strangely vacant

expression on her face. She reached up to pause whatever track she was listening to, her gaze resting on him, although it seemed half seeing.

'Do you want to eat before or after?' he repeated.

'Don't mind,' she said. Her voice was so slow, it was almost slurred. As though she'd put herself in some kind of trance. 'Either. Whatever.'

Paul glanced across at Julia. She didn't seem to have noticed. She had tipped to one side, letting herself lean against the soft pillows.

'Well,' he said, making the decision for all three of them. 'Let's eat after then. It'll still be early enough. Here, Chrissie, have some of these to see you through.' From the tea tray, he threw across a packet of fancy shortbread. Chrissie didn't flinch; she hardly even reacted. It seemed the only real movement in the room was the pounding in his chest. The biscuits landed with a thud in her lap. She let them slide to the side and left them there. Then, silently, she clicked her music back on.

*

At the Barbican, the concert venue, they were soon separated from Chrissie as she was ushered away by the competition staff, a tiny figure in their midst, clutching her violin.

As their daughter retreated, Paul took Julia's hand. An anchor. 'Let's find our seats.'

The concert hall had that smell, so recognizable: velvet upholstery and the wood of the stage and the instruments of the hundreds of people who had played here before. Paul breathed it in, longing for it to comfort him. The auditorium was already packed when they entered and they had to shuffle past people already sitting in their seats, whispering *sorry, sorry*. The venue was huge and the event was sold out. There had to be at least a thousand people in the audience alone. Plus the camera crews for the broadcast. Plus the judges.

Finally they reached their places and Paul let himself sink into his seat. He had done it. He had brought them all to this point. Chrissie couldn't back out now, and success here would further cement her future. Somewhere near them in the auditorium, a man coughed and cleared his throat. On stage, the announcer stepped forwards to welcome them. A hush rippled through the audience.

And someone, somewhere, dimmed the lights.

CHAPTER 23

Julia

NOW

For over an hour, Paul and I don't speak; that whole time my heart beats at the top of my throat. *Forgive me*, I think to myself. *Forgive me, for Chrissie's sake. We have to remain a united team.*

I sit upright, stiff, on the bench in the garden, even when the sun slides away behind thick clouds, even while I grow chilly, then cold. I refuse to let myself relax. Eventually, after an hour and a half, I go looking for him.

I find him in Chrissie's practice room, looking down at an iPad in his hands. His hair is grey across his crown, ageing him. How did I never notice this before?

'What's that?' I ask, softly.

He jumps at the sound of my voice. Guiltily, I think, and all my own suspicions come racing back.

'Is that my old iPad?' I ask him.

Paul nods. 'I found it on the shelf. She was using it to record her practices.'

I take a step towards him.

'I assumed the police would have taken it,' Paul says. 'But maybe they missed it. It was tucked in with all the CDs.'

I cross the room to stand next to him. I so rarely come in here, but the whole place is infused with Chrissie's presence. It smells of her. It *feels* like her. I find myself looking over my shoulder, as though she might be right there behind me. Her violin case is set down on the top of the piano. I don't remember Paul, or anyone, bringing it in from the car, but someone must have done. Maybe I did at some point. Our suitcase has ended up back in our room. We used our toothbrushes from it last night.

It *is* my old iPad, I recognize it now, with its scuffed purple case. Paul has it open on the lock screen.

'I don't know the passcode,' he says.

'Shall I do it?' I say.

'No, just tell me.'

The art of compromise – isn't that what Lynn is always saying to us? I reach over and tap the number in for him without taking it out of his hands.

It opens up on the home screen. It looks pretty much the same as when I last used it: the same dull apps.

Paul moves away to the big bay window. 'It's so gloomy in here,' he says. Outside, the sky is sullen. 'I need more light.'

I let him go. After a beat, I say, 'What are you looking for?'

'Something. Anything.' I approach him at the window. I feel as if I'm following him around the room. 'Anything that might tell us, but I can't …'

He sits down on the window seat and presses a hand to his eyes. I sit down next to him and take the iPad off him. I scroll through notes, photos, the email app, Messenger, but he's right. There's nothing there. Any videos she made of herself, she's deleted. This iPad would probably tell you more about me than about her.

I let the tablet rest on my lap and dig into my pocket instead. 'Paul?' I say softly. 'I'm sorry about before. The way I reacted. But I've been thinking, trying to make sense of all this.'

She was always a smart girl, Chrissie. Quiet but observant, with that shrewd mind whirring away. We should never have called the police, I know that now. We should have dealt with this privately.

Paul lifts his head to look at me and I draw a breath, trying to speak gently this time and not accuse him of anything.

'It's my mother's necklace, but it wasn't her who left it there, was it? I mean, I believe you, and Paul … I think it was Chrissie who put it there instead.'

Paul draws a hand down his cheeks, confused and weary. 'What do you mean? You're saying Chrissie stole it?'

'I don't know. Maybe. The point is, I think she left it behind deliberately.'

'Deliberately, how?'

'I think she planted it. She's leaving clues, Paul. Our own daughter—'

'Clues? That's ridiculous. Chrissie is *missing*.'

'No, I know, but I think she meant you to find this. She put it in the dishwasher for you. It's just that I happened to find it instead.'

Paul laughs, and I don't blame him.

'I get it,' I say. 'I know how it sounds.'

He takes the necklace from me, letting the fine gold chain

run through his hands. That pendant. Chrissie has a necklace just like it, only hers is silver, but I've not seen her wear it once since my father gave it to her.

'Then we'd better get straight back on the phone to the police,' Paul says.

'Paul – no, listen, she's trying to communicate with *us*. We never should have involved the police in the first place.'

'Julia—'

'No. Think about it. The state of her room. The chair.' I can't tell him about that other clue I suspect – the glove – so I present him with these scraps of evidence instead. 'The way it was lying half under the desk? I've been thinking about it. There's no way it would have fallen like that.'

Whatever this is, whatever kind of game Chrissie is playing, it fills me with a jarring mix of relief and terror. If this is all a series of clues – the upended room, the glove, the necklace – then it means that at any moment she could come banging through the front door. Any moment now, she could walk in through our back gate, confronting us with ridiculous teenage demands and accusations. At the same time, it feels like I'm being crushed in a vice. Paul has lied to me, I've discovered that, and I'm being forced to open my eyes. Maybe he's being forced to open his too. But can Chrissie really have understood the consequences? To her, maybe this is all just some game, but to me it's everything: it's my marriage, it's my life.

'All right,' says Paul. He leans against the frame of the bay window, leaning away from me. 'You tell me then. What don't we know? What aren't we seeing?'

But he sounds defeated, defensive, and what was I expecting? That he would come clean with me when I'm keeping all these secrets from him? The words I've been holding jam in my throat, and instead of answering, I look down again at the iPad which rests in my lap. The thought comes to me. *Check the search history.*

Numbly, I open up the Internet app and click the little icon that looks like a book. A vertical tab opens at the left of the screen.

She hasn't cleared it. She *hasn't cleared it.*

The list that appears shows only three web addresses, all different pages of the same main site.

A website I've never been to. A place we've never heard of. *Camp Dìon.* Camp Dìon?

I click the first link. A home page loads: a garish, bright yellow thing. It looks amateur, clumsy, headers shouting in capital letters and clusters of phrases highlighted in bold. The highlighted words and slogans jump out at me: *Community, activism, energy crisis, renewables. 'Our name means protect, because climate change kills!'*

The words raise a rash of goose-bumps on my arms and my neck, and let loose a cascade of emotions: confusion, relief, disbelief, hope. I have no idea if Chrissie meant for us to see this. I have no idea whether this is one of her planted clues. This website seems so random, how did she even come across it? It doesn't seem the sort of thing she'd be interested in at all.

So maybe this is nothing to do with any of it. And yet, what else is there in her search history but this? I click through to the website's other pages, taking in the jumbled mission statement, the poorly cropped 'our daily log!' photos – and, above all, the location details.

'Look at this,' I say to Paul now. 'Look at it.'

He sits up, and I lean against him with the iPad, letting him see while I try to process what I've read.

This so-called camp is in the far north of Scotland – but it's within reach, a place we can get to. The whole set-up looks completely out of character for my daughter, but then her disappearance is as out-of-character as it gets. I shouldn't get my hopes up, because this might turn out to be nothing.

But if it *isn't* nothing, if it really is *something*, then ... is it possible that we finally know where she is?

CHAPTER 24

Paul

ONE HOUR BEFORE

Brilliant.

She was brilliant.

Beside hers, the other performances dimmed. There were five contestants in this round, the winners from each of the Category Finals: a flautist, a pianist, a drummer and a trombonist.

Sure, they were good. Very good. Paul could recognize the lengths they must have gone to in order to play their pieces so proficiently, and the courage it took to stand in front of an audience like this. The drummer who was wild and passionate, creating a wall of sound that felt as if it could flatten you, hands moving so quickly that they were little more than a blur. A trombonist next, pomp and bravado, the sound cracking once, twice on the high notes. The flautist with an assurance in his playing and a feel for the music, something akin to what Chrissie herself had. And then a pianist, in the slot before Chrissie. A girl whose hands were perfect for her instrument, fingers long and flexible. Paul knew a natural pianist when he heard one. She was lovely and she played beautifully. But she wasn't Chrissie. None of them could touch her.

Finally it was her turn. Hers alone. As his daughter touched her bow to the string, Paul found himself close to tears. As she played, he shut his eyes, aware of nothing else but his daughter and Julia beside him. Her intonation was perfect, her bowing flawless. The result was a perfection almost too intense to bear, like trying to look directly into the sun. It was so beautiful, so stunning. He knew that Julia could feel it too.

He gripped the arms of his seat, dizzy. It was so much, too much. She had such talent, he had always known it. He had harnessed himself to that; she had been the conduit to realize his own dreams. He couldn't deny it now; the way he felt in listening to her play made it all so clear. He pushed her, focused her, at Celina's behest, for Chrissie's own good. But it fulfilled a deep need within him too. He kept her on the straight and narrow, the way he'd kept himself on the straight and narrow all his life, refusing to let the mess of his childhood or the genes he'd inherited dictate his life. He was doing it for her; she was doing it for both of them. Right now, she was playing better that he had ever heard before. He almost prayed for her to finish because he felt as though his body couldn't take much more. He was shaking, shuddering.

And then it was over.

Her last note faded. His body went hollow, limp. From the corner of his eye, Paul could see Julia's chest rising and falling in short, shallow pants. He understood: he could hardly breathe himself. His tongue felt thick and dry in his mouth.

He could barely lift his hands up to clap. The rest of the audience was slow too; they seemed stunned. He looked over at Julia and his gaze locked with hers.

She did it. She did it.

She'd been beyond extraordinary.

Crashing through the venue, the applause broke like a thirty-foot wave.

CHAPTER 25

Julia

NOW

I'm holding out the iPad to show Paul what I've found, but before either of us can look any further, someone raps at our front door.

Paul looks at me. 'DS Brayford must be back,' he says. 'Do we show her this? It's a bloody *location*. A clue, like you said. Why else is it on here?'

'Show her? Yes. No. I don't know.'

If Chrissie is at this place, Camp Dìon, we have to get to her. The authorities need to get to her, Chrissie is a missing person. But what about everything else, all the other incriminating clues? How can I risk exposing all of that?

'Is she there?' says Paul. 'Do you really think she's there?'

I shake my head. 'I don't know. I don't know, but she might be.'

I take screenshots of the website – why, I don't know – and we go downstairs with me still clutching the iPad.

When we open the door, it isn't DS Brayford. It's the male

police officer from before who's standing there – the one who drove for hours round Oxford for us.

'Hello,' I say, my heart pounding. I hold the door open to let him inside, but he shakes his head.

'Would you mind both coming down to the station? DS Brayford would like to talk to you there.'

'To the station?' I say, disorientated. 'Wait – is there news?'

The officer opens his mouth but then doesn't answer. My stomach plummets. Surely the answer is a simple yes or no?

He hasn't answered and now I feel horrendous. If this isn't good news or nothing, then it's bad news, awful news – it must be. What has happened, what will they ask me, what will they tell me that I don't want to know?

Paul pushes past me. 'What is it? Have you found something? Have you found *her*?'

The officer looks uncomfortable, out of his depth. He shakes his head. 'Just something that's … better discussed down at the station. Can you come now?' He gestures behind him: a blue-yellow-white police car. 'I can give you a lift?'

He's so polite and nice and kind. They are only trying to help. It isn't the police's fault we have so much to hide.

'Yes,' I tell him. 'One second. I'll just get my bag. Paul, I'll fetch your wallet too.'

I find them both in the kitchen, where I also set a bowl of fresh meat down for our dog. The iPad is still in my hands and I set it down for a moment on the kitchen surface to feed Jackson. Once that's done, I pick it up again and squash it into my bag.

Back at the front door, Paul has his shoes on. I hand him his wallet and he crushes it into his pocket. I don't know where my work high heels are – upstairs, I think – so I end up cramming on a pair of running shoes instead.

'This way,' the officer says, and we head to the car. How can we help but feel like criminals? Herded into a squad car in the middle of the street! I try to keep my hands where you can see them – for the neighbours' sake, so they can see, quite clearly, that I'm not in handcuffs. *Our daughter is missing*, I want to say. *You know that. The police are helping us and we're helping the police.* The officer opens the car door for me to get in the front, and gestures for Paul to get into the back.

Fifteen minutes later and we've been deposited in a waiting area – just an office really, people coming and going all around. 'DS Brayford won't be long,' the original officer tells us. 'I'll go and let her know you're here.'

The blood is pounding in my ears. I dread hearing what they've found out. The maybe-a-clue that we found on the iPad feels laughable now. I don't even know why I took those screenshots, as if they were evidence that would help in any way.

I pull the iPad out of my bag and open up the photos, thinking now that I should just delete them. There's one with a photograph of all the – what do you even call them? Residents? Members? They look like slightly grubby university Freshers: young, uninhibited, smiling, clueless. Innocent.

I zoom in. The rows of faces grow larger, clearer. I scan the background too: makeshift log seating, orange canvas tents. Wet clothes hung up clumsily to dry on a tree branch. A door across the office area bangs.

I almost drop the iPad. The answer is right there, like a hammer banging a nail into place.

'Mr and Mrs Goodlight?'

Ms, I want to shout.

I realize as she comes towards us that DS Brayford has another colleague with her. 'We'd like to interview you separately,' she says. 'Mrs Goodlight, please come with me, and Mr Goodlight' – she gestures to her colleague – 'DC Moore.'

'Separately?' I don't understand. I'm so confused. I feel as though I've been slapped round the head, but I find myself just following her and watching Paul disappear the other way.

Interview room.

Plastic cup of water.

'Don't worry,' DS Brayford says, 'all this looks more intimidating than it is. We're doing it this way more for reasons of … sensitivity. Husbands and wives … sometimes they don't share everything.' She gives me an odd smile and suddenly I feel like a rat in a cage, heart scrabbling with fear in my chest.

I want to tell her: *We've found her – I know where Chrissie is!* It seems ludicrous, crazy, a totally random fact, but the evidence was right there in front of me, and the other facts fit. It is possible, and not just possible but real.

Instead, DS Brayford sets a photograph down in front of me. 'Now. Can you tell me – do you know this man?'

I look down. I pick up the photo. This man? *This* man?

I shake my head, but that's more a response to my shock. What is this? Am I wrong? Have I got it all completely wrong?

'Is that a "no", then?' DS Brayford asks.

So many words are crowding in my throat, and I can't seem to say the ones I'm supposed to. I look up at her. 'Chrissie,' I say. 'What are you saying has happened to Chrissie?'

'This man's name is John Francis Maitland. He was seen

with your daughter walking down towards one of the Cherwell towpaths. We also found travel searches on Chrissie's phone. Flights, train routes. That sort of thing. We picked them up on CCTV, from three nights ago.'

'This man was seen with my daughter?' I choke out the words. 'With my *daughter*?' The room is reeling. I feel sick. I feel as though some whole edifice is about to come crashing down. I want to know and I don't want to know anything. I force the words to come. 'Have you spoken to him?'

'No. We haven't been able to. This morning his wife—'

Yet another jolt goes through me. 'His *wife*?'

'Yes. She came into the station to report him as mi—'

A knock at the door. I feel totally speechless. My head creaks on my neck as I turn to look. The other detective slides into our room and whispers something in DS Brayford's ear. She looks up at him and nods a thank-you. The other detective disappears again. I make myself face DS Brayford.

She looks at me with her eyes wide and bright and taps a square fingernail on the photo. 'Apparently, your husband knows him.'

'Sorry?' I say. 'What?' I am horrendously off balance, mentally staggering under the succession of blows. *Oh, Paul. Oh God, what have you done? You really, really should have talked to me first.*

'I'm sorry, wait. You're saying this man – are you saying he hurt Chrissie?'

'Ms Goodlight—'

But I'm shaking my head, stubbornly, violently. I want to haul everything back on track again, and tell DS Brayford, *You're wrong, you're wrong, There's no way he can have hurt her, because we've found her! She left us these website links and look, right here in these photos. We told you she was last seen wearing a navy dress, and that's true, she was, but earlier she was wearing her Jericho Music Academy sweatshirt. And look – here, it's right here! In this place – Camp Dìon. It's hanging right there, in broad daylight! She never came back to Oxford. I have no idea why she's gone there, of all the places in the country, but she has!*

But before I say anything, even before I can draw another breath, DS Brayford throws a total sucker punch.

'No. We're saying, Mr Maitland is *also* missing. Ms Goodlight, we suspect that your daughter left home with *him*.'

CHAPTER 26

Paul

NOW

Paul half tugs, half drags Jackson up the tarmac of the lamplit street, the dog whining the whole way. It's windy, gusts whipping and tugging at them. The forecasters have predicted a storm. Jackson knows something isn't right; he's upset and anxious, doing all he can to protest, and Paul's arm aches with the weight of the bag of cans and biscuits he's carrying: enough food to last Jackson a week.

He has no idea how long they will need.

When he rings the bell of the Fairshaws' tall front door, it's their son Danny who answers. Croaky-voiced, acne-plagued, thirteen-year-old Danny.

'We need a favour,' Paul says breathlessly. 'We have to take an emergency trip. Please can you and your parents look after Jackson for a few days? We wouldn't normally ask, but this really is an emergency.'

Danny stares down at the dog. 'My parents aren't home.'

'Okay … well, I'm sorry we haven't been able to speak to

them beforehand, but can you just take him? I'll get Julia to call Sally later and sort it all out.'

He's already holding the lead out to Danny and setting the bag of food down on the step.

Jackson backs up against Paul's knees, his eyes wide. Paul crouches down, shucking his fingers behind the dog's shaggy ears. 'It's all right, boy, we won't be gone long. Sally and Danny will look after you, you're going to be just fine.'

He stands up and holds the end of the lead out again to Danny, half jabbing it at the boy this time. 'Here, can you take it?'

Danny reaches out, confused and reluctant. 'Okay ...'

'Thank you,' Paul breathes, hands and arms empty now. 'I'm sorry. But thank you.'

He pats Jackson's head and ruffles his ears one last time, then tries to close his own ears to the barking as he hurries away. He simply feels sick. He still cannot believe what he was told: about a man, about *this man*. It's all his worst fears. It's his worst nightmare: it's all the dangers, all her hidden tendencies emerging. His daughter, his oh-so-innocent daughter, *has run off with a man three times her age*. God knows how they even met, but now Paul remembers that evening he got home from walking Jackson to find that scent in the air of the kitchen: woody, peppery, intense – the same scent he'd once been assailed by in the street. He remembers flecks of dried mud on the floor. That man had been there, when only Chrissie was at home. The two of them had been together, alone in Paul's house.

They have told the police nothing about any of this. Paul is half running as he turns out of the Fairshaws' drive, and nearly slips on a damp paving slab, but he's scared that if he doesn't hurry, Julia will leave. She left the police station without him, came back here without him, went online and booked herself a plane ticket without him. If the police hadn't released him so soon after her, he might have returned home to find her disappeared too.

When he confronted her, she was immovable, insistent. *She had to get to Chrissie. She had to go now.* That was when he managed to get out of her what she'd seen in the photo, the online image with the glimpse of Chrissie's sweatshirt, and still she refused to let him call the police. She almost screamed at him the moment he said it.

Please stop talking!

Jesus, Julia! We shouldn't leave without telling them. We should inform DS Brayford at least. I get it, I feel as desperate as you do, but the police know what they're doing. We should just let them help.

You don't understand.

You're right. I don't. So tell me. He tried to grab her arm, slow her down, hold her, but she was too busy throwing clothes in their case.

Stop it, Paul. I need to go. Please.

He didn't get it. He couldn't grasp how she was thinking. He couldn't understand why she hadn't shown the photograph to Brayford – incontrovertible proof that their daughter is there. *He* would have told DC Moore, the officer who interviewed him, but segregated in the small room without Julia, how could Paul even have known?

Now Julia had bought plane tickets and was planning to leave for the airport in less than an hour. He was unable to reason with her or get her to think straight, so what other choice does he have but to go with her? And still he thinks, if he hadn't come home in time and caught her, would she just have left him completely in the dark?

Julia is already loading their suitcase and bags into the boot of the car when he gets back to their driveway. It's the same suitcase they took to London just twenty-four hours ago but everything will be different with this.

'Did you do it?' she asks. 'Is it sorted?'

'I gave him to Danny,' Paul says. 'It was Danny who answered. We're going to need to call Sally and let her know.' Poor dog, poor kid, what the hell are they doing?

Julia nods. 'Okay, fine. I'll do that. Have we got everything? Are we ready?' They've packed so quickly, he's really no idea. Barely two hours since they left the police station, seven o'clock that same evening, but there is a plane they can get on at ten p.m. that will fly them straight to Inverness. And from there, a hire car, and from there … Well, from there, Julia has said, they'll do whatever it takes.

'I think so,' he says, though nothing about this feels right.

Julia hands over the car keys. 'Can you drive?' she says. 'I'm sure of it now. Chrissie left her light on.'

'What?' The two statements don't seem related at all.

Julia points behind him, up at Chrissie's window. 'She left her bedroom light on before we left for London. We wouldn't have noticed when we were leaving. Now that it's growing dark, it's different. But at that time, we wouldn't have seen it from out here, with the sun.'

He turns to look, and realizes she's right. He remembers that sunny afternoon, the three of them getting into the car; he can picture it: with spring sunshine bouncing off the windows, you'd never be able to tell if a ceiling light was on inside.

'She was the last one to leave the house,' Julia continues. 'She smashed her phone screen, tipped her chair over, unlocked the French windows, all before we left for her audition. You get it, don't you? Forget the police, Paul. She left all those clues *for us*.'

It fits, but at some level Paul still can't make sense of it. All these signs Chrissie allegedly left – why do any of that? Why run away – practically *elope* – with some man, and then leave a trail of clues in your own wake?

Julia climbs into the car, and Paul gets in on the driver's side, the wind almost wrenching the door from his grasp. He yanks the gear stick into reverse and releases the handbrake. He truly can't believe they're doing this.

As they follow Woodstock Road, their route out of Oxford, he tries again. 'We don't have to do this, Julia. We can turn back.'

Julia shakes her head. 'I can't. We can't. It's too late. Listen, we know where she is now. We just have to get to her.'

They're on the slip road now, heading east. Towards Heathrow. Julia leans forwards, forehead on her knees. *Breathe out. Slow down.* He's scared to challenge her, he realizes. In case he completely capsizes their boat. Paul thinks of his own fat secrets squatting inside him. The boarding school, the investment. Okay. All right then. He concentrates on the motorway lanes in front of him, gripping the steering wheel as the wind buffets the car. There has to be a way to make this come right again. He'll just explain to Julia how he was trying to help Chrissie; he can explain to their daughter why he thought it would be best. If they can just get to Chrissie and bring her home again, all agreeing to put everything behind them, then maybe they can re-establish their family without everything blowing apart.

Julia sits back up, hands clasping her knees now. 'I'm going to call Sally. No – I'm going to text her.' She fumbles for her phone. 'We'll call the police as soon as we've got her and we know for sure.'

'But why not now, Julia?' If she would just explain, maybe he'd get through to her. He can talk her down, the way he's done before.

'Because you told them you knew him,' says Julia. 'Francis.'

'What? Of course I did. He was a guest in our *house*.'

'I know. I told DS Brayford that as well; I had to. I knew you'd have said he was at our party.' Julia places both her hands on the dashboard, leaning her head down between her thin arms. 'But—'

'But what?' He needs to keep his hands on the wheel. His eyes on the road.

'I didn't want them to think …' She exhales, violently. 'I didn't want them to assume we were part of it.'

'For God's sake, Julia. Part of *what*?'

'Part of whatever has happened to Chrissie! I said he must have been a friend of a friend.'

'Julia …?'

'I panicked. I said I didn't know him, Paul. I lied.'

CHAPTER 27

Julia

EIGHT WEEKS BEFORE

When Chrissie came into our bedroom that morning, shaking Paul awake for their run, I was already awake. Of course I was. I had barely skimmed the surface of sleep all night, my body shivering, my skin half-burning. It had happened. It had truly happened, and whatever I had wanted, there was no going back now.

I lay completely still as I listened to their whispered conversation, and I remained equally still as I felt the slide of Paul's arm across my waist. It amazed me that he couldn't feel the ripples of feverish energy coming off me. Could he really not sense anything at all?

I stayed there through the roll-and-bounce of him getting up, and on through the whine of the smoothie-maker downstairs. I pictured Chrissie, bright and shining, moving about below me in our kitchen. I had been in such a state when she arrived into this world – broken, stunned, frightened – but it had never stopped me loving her, despite all the ways in which

I had failed. Still, in my own way, I kept trying to protect her: trying to stop the things in *my* life from spilling into *hers*. I went on lying there, picturing the two of them – my lovely daughter, my faithful husband – until I heard the slam of the front door.

I only got up once I knew they had both gone.

Jackson came scratching at the bedroom door as I pushed back the covers, and he pushed himself against my knees as I made my way to the bathroom, as happy and enthusiastic as ever. I had showered last night, at one thirty a.m., but could he still pick it up on me now? I crouched down and took his shaggy head in my hands, looking into those big, trusting brown eyes. 'You love me, don't you?' I whispered to him. 'You don't hate me?' He panted back at me, wide mouth smiling.

In the bathroom, standing at the sink, I tried to get a grip on the myriad sensations and parse them out into separate details. The fizzing and burning of my skin was *psychosomatic* – for want of a better word. A physical manifestation of an emotional state. I'd had it before, only once, maybe twice in my life, but I recognized it again now: a sort of terrified, euphoric shock. Only a matter of time before that wore off.

The fizzing in my nostrils was real. The skin around my nose was pinked and the back of my throat burned too: no prizes for guessing the reasons for that.

I had a splitting headache as well, but two paracetamol could sort that out easily enough. I searched through the bathroom cabinet to find them and swallowed them with a mouthful of stale tap water, then stood and looked at myself in the mirror. The fizzing feeling showed in my eyes, which seemed unusually bright, and my lips looked swollen. I hardly recognized myself. I looked like a person suffering some kind of shell-shock. And also like someone who had been taken by the shoulders and shaken. Hard. The way you might to wake someone from a deep sleep.

In the shower, I dowsed myself again with shampoo and soap, shivering in the heat as I washed it all away. I'd done it, and now I was trying to get rid of it. I had needed it, but now I wanted it gone.

By the time I got out of the shower, there was a text waiting for me on my phone. I read it, slowly, each word marked by the pounding in my head. I towel-dried my hair and smeared Vaseline onto the raw skin around my nostrils. I knew I would need to get to the office early, and go in tomorrow probably too. Slowly, I got dressed, my hips aching as I pulled on my tights. The muscles of my inner thighs ached, too, as I reached round to do up the zip on my skirt. As I buttoned up my blouse, my phone yelled at me again from my bedside table.

This time, I answered the message with a quick reply: *Yes, I'm coming.*

Then I read the previous message, the one that had arrived while I was still in the shower, for a second time. Despite my best efforts, despite everything, as I read it, I couldn't still the thumping in my chest.

*

Downstairs, in the kitchen, there were strawberries in the fridge, staring out at me when I opened the door, their smell intense despite the cold. Strawberries in February. Somehow they summed things up perfectly. Perfectly wrong, and yet

191

beautifully right. I hadn't bought them; they had been given to me as a gift. You know you can buy strawberries in the middle of the night. I ate two. I should probably have been ravenous, but I wasn't. I remembered that side effect now, so welcome to me when I was at university and for a few years beyond. Back then we had all been young and skinny and beautiful and stupid, and now I thought: *well, and which one of those descriptions is still the case?*

I made myself a cup of tea and drank it while I waited for Paul and Chrissie to come back from their run. How far would they go? How long would they be gone? I hardly knew what to do with myself, alone for a change in our big, handsome house. I should have felt at home here, satisfied and settled. It was exactly the sort of place I'd expected to live in, its features signifying luxury and worth: the elaborate cornicing that bordered our ceilings; the antique dining chairs that my parents had bequeathed us; the huge Persian rugs draped across our floors. Instead, I'd look around and think: *is this really who I am?*

I sat at our breakfast bar – solid oak and marble, with designer stools to match – and watched the clock on the microwave flash and then tick over. Jackson came downstairs and flopped in his basket, grunting softly. Paul, or Chrissie, had evidently fed him already. Little flashes from last night flickered through my mind, and yet now, in the daylight and the ordinariness of our big, bright kitchen, it all seemed so unreal. For a moment or two I really did wonder whether I had dreamt it. It wasn't unusual for me to have dreams as vivid as that, dreams that sometimes turned into nightmares. I touched my nose where it burned, tingled. It seemed quite possible that none of it had ever happened, and for a moment I was hit by a shuddering wave of relief.

And then when I recognised that, of course, it was real after all, it was as though a strange type of splitting happened, and it felt as if I could become almost two completely different people.

The one who came home at one a.m. last night. And the one standing here now, making herself another cleansing mug of tea, and turning as the front door banged to greet her beautiful daughter and her handsome husband, who came into the kitchen carrying fresh milk and orange juice. The wife who leaned in lovingly as her husband kissed her cheek.

Julia, I said to myself. *How can you think of hurting this man?*

CHAPTER 28

Paul

NOW

Outside Heathrow Airport, it's heaving. Paul can't believe they are really doing this. Queuing behind a dozen other vehicles, red taillights strung out in the dark, they inch towards the long-stay car park, where Julia purchases a ticket for three days. We go there, she tells Paul, we get her and we come back. If we need longer, she says, so what? We'll pay for an additional ticket or the excess or the fine.

She still isn't telling him everything, he feels that in his gut. But he hasn't told her everything, either. Her money, the investment. He is simply choosing to trust her; the blind leading the blind to make things right.

Now they are standing in the queue for check-in, Julia rigid, half a pace in front. The line is moving agonizingly slowly. Julia keeps checking the time on her phone.

'Did you call Sally?' Paul asks to break the tension, knowing he's probably only making it worse.

'No.'

But she was fiddling with her phone in the car the whole way here. 'I mean, did you text her?'

Julia shakes her head again. 'No.'

Paul's stomach clenches as he grasps Julia's shrewd reasoning: better to leave poor, confused teenager Danny to explain it, because he will give some muddled, stuttering story, and it will be better for that to be all Sally knows.

'She tried to call me,' Julia says now, 'but I didn't answer.'

So this is what they're doing now, is it? Hiding from their friends as well? Julia hasn't even contacted her parents yet, and the fact leaves Paul suffused with both guilt and relief. They deserve to know that Chrissie is missing, but at the same time, Paul can't bear to think how Celina – or Celina and Duncan both – will react to what their beloved granddaughter has done. Paul was supposed to be watching her, protecting her, supervising her. He recalls Celina's words, her sour breath on his face. *You can practically smell it on her* – as though lust, sexuality, wantonness had its own unique scent. The words shocked him at the time, and he had wanted to correct Celina. He'd meant to stand up and say to her, *what are you talking about? Your granddaughter isn't like that.* But he didn't, did he? Because he recognized something in what his mother-in-law was saying, as he set her words against those WhatsApp pictures Chrissie had posted, and all those crude messages that cluttered up her phone. *It's not like that*, Chrissie had told him, and he had tried to downplay it, making his clever plans for her schooling, thinking he was doing such a good job. But what did he know about teenage girls and how they felt and what they were capable of? *Celina* had known. Celina had warned him, but what good had it done? He thought he had ferreted out all Chrissie's little secrets, and instead she has completely, disgracefully deceived him

When they finally get to the check-in desk, the woman on hand is pristinely dressed and full of smiles. They hand over their passports and tickets, and Paul lifts their modest suitcase onto the conveyer belt scales.

'You're in first class,' the attendant says, and Julia nods. Paul wonders why he's surprised. Julia has always flown first class, whether for business or pleasure; she was shocked when Paul told her that he'd only ever flown economy. She wouldn't have thought of doing it differently now. And for the first time, Paul wonders how Chrissie got to Scotland herself. Did she fly there or go by train, or coach, even? The police, he thinks again. They could easily discover that. Why are we doing this on our own? But Julia has made it practically impossible to do otherwise, lying to the police, claiming she didn't know this *Francis*. Even though he was *in their home*.

The woman on the desk hands their printed reservations back, the boarding passes now tucked neatly inside. 'Boarding starts in forty-five minutes, gate twenty.'

And that's all it takes.

'Should we do it now?' says Julia. 'Go straight through security?'

He understands her thought process perfectly. Surely, if anywhere, that's where they'll be stopped.

'Yes. Let's do it.'

They head through the airport to join yet another queue. This one is shorter and moving faster. They are almost at the scanners when Julia's phone rings, making Paul's heart leap in his chest. 'Sally again?'

Julia is checking the phone screen. She shakes her head.

'Who then?'

She answers the call without telling him. A security guard is waving the next passengers forward.

'Hello? Hello … yes, this is Julia.'

Under the harsh lights, Paul checks his pockets for loose change or shrapnel or stolen jewellery or bullets. It feels as though he could have anything in there, as though *criminal* is written right across his forehead.

'No, no,' says Julia. 'We aren't at home at the minute.'

So where are they meant to be then? It's almost ten p.m. Paul's feet in their socks are sticky against the airport floor, sweaty.

'No, we're visiting my parents for the night.'

Paul is amazed at how easily the lie comes to her, in the same moment that he realizes that she is talking to DS Brayford. And the detective is calling them late at night.

'Tomorrow? Yes, that shouldn't be a problem.'

The security guard is calling them forward now. Paul dumps his phone, his money, his belt and shoes in the tray.

'Yes,' says Julia. 'That's fine, thank you. We still haven't touched her room.'

'Madam?' says the guard. 'You'll need to hang up now.' Paul can imagine what he must be thinking: rich woman, entitled, glued to her phone.

'No,' says Julia. She's placing her own items in a plastic tray. 'We haven't heard from her. We keep checking our messages but there isn't any more news.'

Lies, lies, lies. They just keep tumbling out of her. She lied back at the police station, and she's lying again now. How, Paul thinks, can this do anything but make things worse?

'*Ma'am?*' The security guard is impatient now. He's waving at her; she needs to hang up, put the phone down, move through.

Paul reaches out for her.

'Step up,' the guard says. 'Yes, you, sir. Step up.'

'I have to go now, DS Brayford,' Julia is saying. 'Yes. Of course. Please let us know everything.'

The guard is waving Paul through the scanner. He fully expects the alarms to go off. *Guilty*, he hears them say. *Guilty, guilty, guilty.* And the security guards would demand of him: guilty of what?

But a moment later and they are both on the other side. Cleared and swept onwards into the glossy maze of duty free. Bottles of whisky and perfumes and cigarettes. Just the sight of them makes Paul feel sick.

'Let's find the gate,' he says. 'I just want to sit down.'

There are hard chairs and a vending machine by gate twenty. Paul sits, his knees weak, trying to stop the name *John Francis Maitland* from pounding in his head. He pushes away the intrusive thoughts of the two of them together, the stark images of what that man might be doing with their daughter. He tries to focus only on thoughts of finding her, rescuing her, but at the same time he feels himself shivering and shaking, an alarm bell ringing somewhere deep inside, like that shrill fire alarm that went off only last night. It feels as though his insides are bruised. And he thinks as well about the things he is carrying himself, his own secrets. He has committed his own forms of betrayal, and all of this they will be taking with them. He is so aware of Julia sitting next to him, their arms almost touching on the armrest. As he tries to tamp it down, stamp it out, it hits him fully, for the first time. This flight, this journey, this mission to find her. Julia and he will be together non-stop.

They are leaving, running to find Chrissie, wherever she's escaped to.

But from each other, there won't be any escape at all.

CHAPTER 29

Julia

EIGHT WEEKS BEFORE

At a quarter past eight on Saturday morning, the office was almost deathly quiet. Peter was there, though, waiting for me and looking much better rested than I was. He had already switched my computer on so it could churn through its updates, and he had made coffee for both of us.

Caffeine, caffeine and more caffeine.

'Here you go,' he said, handing me the mug. 'You look tired. Are you feeling it?'

'I'm fine. It's always like this with these kinds of cases, isn't it? I'll survive.' Far better to let him assume that work was the reason for my appearance; an easy assumption for him to make. Peter had studied law at LSE, graduated first in his class. He worked harder than almost anyone, this career his priority, the way it so often was mine. It was like speaking the same language, sharing a mother tongue. There were certain things you didn't have to explain.

'Thanks for the coffee. Are we working in here today?' I tried to relax as I sank into my desk chair. My office was a fraction bigger than Peter's, a mixture of classic and modern, sleek lines, nothing cheaply ostentatious or glib. No windows, but the lighting made up for that: bright yet subtle. Clients loved it. You saw it as soon as they entered the space, reassured by the solid yet discreet display of wealth.

'If you don't mind,' said Peter, 'I already brought the boxes through.' I spotted them stacked by my desk. The case we were working on was a vicious dispute over a mendacious manslaughter charge and one of the biggest the firm had landed. I knew that Peter was gunning for partner; he knew I'd be in line for the same thing next year. It was a reciprocal arrangement. If we pulled this case off well, we'd both benefit; that was implicit.

I leaned over and prised the lid off the top box. 'They're playing hardball, aren't they?' My arms felt shaky as I lifted out a first stack of files. We had received this new release of materials just yesterday: thousands of pages we'd need to painstakingly review in order to submit a summary on Monday. Of course the files had been sent to us late.

'You could say that. Gimme. I looked earlier – those ones are the worst.' He lifted the heavy pile from my arms, generous, chivalrous. There was a strange intimacy to being here on a weekend. I wondered sometimes whether Peter felt it too. With clients, I often felt it. In the way we worked, there was an accepted blurring of the professional boundaries. We went with clients for lunches, for dinners, for drinks …

I took a mouthful of my coffee: bitter, black. It needed sugar, but I'd do without. Right now, the harshness felt right. 'Okay. Let's get to this.'

Peter uncapped a highlighter. 'See you on the other side.'

For the next two hours we worked almost in silence. I was used to this. I was good at my job. I knew how to pull together whole swathes of information, immerse myself in the detail and then pull out exactly the targeted arguments required. There was a point at which you were dealing with evidence so voluminous and diffuse that it would be easy to get lost in the weeds. I never let that happen, though; I was careful never to lose focus. Not in this area of my life.

There was a flow that came to the work sometimes, when I would find myself almost hypnotically absorbed in my task. Hours could simply disappear, and there were many times I had come home late because of it, letting Chrissie down. And Paul. The number of times I had come in, apologizing, too late for dinner or to help Chrissie with her homework or see the TV show Paul had wanted to watch.

I would try to make it up to them, leaving the office early the next day to meet Chrissie on her walk home from the academy, offering to carry her bulky violin case along the banks of the Cherwell. But the secret, hidden truth was that it suited me. It was safe, familiar. I'd never learned how to be Chrissie's mother. I'd never fully felt I had a right. From the beginning – during all those weeks when I was recovering, marred by bruises and fractures and contusions – my honourable parents were the ones who stepped in. *They* were the ones who looked after Chrissie, changed her, dressed her, rocked her to sleep. It went on like that for months, even years afterwards.

They took her in, and I stayed apart.

Come half past twelve, Peter began to stack the ring binders back into their boxes, clearing my desk of the work we had done. I gathered up the handwritten notes we'd made: all the points our opponents would have been hoping we'd overlook. We still needed to summarize our findings – another half an hour's work at least – but my muscles were twitchy, the headache starting up again behind my eyes, and the thought crossed my mind: go to the bathroom, take another dose.

Crazy, reckless, stupid thinking. I rubbed my eyes.

'Here.' Peter was holding out a hand. 'Give them to me. I'll type the summary at home tomorrow, have it ready for you Monday, first thing.'

'No,' I told him. 'Honestly, it's fine. You've got the Defraine case to deal with. This will only take me twenty minutes and it's easier to present when I've written it myself.'

'You sure?' Peter looked grateful.

'Absolutely.' I closed the last ring binder and logged into my computer, ready to translate our notes into type.

'All right then,' said Peter, slipping on his navy coat. 'See you on Monday. Ring me if there's anything you need. Phone's always on.'

'Ditto,' I replied, as he lifted his hand to wave me goodbye.

A cleaner arrived just as he was leaving. 'Sorry,' she said. 'I wasn't sure anyone would be here.'

'Not a problem,' I told her, typing quickly in a new Word document. 'I'm just writing up a few notes, and then I'll be away and out of your hair.' It was close to one o'clock now. Peter and I had been here for nearly three hours. I was hungry, my appetite finally kicking in. Plus, we were due at my parents' tonight.

I would finish this summary, go home and spend time with Chrissie. I could make her lunch and then we could … I wasn't sure what she'd have time for. Watch a film, go for a walk?

The cleaner started up her Hoover, an inevitable distraction.

Maybe I should finish this at home. I emailed a copy of the document to myself, then sent a text to Paul, asking if he needed me to pick up anything on the way. He didn't reply, so perhaps he and Chrissie were still practising. I hesitated, then opened up my personal email. I might as well get this task done as well. I thought back to what I had read in Chrissie's diary this week, my narrow window into her life. It was always serious, always innocuous: details of her practice, her school work, sometimes a little about Reece. For a teenager, she was so innocent, so different to me. I knew it was Paul's influence that had made her like that. Once a week I would comb her pages in secret while Chrissie was watching TV, or practising, or taking a bath. I was always careful to replace it and the floorboard exactly so, then I summarized her entries in emails to my father, sending him updates every two weeks. This had started years ago, when I began taking care of Chrissie properly again. Once Paul was there to help me and I had my life back on track. To begin with it was just part of the … handover, but it had kept going, and over time it had become something different. It remained a form of supervision: of me and of Chrissie. And at the same time, it was a way – *an essential way* – of keeping my father at arm's length.

This update wasn't very long; I mentioned her next audition. I mentioned her school successes. I wrote, *Chrissie sends her love.*

Once it was done, I switched off my computer, got up stiffly and pulled on my coat.

'Thank you,' I said to the cleaner. 'Have a good weekend.'

She nodded at me and went on Hoovering, and then she shouted, over the racket. 'Oh! There's someone waiting for you downstairs. A man.'

CHAPTER 30

Julia

EIGHT WEEKS BEFORE

He was sitting in the lobby of our office block. When he saw me, he got to his feet.

'What are you doing here?' I asked in shock.

'What do you think?'

I hitched my bag. I felt like I was naked. 'Who let you in? The cleaner?'

'She was so sweet. I told her I had an appointment with you and she agreed to let me sit here.'

'But how did you even know where I was?'

'You said you're here most of the time, didn't you? Lucky guess, I suppose.'

I shook my head. 'You can't be in here.'

'All right then,' he said reasonably. 'Let's go outside.'

I pushed through the heavy glass doors of the entrance and he followed me out, across the car park to my car. 'You know, you still haven't said what you're doing here.'

'I've come to see you. Let's go for a walk.'

I blipped the car open. It wasn't raining any more, but it was still cold. 'That's silly. I can't. I'm on my way home.'

'Really?'

'Yes. They'll be expecting me.' I was careful not to use their names. 'Listen, I'm sorry, I never intended—'

He spread his arms out. 'But Julia! I've come all this way.'

My heart was doing it again: *thump thump thump.* I could feel that burning again on my skin. 'You shouldn't have come here. Really.' I wanted and I didn't want it. I needed it, yet it was so ugly, so wrong.

I opened my car door, telling myself actions spoke louder than words, and yet my breath was hitching in my throat. Peter was long gone by now; he was hardly going to step in and rescue me, and the windows of the offices were all blank: no sign of the cleaner. There were people passing us by in the street, going about their everyday business, not even noticing us, and I felt that split inside me again: Julia one and Julia two.

I could hear my mother's voice looping in my head. *What's wrong with you, Julia? What on God's earth has made you like this?*

I don't know, nothing, I found myself answering. *Or … you? Is that where it comes from? Do I have your own errant traits in my blood?*

He was still standing there. Just his physical presence was almost like a pain. I looked up at him, following the line of his shoulders, his neck. His arm was resting along the top of my car door.

'I brought this for you.' He reached into the inner pocket

of his jacket and palmed out a tiny see-through bag. '… In case you fancied it.'

'I can't,' I told him again. 'I really need to head back.'

It was pointless though, and I knew it even as the words were leaving my mouth. He already had me; I had fallen so fast. I was like a puppet, dancing, light-headed, feet lifting off the ground. Willing to throw myself off the cliff.

I said it again, anyway, as though for the record. 'I can't.'

'Julia,' he said. 'Julia …' It was almost like a lullaby, the soft way he repeated it. 'Julia. You can do anything and everything you want.'

CHAPTER 31

Julia

EIGHT WEEKS BEFORE

That evening did a lot to harden my resolve. I knew on the way there how it would affect me: dinner with my parents, in my old childhood home. As soon as I walked in the door, it was like stepping backwards, like finally seeing the danger signs up ahead. What are you doing, Julia! What are you doing! *Use it*, I told myself. *Grasp these feelings.* Like grasping a nettle bush to stop yourself falling off a cliff.

It went all right too, through drinks, starters, main course. There was good news to report; the conversations stayed light. I could forget all about the other night. Then between the main course and pudding, Paul excused himself and my mother disappeared to oversee the desserts. In the space that remained, it was just the three of us: Chrissie and my father and me.

We sat with the tinkle of classical music in the background: an old choral record he liked to have on. In the lull, replete from our food, I took the opportunity to quietly size up my father. He was older, but he never quite looked old. There was still always a strength in him.

'So, Daddy,' I said, keeping the tone of my voice light and easy. 'We haven't chatted much yet tonight. How are you?'

He raised his eyebrows. 'I'm well.'

'Are you and Mummy looking forward to your holiday? It's Kenya, isn't it, that you've booked this time?'

'That's right.' He let the rest of my question slide, directing his next words to my daughter instead. 'Chrissie,' he said, 'get up and have a look what's on the sideboard.'

She looked up. 'The sideboard?'

I followed the jerk of my father's chin. I hadn't noticed it before, but there was a small wrapped box on there.

'Go on then,' he said.

Chrissie unfolded herself from her chair, stepped over and picked it up. 'What is it?'

'What do you think?' My father rotated his glass, slowly swilling the dark wine inside.

She smiled shyly. 'A present?'

'Exactly.' He smiled in return.

Chrissie brought the gift back to the table and set it down in front of her.

'You can open it, you know.'

She glanced at me as though seeking permission, and I gave her a tiny nod, but my stomach was so tight. Where had my mother and Paul got to?

'Daddy,' I said. 'You didn't have to.'

My father held up a hand, his simple gesture for silence, while Chrissie tugged at the slim ribbon, unravelling the bow.

The thick paper fell away easily and revealed a dark blue box. Jewellery.

I couldn't help saying it again. 'Daddy, you shouldn't have.'

'I can't reward my granddaughter?'

Chrissie cracked open the box. 'Wow,' she said. 'It's lovely.'

A silver chain glinted in the light from the chandelier. The thing was expensive, no doubt about that. And familiar.

My father leaned back in his chair. 'You like it?'

'Of course.' She touched a finger to its pendant.

'It's for doing well in your competition. I told you, I'm proud of you. Here. Come over here.'

I had been watching him all evening and he had drunk very little, yet his focus seemed to waver. Chrissie stood next to his chair at the head of the table with her back to him, hair lifted, neck exposed.

'Keep still.' The chain looked more delicate in his large hands, and I felt a shudder run through me as he fastened it around her neck. I couldn't recall him ever touching me like that. *Stop it*, I told myself. *It's lovely. It's a beautiful gift.* But I couldn't stop my eyes returning again and again to the doorway. Why on earth was Paul taking so long?

'There.' He pressed his hands to Chrissie's shoulders. I was surprised he'd been able to do up the clasp so quickly.

Chrissie was smiling, her cheeks flushed. She held the pendant between thumb and finger, examining it. 'It's so pretty.'

'Mmm-hmm. Like you.' He released her, directing her back to her chair. 'Your grandmother has one just like it, you know – you've probably seen it. It's exactly same as yours, only your grandmother's necklace is gold. Otherwise, you're perfectly matching. My wife and my granddaughter.'

Chrissie looked at me as she returned to her seat. 'Does Mum have one too, then?' she asked my father. He didn't answer. Chrissie looked across at me. 'Do you?'

She didn't get it. She had no idea. Stiffly, I shook my head. 'No, I don't. Not one like that.'

'The pendant,' my father went on. 'You know what it means?'

Chrissie shook her head. Her voice was quieter this time. 'No ...'

'Look at the engraving. It's a symbol.'

'Oh! Okay ... of what?'

My father closed his eyes, as though sleepy, then opened them again. 'What do you suppose, Cee-Cee?'

Cee-Cee? Celina? I jerked. 'Daddy? This is Chrissie.'

He turned his gaze to me. 'What?'

I shook my head. 'Nothing, Daddy. It's fine.' Surely it *was* fine. A simple mistake, a slip of the tongue.

'Well?' My father turned back to Chrissie, still waiting for his answer.

Silence. 'I just ...' Chrissie said. 'I don't know.'

I couldn't tolerate the quiet any longer. I felt as though my father could see right inside my skull. *It's a coincidence*, I told myself. *A total coincidence.* 'Chastity,' I said to Chrissie. 'It symbolizes chastity.'

'Oh!' She let the pendant drop against the ridges of her collarbone. 'Well ... thank you. It really is lovely. And special too. Because of Grandma.'

'Then you'll look after it, won't you.' An instruction as opposed to a question.

'Of course. Thank you, Grandpa.'

I pushed myself to my feet. 'Here, we should clear all this up.' I tried to gather the dirty plates, the heavy cutlery, empty glasses; I didn't know where the young woman who had served us earlier was, and anyway I was just desperate to disrupt the conversation. I knocked against the table and a knife slipped off one of the white saucers and went bouncing onto the carpet at our feet.

'What are you doing?' my father said. 'Julia. Leave that.'

I bent to collect the knife, which was lying with its blade right under his chair. 'It's all right. I've got it.'

'For heaven's sake, Julia. Leave it and sit down.'

I abandoned the knife. My jaw was rigid, my mouth dry. I hadn't heard that tone of voice or seen that expression on my father for a very long time. Not for years. Not since …

'Sorry,' I said. 'I'm sorry. Chrissie, sit properly.' My daughter was angled sideways in her chair.

My father didn't look right: he was flushed, his eyes darting. What was wrong with him? He was irritated with me, I understood that, but there was something else too – was he drunk? He seemed agitated but disorientated as well, a combination I'd never seen in him before, and one that sent a brand-new pang of fear through my gut. We were visiting for dinner; I shouldn't need to be fearful. Not now, not like this, not with Chrissie. I reached along the table and took her hand, to comfort her or myself or hold her still, I wasn't sure. A second passed, then another, then another. We were like a tableau, frozen.

It was the clatter of my mother's heels in the hallway that released us, sending me weak with relief. I would never have thought I would be so glad to see her, but here she was, and then Paul too, not far behind.

Chrissie let go of me to rise to her feet. 'Dad! Grandma! Look.' She lifted the necklace.

If my mother understood, she didn't show it. Neither did I; I kept my eyes fixed firmly on Paul.

Because Paul wouldn't understand any of this, and he didn't need to. And to that, all I could think was, *Thank God. Thank God.*

CHAPTER 32

Paul

NOW

Boarding is much quicker when you fly first class, and he and Julia are being called up to board before Paul has even fully adjusted to being at the airport.

He steps with Julia to the front of the queue, handing over their boarding passes and letting the flight attendants smile them into the close tunnel that leads to the plane.

Inside, the first-class cabin welcomes them with comfort, privacy, ease. An attendant lifts their hand luggage – Julia's handbag, a small rucksack of his – into the rack, and Paul drops into the deep, wide seat. He sits next to the window, Julia by the aisle. Trains, planes, it doesn't matter. They have always travelled that way.

They don't speak. What is there to say right now? They are on the plane, poised on the runway, suspended between all they've left behind in Oxford and everything that awaits them up north.

It takes twenty minutes for all the passengers to embark. While they wait, Paul creases the pages of the glossy magazines in front of him, scoring through the promises of entitled, privileged lives. Julia has dark sunglasses pulled down over her eyes, even though there's no sunlight showing through the porthole, just black sky and the grey pall that foretells the growing storm.

They sit and wait, and the plane doesn't move.

When the announcement of a delay finally comes, it's almost a relief, it was so inevitable. Paul fumbles to undo his seatbelt; after all, the warning signs are now turned off. He's so stiff it's as though he's already been sitting on the plane for hours. He accepts the attendant's offer of free water and orange juice and a cereal bar and fruit.

'There'll be further announcements,' she tells them. 'We'll keep you updated on everything we know, and if you have any questions, then please do just ask. We are truly sorry for all the inconvenience, but we're assured the storm will be moving north very soon.'

She moves up the cabin and Paul hears the same words, repeated verbatim, to the next passenger along.

'How long do you really think it will be?' asks Julia.

Paul cranes to lookout of the porthole, where a tow truck buzzes across the runway. He shakes his head. He doesn't know. Julia pulls out her phone to check the weather, as though the Sky news app will have more information than the airport itself. 'It says the same here, the storm's moving quickly. So I'm sure it won't be long. Forty-five minutes, maybe? An hour?'

Paul hopes so. Being stuck here like this, when he feels so wrong about the trip anyway, feels like a sign: *they shouldn't be going*. He imagines saying as much to Julia. Change of plan. Let's call DS Brayford. The Oxford force can contact the police in Scotland and they can go straight out to this place and find Chrissie. Maybe arrest Francis. Instead he bites his tongue. Sitting in a grounded plane at Heathrow Airport they are no good to anyone, least of all themselves, but he knows Julia won't turn back now.

The man in front of him has his in-seat TV tuned to a news channel, headphones on. Reports flicker across the screen, the silent images mesmerizing, and Paul can't look away. He almost expects to see coverage of Chrissie on there. Maybe of Francis Maitland's disappearance too. But the police said it wasn't time for that quite yet; they were planning to give it at least one more day.

If he closes his eyes, the cabin feels as if it's spinning. As though someone should be shouting at him: *brace, brace, brace!* He has to keep his seat back upright to avoid the nausea, even though he longs to lie back. Julia has reclined her seat as far back as you can without making a bed. He longs to claw back some sleep on this plane, but for the life of him he can't seem to switch off.

If only they would *get going.*

He pulls out his phone and checks the share price, despite how irrelevant it feels now. But it isn't irrelevant, why should it be? In fact, maybe it's even more important than ever. They'll find Chrissie, yell at her, ground her maybe for the rest of her life, but after this whole mess she's made, this *scandal*, there's more than enough reason to send her to the Royal Institute. Not as a punishment but *for her own good.* Her behaviour has escalated in a way Paul never imagined, despite everything Celina always said. This *thing* with Francis – whatever it is – is hideous. A total deal-breaker, and a shocking justification for what – until now – a tiny, naïve part of him has resisted.

He looks up again. An attendant is leaning over the passenger in front, temporarily blocking Paul's view of his TV screen. Beside him, Julia shifts in her seat.

When the attendant straightens up, Paul feels his blood run cold.

The images are showing a footballer. The tickertape mentions post-Brexit tensions in Ireland, and then this:

Leaked documents show extent of governmental corruption ...

In the perfectly regulated air of the cabin, Paul's breath freezes in his throat.

The pilot – smooth, patronizing – announces that their flight will be grounded for another two hours. Paul's forehead, his armpits, grow slick with sweat. An attendant smiles at him, unaware of his horror. He swipes open his phone, tipping his screen away from Julia – behind those dark glasses, he can't tell what she can see – and finds the full coverage on the news app. He cannot bring himself yet to look directly at his investment. He cannot take in the full facts of that yet.

The news app confirms it, though. The name of his company is explicitly listed. *Fraud over illegal awarding of governmental contracts ...*

Paul swallows, choking down the taste of disaster. He glances again at Julia, who has removed her sunglasses now, lying back with her eyes closed. He already knows in his bones there's no recovery from this. Not in the share price, and in his marriage – God knows. Now, finally, he opens the investment app, but only to confirm what he already knows. It's right there: an almost vertical, aircraft nosedive.

His shares are in freefall. The money is gone.

CHAPTER 33

Julia

SIX WEEKS BEFORE

When the details of Chrissie's next audition round came through, I took the day off work. I couldn't remember the last time I had done that, but I decided on it right away this time. Chrissie seemed fine; she didn't particularly seem to need me. Maybe, instead, it was the other way round. Since that first crossing of the threshold, I had fallen more than once, skin burning. Sometimes it seemed like exactly what I wanted, but increasingly it felt like dangerous quicksand. On the other side rested my ordinary life: still there, still waiting for me. I felt the need to claw my way back to it. I pictured hitching myself to my husband and daughter, the way a rock climber judiciously secures their harness and rope.

Get back to them. I repeated that to myself as I sat with Paul in the kitchen on the morning of her audition, waiting for Chrissie to get herself ready and come down. We sat and looked out at the garden together, and it was a pretty day, bright and sunny, and Paul had made me coffee the way I liked it: two sugars, no milk. I pictured kissing him and tried to remember the way we had kissed when we'd first met, when we were so much younger and in love, because it felt like he was rescuing me, and he said I'd rescued him.

You're still in love, I told myself. *You can still be rescued.*

I complimented him on the garden, trying to fill up the space between us with breezy conversation. Later, in the car, as we crossed the border into Wales, I leaned my head against the window and watched the edges of the motorway slip past, the smell of Reece's aftershave in my nostrils. *I love them*, I told myself. *I love them*. It felt good, the four of us there in the car, on a journey together, celebrating Chrissie. From here on, I would give them my undivided attention. *Julia*, I said to myself. *What an idiot you have been.*

*

Another week on, though, and I was still in it, letting it become more complicated than ever. I don't know why I let him convince me. Clearly, there were still all sorts of things going on with me that I didn't understand or couldn't even recognize at the time, which was why so many of my choices hardly seemed to make sense. I desired him, and I didn't know why. I didn't want this relationship – and yet I did. And because I was confused and always vacillating, it was easier to simply go along with his suggestion about the party. The idea was crazy, reckless, but maybe, I told myself, that was exactly what I needed. Maybe I was seeking a way to bring this to a head.

I suppose I hoped that by inviting him, I would be giving him a message: *We can't keep doing this. Look at me: I have a husband, a family, a whole life*. Then later, as I got dressed upstairs, Paul doing up his shirt cuffs beside me, I began to disbelieve that he would actually show up. Surely, in reality, there was no way both of them could ever be in a room together. I had kept these two sides of my life – these two sides of myself – so incisively separated that bringing them together would feel like trying to break the laws of space and time. The more I thought about it, the more the very idea felt unimaginable, close to horrifying.

He wouldn't come, I convinced myself. In fact, as I pushed the Saint Laurent earrings through the flesh of my ears, I began to pray that he would not. Surely he could see how inappropriate it would be, how potentially humiliating for us both. In the end, he would sensibly stay away, and my invitation would simply have had the effect of forcing his hand, paving the way for the conversation I knew we had to have. *You see*, I would say to him later. *It doesn't work, does it? I'm sorry but I don't think there can be a future in this. I just don't think I can keep you as part of my life.*

I really thought I would be able to say that. And I honestly never expected him to show up.

By the time the first guests arrived – Sally and Stuart – I was feeling calmer. While Paul went down to open the door for them, I blotted and reapplied my lipstick and looked at myself for a final time in the mirror. I looked good. I looked just the part. But at the last minute, I took the earrings out. Then I smoothed my skirt and went to check on Chrissie. She was hunkered up in her bedroom.

'The guests have started arriving,' I told her. 'If you want anything from the kitchen, now's probably the time.'

'I'm fine, Mum,' she told me. 'Have a good night.'

Downstairs, the place looked lovely. Paul had done a great job of setting up. Stuart kissed my cheek; Sally hugged me, gushing compliments about my dress. The other guests began arriving quickly after that. Before long, I had a drink in my hand, then another. Wine, music, friends, laughter.

I realized I'd needed this for a long, long while.

An hour later, the atmosphere was expansive, tipsy, relaxed. The room was stuffed to the gills with guests, the volume of conversation rising all the time. I liked the noise – the chatter, the tinkle of glasses, the laughter – blocking out the chatter in my head. I weaved through the knots of people to turn up the volume on the stereo. The wine had loosened me; I'd almost forgotten the dangerous possibility of Francis showing up. Until I turned around and saw him standing there, in the centre of the room.

It was half past nine; had he only just arrived? Who had let him in? He was in a group with three other guests – associates of mine from the firm plus a visiting lawyer from the States.

When he saw me, he held my eye and raised his glass. 'Well, good evening, Julia.'

A mistake. A total mistake. I felt as though I was standing there naked, as though the black gown I was wearing had fallen off, leaving me completely exposed. I could have burst with relief when Sally tapped me on the elbow, unaware, it seemed, of what was going on.

'Come with me,' she said, drawing me away from him. 'There's someone I need you to meet.'

I managed to lift my own glass and nod and murmur his name in response, playing the good hostess, before Sally led me away to a corner of the room where some friend of hers was waiting for us.

I felt his eyes on my back every step of the way.

I have no idea what he told the people he was talking to that night. How had he explained who he was, how he knew me? He must have told them something they easily swallowed – or perhaps he had told them nothing at all. He had such a charm; I didn't know what else to call it. When he looked at you, it was as though the rest of the world fell away.

At least, it did for me.

Apart from that small, singular greeting, I didn't talk to him all night. I spoke to everyone else instead. Brightly, loudly, though it nearly killed me not to let my panic show. I circled the room, talking to anyone and everyone, but always making absolutely sure to avoid *him*. I felt manic. How could I have risked this? I was operating on an arcing wave of dread. I thought of my daughter upstairs in her bedroom, unaware of any of this. What would she think if she knew what was happening? What would she say if she saw us like this?

As I looked up from the group I was talking to, my heart faltered. Paul was over there next to that group, *his* group, holding a half-empty bottle of wine. He set it down and stepped forwards towards them. He seemed to be listening intently to their conversation, and my heart lurched at the possibility of what was being said.

My voice rang out across the room, bright as ringing glass, calling him to me, calling him away from there. 'Paul! We've missed you! Where have you been?'

*

He disappeared not long after that. I assumed he'd left, without saying goodbye. He had bettered me; he had thrown back my challenge. *See,* he'd seemed to say, *I can fit into your life just fine. These people love me, they feel as if they already know me. And your husband? My God, Julia, does he really not know?*

I should have been angry with him, humiliated, furious. And I was. But I couldn't help how else he made me feel too.

It was later – maybe ten minutes – that I spotted him leaving. I desperately needed water and was crossing to the kitchen to get some when I spotted him in the front hall pulling on his jacket. Where had he been? Outside? In the kitchen? Or … my heart swallowed – upstairs? I imagined him peering into my bedroom, the master suite that I shared with Paul. What would he think of our bed, our decor, all our precious, personal things? The domestic life I was in danger of shattering because of him. It's only now that I think of Chrissie being up there, too.

'Julia,' he said, in a tone that said, *there you are.*

'You're leaving?' The words fell from my mouth before I could stop them.

'I am. I couldn't wait around for you all night. Still … It's been a great party.'

I shook my head. 'Listen, I'm sorry. I shouldn't have asked you.'

'Why not? I've had a great time.' He grinned and I had the sense he was taunting me. Well, I deserved that, didn't I? For trying to taunt *him.*

I became aware of someone – Sally? – in the hallway behind

us. Francis stepped forwards and pressed a kiss to my cheek. 'Really, Julia. I've had a wonderful evening.'

I didn't have a choice, did I? Not with Sally standing there watching, curious as ever about other people's lives. I had to play along. 'Thank you for coming,' I said brightly.

This time his grin looked almost wolfish. It was as though he saw all this as nothing but a game, and he knew that he'd come out the victor tonight. 'The pleasure was entirely mine, Julia. Goodnight.'

*

Just a couple of days later, Paul and I had our final appointment with our therapist. The three of us had planned this ending a little while back, and I had been counting down the weeks until we could bring these sessions to a close and I wouldn't have to worry any more about what I might blurt out. God only knew how I had got through all those other sessions before, splitting myself in two.

With Lynn, we had talked about my upbringing, my parents, Paul's upbringing, Paul's parents. We'd talked *languages of love*, the art of listening and reflecting back, and how to address our words in session to each other, rather than to Lynn.

'And how are things?' she asked us now as we settled ourselves down on her familiar sofa. Her room had a funny smell: it had taken me a long time to pin it down. Then one day, when Paul was cooking bolognese at home, I had nailed it: oregano. Which had only opened up a whole new swathe of questions.

Paul looked across at me. 'Mostly good, I think,' he said.

'Yes,' I echoed. 'Good.'

The little clock on the side ticked along.

'We've been arguing much less,' I added. That was true, but at the same time I had no idea when I had become this good an actress, both here and at home. Now, as I sat compliantly across from our therapist, I wondered if Lynn knew anyway. I wondered if that was part of her expertise: an ability to read a dynamic and see right through it.

If she did, she didn't say anything.

'I know in the future,' Paul was saying, 'we'll have further decisions to make, depending on what happens with Chrissie's career. Whether I go back to work, for example. But for now, I think we've come to the conclusion that things are best as they are.'

That had been the question we had initially come into therapy with. Was our unorthodox situation really working out for us? We had talked so much about that, looking at the expectations each of us had brought into the marriage, our expectations of career and family life and parenthood. We had talked about how I didn't want more children, because the difficulties around Chrissie's birth were something I'd never want to go through again.

Maybe Lynn really thought we were addressing the *big stuff*. But we had never really scratched the surface. Or at least I never had.

We had really just talked in simple practicalities, like the best ways for me to let Paul know if I was going to be late, or ways I might still contribute to some of the household chores. How Paul might ensure he found a sense of value and purpose, even within his role of being just (*don't say 'just'*, Lynn would chide) a stay-at-home dad.

But other than that, I had mostly lied.

And what about Paul? Was it possible that Paul had lied too? I looked across at him. These last few days, he had been twitchy and jumpy. Stressed in a way I had never known him to be before. I had felt him tossing and turning in bed next to me in the night, and when I asked what the matter was, he said he was worried about the competition. Yet it was out of character for him to show performance nerves like that, which meant either there was more to this competition than I had realized or there was something entirely different going on.

'Julia?' said Lynn, interrupting my thoughts. 'Do you agree?'

I nodded. 'Oh – yes. I know it's often difficult. Especially right now. I'm working very long hours again. But it won't be for ever. It's just this current case.'

'And Chrissie is doing exceptionally well,' said Paul, as though that was the deciding factor, the litmus test.

'Definitely,' I echoed. 'She is.'

You'd think that here in the safe space of therapy you would be able to lay all your cards on the table. You'd hope that you could be truly honest, peel your lives bare and say things that might be wounding and hurtful, but ultimately productive and true. I'd always thought I would be a good client in couples therapy. When Paul and I had signed up last year, I'd thought I would step up to the challenge quite brilliantly: straight-A student all the way. I would take whatever blows Paul might deliver me with humility and grace, retaining my reason and composure whatever might be said. We would weather the necessary storms together and come out the other side with a love that was stronger and truer than we had had before.

Instead I had sat here and lied and lied and lied.

'Well,' Lynn said, clasping her hands. 'That's good to hear. You've both worked hard here and taken a lot on board.'

For a moment I desperately wanted to appeal for her help. I wanted to say: *you're a professional, you're trained, would you be able to explain what's wrong with me? Tell me why I'm doing this. Tell me why I'm choosing such disgrace for myself.* But it was far too late for that and that was utterly my own fault. I hadn't told her anything of use, for me, for any of us. I'd wasted all this money, I'd wasted all this time. And still I found the words balancing on the tip of my tongue.

'Well then,' said Lynn, 'I just have some questionnaires for you both to fill in. You know, to follow up on the ones you did at the start.'

'Sure,' said Paul, already leaning forwards. 'No problem.'

Lynn handed us across the sheets of paper, and a clipboard each to rest on our laps.

I tried to think back to the way I had answered these questions at the beginning. *Is your relationship boring, fragile, happy, honest? Rate on the scale.* I couldn't remember; I found myself unable to form a judgement now. In the end, I just put in positive ratings for all of them, though not so high as to look patently false.

At the very end was a box for 'any other comments'.

I stared at that empty square for a long time, Paul still scratching away with his pen beside me. This was my last chance: I could write it here. *I'm sorry. I've lied to you. I've been unfaithful.*

At least then I would have made some sort of confession. I would have come clean with Lynn on the bare facts.

I'm sorry, I managed to write. I stared down at those words. I had no proper thoughts – just a sinking, angry, defeated feeling: car upended, nose in a ditch.

You made your bed, Julia.

You made your choice.

What would Lynn do if I handed such a confession to her, when she came to tot up our questionnaire scores and discovered it? Would she call us in for a follow-up session and make me say it straight to Paul's face? Surely she couldn't overreach herself like that.

Beside me, Paul sighed and turned to his last page. Lynn was sitting silently in her seat and when I looked up and caught her eye, she gave an encouraging smile. I bent my head back down to the page and scribbled those last two words out.

Then I wrote them in again, and simply added: *I'm going to be a better person from now on.*

CHAPTER 34

Julia

THREE WEEKS BEFORE

My father called abnormally early the next morning. Out of the blue. If either of my parents called us, it was almost always my mother.

'Just stay there,' I told him. 'I'm coming right over.'

I hardly allowed myself to think as I got in the car, allowing nothing into my mind beyond strict reassurances. These things happened. Misunderstanding, frustrations. My father was older now, and impatience, impulsivity – these things could be natural in old age. And then my mother … It wasn't as though I hadn't noticed her drinking. Or rather, her *drunkenness*, which was perhaps worse, because while we had been there at dinner the other weekend, she had drunk very little but she had been visibly inebriated, even so. Which meant she'd had God-knew-how-many drinks beforehand. Take someone who was old, and could be grumpy and impatient, and someone else who tended to get a bit drunk, and it was inevitable, wasn't it, that sometimes they would clash? Somehow they'd managed to get into it at five in the morning. But these things happened, even with the best of couples. It would be fine, I could sort this.

Just so long as he had let her be.

*

I was shaky when I got out of the car in front of the house. I had driven fast and I'd had nothing for breakfast, I realized now. I tried to walk straight in through the front door but one of them had locked it, so instead I had to knock and ring the bell.

It was my mother who answered. She swung the heavy door open. 'Julia!'

I looked over her shoulder, trying to glimpse whether anything in there appeared amiss. 'Are you okay? You know Daddy called me.'

'For heaven's sake, Julia, I'm fine. You didn't have to come.'

I tried to size her up. Were her eyes glassy, her speech slurred?

'It's okay. I wanted to, and I don't have to be at work until later.' Neither part of that sentence was true. 'Can I come in, then? Where's Daddy?'

'Your father's gone out for a drive.'

'He isn't here?'

'No. Not right now.'

My stomach dropped. I couldn't pretend any more that I didn't know what we were dealing with. I recognized the pattern, even though it occurred so rarely: once a year maybe, or once every two – always the exception, never the rule. But hadn't it happened just a month or so ago, as well? That was worrying. That was new.

A strange thought jarred me. 'Daddy hasn't gone to our house, has he?'

My mother looked at me. 'No. Why would he? Presumably you told him you were coming here.'

'Well, okay. Shall I come in, then? Have a cup of tea? I can stay with you until he gets back.'

I anxiously wanted my mother to let me in, and at the same time, I wanted nothing to do with this. I wanted to get back in my car and drive away, drive home, drive to work. To my own place, my own life.

'Oh no,' my mother said, 'that really won't be necessary. I appreciate you coming, but for heaven's sake, Julia, we're both fine.' She was repeating herself, and I could feel already that she wanted me out of there. She never welcomed my input – why hadn't I learned that? Every time I tried to help, or even just talk to her, she only ever wanted to pretend everything was fine.

I gave it a beat. Two. 'I'll call later then and have a talk with Daddy. I've been a bit worried, Mummy, that he isn't all that well. His mind, I mean. It seems to slip sometimes, have you noticed? Maybe it's something we could consider getting checked ...'

My mother shrugged a tiny, elegant shoulder. 'If you really think that's necessary.'

I just wanted to try *something*. 'Well, what do *you* think?'

She sighed. 'Oh, *I* don't know, Julia.' It made me want to shake her. It made me want to cry. I was so aware that I was still on her doorstep and hadn't even managed to set one foot inside. The house was so big, huge and empty behind her. Anything could be going on with her in there, and who would really know?

'Listen. I will. I'll try and speak to him later. Why don't you let me know when he's back?' I didn't know how to say the next part. 'And in the meantime, Mummy ... please try ... please try not to *do* anything. I know you don't mean it, I'm not saying it's your fault, but you have to try – try not to ... *contribute*.'

An iciness washed over us then. I shouldn't have said anything. My last words had touched too close, pierced too deep. I shouldn't have said them. We both knew how this worked – I had been living my whole life by it – but I shouldn't have named it. That was how our family continually navigated this minefield: by never acknowledging the things we all knew.

I tried one last time. 'Are you sure you don't want me to stay, Mummy?' But the answer was obvious. I was already stepping back off the step and my mother was already easing the door closed.

'I don't think so, but thank you, Julia. Really. I do appreciate you coming all this way.'

CHAPTER 35

Paul

NOW

In the turbulence of the plane, everything is shaking: the seat, the tray-table, Paul's heart.

Julia pushes herself upright, fully awake now. 'Are we landing?'

Paul nods. The turbulence eases, but then starts up again, and his stomach lurches as the plane starts to bank. Surely the angle is far steeper than it should be. Surely this isn't normal – they are out of control, they're going to crash …

They were delayed on the Heathrow runway for close to three hours in the end, before the pilot finally had clearance to take off. By now it's close to three a.m. and they have been in their seats for nearly five hours straight. Paul is still thinking about what has happened to his investment. He feels as if he's still in some kind of shock. While they waited for take-off, phone screen hidden from Julia, he desperately scoured the Internet forums, trying to glean advice on what to do. All the posts said pretty much the same, because to be honest it was obvious: in his position, the only sane option was to *offload*, and as soon as he could to minimize the hit. But he hesitated, paralysed, and now that he's finally made the sale, the shares have dropped to almost nil.

Another announcement comes over the PA, respectfully softened here in first class. First in English and then – what is that, *Gaelic*? They are clear of the dense clouds now, flying underneath. Through the porthole, he can make out patterns of white and orange lights, strung out in irregular lines along roads, clustered like explosions. He's exhausted. He just hasn't slept. All he wants is to get to Chrissie, give her a good shake and nail her back on track.

The plane rights itself, flipping level again. This time when he looks out of the porthole, he glimpses the runway and the big letters of the sign itself: *Inverness Airport*. Minutes until they land now; seconds.

We are coming for you, Chrissie. We're coming.

He closes his eyes and feels himself brace as the juddering plane collides with the runway. The engine roar softens as the plane slows to a coast, and Paul draws a lungful of air-conditioned air.

All good. They have landed safely.

But what now? he thinks. *What next?*

*

The wind whips about him as he navigates the landing steps in the dark. Julia is in front of him. The storm is raging up here as well, making his every step unsteady. He has visions of toppling forwards, crushing his wife in the fall. Freezing rain blows straight into his face as they cross the wet tarmac to the small, hangar-like airport. Inside, it's little more than one big corridor. It's like they've landed in a shiny, converted cow barn, a Tinkertoy version of international life.

'This way,' Julia says, tugging him by the hand. Her hand-clasp feels like handcuffs now, to be used to pull each other this way and that. But Julia is right; she's pointing to a sign: Arrivals/Baggage Reclaim.

She drops his hand to dig in her bag for her phone. Meanwhile, he checks the address of the hotel they are staying at – Inverness Palace Hotel. Base camp, though hopefully for no more than two nights. He tilts his face up to the corrugated ceiling, trying to tune out the clatter of wheelie suitcases passing by. He counts to twenty to ground himself.

It's as he waits for their suitcase to appear that he sees it: on one of the tacky billboards that hangs in the arrivals area, in a line of adverts that fills the space.

He reads the words: *Maitland Renewables. British design for our global future.*

He grasps Julia's arm. 'Look!'

'What?'

He points. 'There. That advert. There's a company here, it's under his name. *Maitland.*'

It's *the* company. It's the one Paul has invested in. But Julia is shaking her head. 'It's a common name, Paul. That could mean anything.'

The conveyer belt is moving now, a jumble of luggage making its slow circuit. 'But don't you remember …' He pulls up short. Of course she would have no idea what he overheard at their party. She wouldn't know about this company that

Francis has connections to, the one Paul recklessly invested in – and how can he explain any of that to her now, when thirty thousand pounds of her money has been completely lost? Instead, he can't do anything but go on lying to Julia the way she's lied to him.

And so is it salt in the wounds or a helpful clue, that evidence there on the billboard sign? Even proof. It seems there has to be a connection between Camp Dìon and Maitland Renewables. It's all part of the same thing, isn't it? Finally it's beginning to make sense. 'Never mind,' he says to Julia. 'But listen – we thought this location was so random, but I really do think you're right. I think Francis is here.'

Until now, he hadn't fully been able to put the two of them together: that man, Francis, and his precious daughter. But he is being forced to picture it now, deal with it as a reality. It is jarring, sickening: a dislocated shoulder being snapped into place. Despite all his efforts to curb that part of her, he never imagined it would show up like this.

'There's ours.' Julia is pointing; their little black suitcase lies slantwise across the conveyor belt. He reaches it just before it passes by for another circle, and wrestles it off, the sharp edge of it nicking his shin.

'Here.' He makes his way back to Julia, and pulls the handle up, setting the thing on its wheels. 'Go ahead. I'll follow you.'

Outside, the taxi rank is poorly sheltered, and it's freezing up here, the wind blistering, so much colder than he could have imagined. Again he has the urge to reach out to his wife and tell her, *Julia, we don't have to do this. If Chrissie is here, why don't we call the police and tell them? Let them help us. Surely we only risk making things worse.*

But now a car with a lighted sign on top is pulling up. The driver lowers his window. He is chewing on something – gum or a sandwich crust – and he says something in a blurry accent that Paul struggles to understand.

Julia shows him the screenshot of their hotel address – the Inverness Palace Hotel and Spa. The place has a swimming pool, a leisure club, a five-star brasserie. 'Can you take us here?'

'Sure, hen. Hop in.' From inside the taxi wafts the smell of chips.

'Are we good?' Paul asks. 'Will he take us?'

'It's fine.' Julia nods. 'Let's get in.'

The driver heaves himself out of his car, which bounces up without his weight. He gives a grunt as he lifts up their luggage, still chewing as he loads their suitcase into his boot.

Inside the taxi, they are finally shielded from the wind. Paul leans back in the sticky leather seat and fights the waves of exhaustion rolling through him. He is dizzy with fatigue, but feels a need to stay alert. It's as though everywhere he looks he's searching for clues – some kind of insight into what is really going on. It's dark outside, but he can make out some things: they are driven down a long, straight A-road, then into the city with its grand houses, grey sculpted stone, such a sense of the historic. He glimpses the tall towers of what looks like a cathedral, and then a flash of river shining in the black. He feels like such a foreigner, with his obvious English accent. They have their own language here, their own currency, their own flag. He's never been to Scotland before, and he never imagined a visit like this. This isn't a family excursion or a romantic anniversary weekend; it's a mission to find their missing, wayward child, without the consent or even knowledge of the police.

His face is cold, but his skin feels windburned. Julia is fiddling with her phone and it beeps. Paul turns to her. 'Did you hear from someone?'

'It's just a provider update.' She stops swiping, but keeps the phone clutched in her lap as if she's waiting for a call.

After twenty minutes, the taxi comes to a halt. The driver parks on a diagonal outside the turreted front of the Palace Hotel. The walls are a pinkish-grey stone with wide bay windows. In the gloom, Paul can make out a sign with the word *Welcome*, and feels an unexpected shudder of relief.

Julia asks him for the reservation printout, as though she wants to double-check that this is the right place, and Paul hands it over, even though it's quite obvious that it is. He can't think of anything but simple phrases to say to her right now. For the moment, all their communication has been stripped back to simple basics: problem solving, transactions, survival, ignoring the bigger picture of what they are doing here and whether any of this is legal – or right. Paul tells himself he simply has to trust her. She's a lawyer, after all.

He gets out, scrabbling in his wallet, and pulls out a bundle of cash. He pulls out another two notes to add on top for a tip. When he hands over the money, the driver squashes it into the pocket of his shirt.

The Palace Hotel is right on the riverfront. If this had been a normal trip, one where they weren't checking in at four a.m., they might have had a shower and then gone for a stroll, holding hands along the scenic waterfront. Instead, Paul has no idea when he'll next get some rest.

The driver retrieves their suitcase from the back and sets it down on the tarmac. The car bounces again as he climbs back in, the slam of the door loud in the quiet of the night. 'Enjoy your stay,' he says through the window before driving off, taillights winking a nonchalant goodbye.

Inside, the hotel is glistening and spacious, like a plush, cream box. There are sculpted white pillars and a wide, polished reception desk. There's no one else here though, at four o'clock in the morning.

'Is there a bell?' Julia says, but the wide reception desk is empty.

Paul feels exposed, at any moment expecting a police officer to emerge, but his wife steps forward – that ingrained confidence again – and calls out loudly: *'Hello!'*

Her voice sounds impertinent in the space, but it does the trick. A moment later, a young woman appears, brightly awake, and she looks so like a typical hotel receptionist that Paul feels himself give another exhale of relief.

Five minutes later they find themselves in the hotel room, the heavy door easing itself closed behind them. Now the relief is overwhelming, because this room is exactly what they need. Spacious, quiet, comfortable, pristine. They are on the third floor, with a tiny balcony and views out over the river. White dressing gowns hang on the back of the door; there's Twinings tea and Scottish shortbread, and a thick stack of towels on a shelf in the en suite. Julia adjusts the heating upwards, filling the room with the warmth Paul craves.

She sits down on the edge of the bed and rests her head on her knees. She has a headache; Paul can see that. He knows she always gets them when she flies.

He still can hardly grasp that they are here when less than thirty-six hours ago they were cocooned inside the Barbican's dusky hall. He cannot believe the things that have happened since then: wild, unimaginable things. *My daughter is missing, she ran off with a man old enough to be her father, a man we invited into our own house.*

For now he tries to focus simply on the practicalities in hand. 'Do you want paracetamol?' he asks Julia.

'I'll be fine in a minute. I might go out on the balcony for a bit.'

The balcony? It's pitch black and blowing a gale out there.

She doesn't move though, and for want of anything better to do, Paul opens their shared suitcase and starts to unpack, sliding shirts onto hangers and underwear into a drawer. He knows it probably isn't even worth it, since they've already missed most of their first night due to the flight delay, and their plan is to stay here at most one more night. The hire car they've booked will be ready for them at half eight in the morning, and the website says the camp is a two-and-a-half-hour drive from here, so it's doable, surely. They can get to Chrissie, drive her safely back here, get her on a plane home then work out what the hell to do next.

If she's there at the camp, that is. Even now the idea of the two of them, Chrissie and Francis, together in this place, this camp, seems ridiculous. Squatting with a bunch of hippy-activists in the woods – is that meant to be charming? Is it some kind of skewed idea of *romance*?

'Shall I put the kettle on?' he asks Julia. 'Do you want a shower or something to eat, or what?' He doesn't really know *what* she might want.

'No. It's all right. I'll just get some air.' Julia pushes herself off the bed, wincing with the movement, then unlocks and tugs open the balcony door. Her action lets a vicious gust of wind into the room, chilling the air at once, but before he can stop her Julia is outside, banging the sliding door shut again behind her. Maybe she wants that. Maybe she needs it. In the wind, her short, dark hair whips about her head. He carries on unpacking their suitcase, putting Julia's pants and bras in a drawer. He clicks the kettle on, though he doesn't want tea either, and moves on to sorting through their hand luggage too.

He can see Julia's silhouette, out on the balcony, a flickering shadow behind the thin curtains and the glass.

He lifts her handbag onto the luggage rack and unzips it to look for some painkillers. She doesn't like taking them, but under these circumstances who wants a blinding headache as well? Her purse is in here, and some make-up and a tiny bottle of shower gel. Packets of tissues, hand sanitizer, the slim case for her glasses. And something else, crushed right down at the bottom, almost lost or forgotten, in a dark corner of the bag. A business card? What is it?

He recognizes the logo and the name. *YSL*.

He can still hear the wind roaring outside as he sits down on the hard, clean bed, and smooths the little card out on his knee. *YSL*. *Saint Laurent*. With a rush of nostalgia, he thinks of those earrings, sparkling in the mirror of the vanity as she dressed. How beautiful she looked that night. But it was also the night that Francis was a guest in their house. The man who induced Paul to invest tens of thousands of pounds in a get-rich-quick scheme that Paul wasn't savvy enough to profit from, a man whom Julia foolishly lied about knowing but who is somehow terrifyingly tangled up with their family, and who – through fate or coincidence or God-knows-what – now seems to single-handedly be ruining Paul's life.

Paul turns the card over. He stops. Almost chokes.

The balcony door clunks as Julia comes in again, half brutalized by the wind. She doesn't seem to notice that her handbag lies open and part-disembowelled on the stand. Her eyes are watering, her cheeks reddish-blue. 'Actually,' she says, 'I think I need that paracetamol after all …'

Paul gets to his feet. Julia trails off as she sees him standing there. Now she is looking at him properly, seeing him and what he's holding.

So now they both know.

She goes pale. He holds the card in his hand like a bomb.

'Julia …?'

No escape. They stare at each other. He holds the creased card out to her, like an offering.

To my Julia, love Francis, it says.

CHAPTER 36

Julia

He wasn't a work associate. Never had been. I first met him at Duchelle's, a private members' club in Oxford. Rather than going home to my family after work, one evening I went to the bar there, alone, instead.

Most people in Oxford wouldn't even know Duchelle's existed. It was perfectly selective like that. But I knew this place – I had first come here at the age of seventeen. My father had taken me and bought me a vodka martini, a drink I've always chosen ever since. He taught me to drink it like a perfect lady: in tiny sips, with restraint. No one cared that I was underage; my father was paying. We spent a whole afternoon there. It was his way of teaching me where I belonged and how I should comport myself. Where I fitted in this world. He was showing me the kinds of people I should mix with and the sort of places I should frequent. Not just anyone and not just anywhere. Only people and places like *this*.

I hadn't been there for years, though. It so happened that I had never come here with Paul. Maybe that was why I picked it that night: as somewhere my husband had never been, it felt like it represented all the things he couldn't know. At the time,

I was just aware of the deep association with my father. It was only later that I came to realize the profound symbolism in that too.

How ironic then – or how perfect – that this was the place where I first met him, in a scene that was almost a perfect cliché. I sat at the bar. I didn't have a book, I didn't fiddle with my phone; I made it clear I wasn't waiting for my 'date'. The vodka martinis I ordered tasted exactly the way I remembered from twenty years before with my father. I sat and waited to see who would approach.

It took half an hour, perhaps only twenty minutes.

From the moment Francis Maitland walked in and set eyes on me, something sparked within me. It rose up from deep inside – not quite an emotion or a sensation or a memory. More like recognition, or an echo. Something that felt like history on repeat.

When I introduced myself, he repeated my name back to me. *Julia Montrose.*

Hearing those words, in his rich voice, and it was as though part of my self came back to me. *Montrose*, I'd told him. Not *Goodlight*.

He bought me a drink: another martini. Brazenly, he offered me cocaine, which I took.

He seemed to know exactly what I wanted.

He would turn out to be perfect for me. The perfect way to break myself.

He didn't know it – and at the beginning, neither did I – but Francis Maitland would turn out to encapsulate everything I craved.

CHAPTER 37

Paul

NOW

He should have known. The clues had been there, almost textbook. Was this ever really about Chrissie at all?

It's five past nine in the morning and they are standing out in a freezing, rain-puddled car park and Paul has the keys to the hire car in his hand. He is still completely reeling from the shock. They've filled out all the forms, paid the cost, paid for insurance. There's nothing left to do now but get in and drive. The two of them. For nearly three hours straight.

The car smells of pine air freshener and cheap leather and carpet cleaner. It only makes the nausea in Paul's stomach worse.

'I'll drive,' he says. More than ever now, he feels the need to be in the driver's seat.

Beside him, Julia is awash with anxiety and remorse. He can feel it coming off her in waves. He's so angry he could drive this car into a ditch. Back at the hotel, he was unable to speak to her. He literally couldn't look at her or find a single word. The only thing he could manage to do at that point was climb into the hard, crisp bed and try to block everything out until daylight came. He wasn't going to sleep; they both knew that. But there was nowhere else to go. He was trapped here, with Julia. Now, finally, he has found his voice, in the action of moving, driving, holding the wheel.

'You lied *deliberately* to the police,' he says. The road that they're on is wide and smooth but the landscape is wholly unfamiliar: bracken and moorland and distant, craggy hills. It makes his whole sense of disorientation worse. 'You told them you didn't know him when you were having an *affair* with him. And, what – now Chrissie too? *Both* of you? What kind of twisted situation is that?'

'No, Paul. Stop. I don't think it's like that.'

'Then what is it? Chrissie and Francis are clearly involved with one another. Or do you think she's run away with him like this just to, what – mess with your head? Spite you?'

'I didn't even know that Chrissie knew him.'

'Well, she did. Clearly.' He is disgusted, sickened by both of them. 'You know what, Julia? He came to our house.'

'I *know* he did. Because I invited him.'

'No, not then. Not at the party. Another time. I came home to the reek of his cologne in our kitchen, just days after that evening when Chrissie ran off.'

He cannot believe what they've got themselves into. What *Julia* has got them into. He wipes sweat from his forehead with the back of his wrist, then places his hands back on the steering wheel: ten to two, as though following the rules and doing things properly could somehow fix things.

'And you didn't tell the police *any* of this, Julia.'

'I know. I'm sorry. They pulled out his photo and I was

246

just so shocked I couldn't speak. And then they told me *you* knew him.'

'So you were going to leave for Scotland without me? What a perfect way to cover your tracks.' He can't keep the sarcasm out of his voice. 'You were never going to tell me, were you? You did all this so you could keep up your lie.'

Paul wants to pull over and cover his ears. Part of him wishes he'd never said anything and had simply shoved that damning piece of evidence back into her bag, fed her paracetamol and water, and pretended none of this was real. But Julia realized as soon as she saw him. The look on his face. You can't be married for eight years and not be able to read each other like that.

So now it's out in the open. There's no escape. For two hours, he has her: he can ask her anything.

'Which way,' he says to her. They are coming up to an unmarked junction and Julia is navigating. 'Which *way*?'

Julia taps the screen of the car's complicated sat nav. 'Straight on – no, wait, left. Follow signs for Laggan and then for Kilgarry – that's the town just outside Camp Dìon.'

It's raining as well now: thick, heavy drops spattering the windscreen. He turns on the wipers, but almost at once the rain evolves into a deluge. Even on the highest setting, the wipers struggle to keep up.

'Slow down,' says Julia. 'We can hardly see anything!'

He has to drive at thirty-three miles an hour on this straight flat A-road, the windows steaming up, the car feeling more claustrophobic than ever. They're both dead silent as he navigates another junction, peering at the signs that have letters half scraped off. When they find themselves on the right route again, it's Julia who is the first to speak.

'You have to believe me,' says Julia. 'Paul, it was over.'

'*Over?* Really? How on earth am I supposed to believe that? Over – or he just moved on to Chrissie?'

This man! He seems to have infiltrated every aspect of Paul's life, torn it apart, like ripping whole beams from the wall. Julia shakes her head. 'Stop it. Stop saying that! Jesus, Paul, you've got no idea. Listen, I broke it off with him weeks ago. Honestly, I did. I mean, I tried.'

'Tried? You *tried*? What's that supposed to mean?'

He is hit suddenly with a sheer wave of grief. He cannot believe this has happened to him. Yes, of course, he knew he and Julia had problems, that she was unhappy. He'd sensed that she had been losing her way. But they had been going to *therapy*, goddammit.

'So with Lynn, then,' he said. 'You were lying to her too?'

'Here,' says Julia. 'This is the turn-off.'

Oh, the irony of it. Being stuck in a car together, having to work as a team. He hates this; he is overwhelmed by these roads, the wind, the rain, the navigation. How can they also be having a conversation like this?

As though in answer, Julia's phone rings.

'Shit,' she says. '*Shit*. It's DS Brayford again.'

'You have to answer it. Let me pull over.' Even through his anger, the practicalities push through.

'No, don't stop. I can't bear another delay, just keep driving.'

'Then put it on speaker. I need to hear as well.'

She swipes to answer and does what he says.

'Mrs Goodlight? I mean, *Ms*?' DS Brayford's voice is crackly. It's hard to hear her over the battering of the rain.

'Yes, this is Julia.'

'I'm outside your house, Julia. Are you not home?'

Shit, shit, *shit*. It's another jolt of complete disorientation. They are supposed to be hundreds of miles away in Oxford, surrounded by the dreaming spires and no doubt just a light drizzle of English rain. Not way out here in the back of beyond, in a sleeting downpour. What are they doing here, what has happened to his life? Paul almost feels like bursting into tears, picturing their house, their driveway, their street. The familiar landmarks of his precious world. Thinking of Jackson, their faithful dog. They are so far from home right now. But more than that, he can't remember ever feeling further away from himself.

'DS Brayford, I'm sorry,' says Julia. 'We meant to come back first thing but we've … been delayed at my parents'.'

'Where exactly are you? It sounds like you're driving. Are you on your way home now?'

Paul tries to keep his eyes on the slick road, but from the corner of his vision he can see Julia as well. She has covered her eyes with her free hand now. As though that makes it easier to lie.

'No. No, we've just driven to the shops. We're in Guildford. Surrey. We … I … just needed to be home for a while. I think we're going to be here for another few hours at least.'

It is making Paul sick to hear the lies coming so easily from her mouth. When did she become so adept at deception? Duncan and Celina are in *Keen-yah* right now, not Surrey. And does DS Brayford really believe her?

'Well,' says DS Brayford, her tone revealing nothing. 'I can understand that. But we're here to do the further search of your house.'

'Yes, of course,' says Julia. 'Yes, that's fine. Please do go ahead.'

'I'll get the key from your neighbour, shall I?' Paul can picture DS Brayford consulting her notes. '... Sally Fairshaw?'

'No! No, don't do that. There's no need to disturb her. There's a spare key under the lip of the dining room window. Use that.'

'You leave keys to your house outside? You never told us that, Ms Goodlight. That could be how someone got in.'

A scraping noise. Faintly, in the background, Paul thinks he can hear the noise of the front door opening. Would the detective notice their suitcase was gone? But then they would have taken it to Guilford, wouldn't they?

'All right,' DS Brayford says. 'We're in now.'

'Okay,' says Julia. Her voice is tight, breathless. 'Okay. Good.'

'You might want to think about coming back to Oxford ASAP. We need to speak with you further about Francis Maitland. And we may release a press statement shortly. I really do think it would be best if you were here.'

'Yes,' says Julia. 'Of course. Absolutely. Thank you, honestly, for everything you're doing. We'll let you know as soon as we're back.'

When she hangs up Julia is pale and shivering, even though they have the car's heating on full blast. Paul grips the wheel and stares at the narrowing road in front of them. He is furious with Julia, but right now, he still needs her. Everything in the rear-view mirror is broken, and he has no idea what awaits him ahead.

CHAPTER 38

Julia

THREE WEEKS BEFORE

Once it began, I seemed to just give myself over to him. Or – not to *him* exactly, but to what we were doing. This *thing*. I kept on letting so many things happen, dumbly oblivious to what was even driving me. What did I need? What was I looking for, why was I letting myself be pulled apart like this? Looking back, I'm no longer surprised by any of the things I found there. All I knew at the time was that it felt like digging my way to the floor of a black hole.

*

Our meet-up that afternoon wasn't so different: we went to Duchelle's again, though these days we didn't do cocaine in the stylish toilets. We did it in a decadent hotel room upstairs instead.

He seemed to be almost glowing when he met me in the

lobby, and I felt myself tumble again. Heart – or something deeper, darker – completely overtaking my head.

'Julia,' he said. He held his arms open as he approached and kissed me. 'How long have we got?'

Not the most romantic of questions, but I shrugged and told him. 'An hour or two at least.'

He kissed me again and pulled me tight. 'Wonderful.' He nodded at my vodka martini, olives close to the bottom of the glass. 'Another?'

I thought about this. I really tried to be honest with myself: what did I want? What had this thing become, what was I asking it to be? We could sit down here, and drink and talk. I could let him compliment me, charm me, respect me as he drank his ruby red wine. I could step back from this. I could tell him, *maybe it would be better for us to just be friends.*

Instead I shook my head. 'No,' I told him. 'Let's go upstairs.'

I had already paid for a room. The staff here had shown no reaction as I held out my credit card.

Upstairs, for a moment again I didn't know what I wanted. Kiss him, hit him, run away, cry. Then he took off my blouse and skirt, and suddenly I did.

It was easy.

It wasn't particularly good. This was our fourth time now, and it was much of the same. His movements didn't fit mine, not the way Paul's had, right from the beginning. Sometimes it felt almost as though I had to fight my way around Francis to get the pleasure I wanted, but I didn't care. What I cared about was being free to move and do what I wanted, having no one tell me *no*, never censoring myself. With Francis, that was the prize I was hunting, ferociously. With him I chased it again and again.

In the hotel room, on top of him, I felt something, cried out. Francis groaned under me. For a moment I hung still above him, then I peeled myself apart from him and lay back, panting. Like Jackson, I thought. Like a dog. I'd introduced Jackson to Francis once, bringing him with us on a walk, and Francis threw sticks for him. That had been in the days when our meetings could involve walking. Walking and talking, as well as the sex.

Five weeks in, and the sex could still make my skin burn, I noted, curiously observing myself from outside as I watched Francis carefully shape two lines of coke. Though I observed as well that another part of me felt cold and lonely and unsure.

What was I doing here? How many times had I asked myself that question? It was becoming clearer now, though, thin thread by thin thread. I sensed that I was trying, in one way or another, to transport myself backwards, all the way to the night when Chrissie was conceived. Yes. *That* night. My mother had refused to throw away the photographs and I never looked at them, but I knew that those images were beautiful. They were *meant* to be beautiful: that's what it *was*. Freedom, liberation, abandon. Splendour, brilliance, bright young things. I was in love with him too – Christopher, Chrissie's father. Or as much as I knew how to love at that age; I was only twenty-one. Everyone was having sex and no one was moralizing about it. We were young and besotted with each other and reckless and rich, but it went without saying that we took precautions. You'd have to be an idiot – or worse – not to. I was better than that; not like some girls. I never took even a single, tiny risk.

So it was *impossible* that I got pregnant. It was impossible that I was that statistic – the woman whose religiously used contraceptive failed. The little packet of pills I'd been inexplicably embarrassed every three months to request. I went on and sat my Final exams knowing nothing, earning my first, with Chrissie growing inside me that whole time. It took five months for me to realize, and another month to tell my mother after that, in one of the most shaming conversations of my life.

We didn't tell my father; he was working abroad then. When he came back, I was seven months gone and there was nowhere to hide. By that point, I had only just told Christopher. He was abroad too, living it up. He said that he would support me once he was back in England again, and settled.

He never came back. It was only a couple of weeks after I told him about Chrissie that there was the awful car crash, and he died.

And not long after that, all hell broke loose.

I was thinking about all this as I looked at Francis, a new awareness growing in my gut.

I said to him then: 'I'd better get going.'

'Stay,' he said, and bent to inhale another line of coke. Then he reached up and threaded his fingers through my hair. I wore it short these days; Sally said I looked cute, like Demi Moore in that old film *Ghost*.

'I can't.' I leaned forward and made myself kiss him, flecks of powder stinging my lips.

Francis shook his head, his fingers tightening against my scalp. 'Stay.'

Afterwards, I told myself he didn't mean it. Drugs can make you do funny things; you aren't always aware of your own strength. Still, the pain was enough to make me lose my breath. It wrenched at something within me, and I found myself pulling at it, like digging with my hands, dragging something up from the depths. Fear and memory and recognition.

'Ow,' I said, and even managed to laugh, even as I was holding my head and neck rigid. It was a joke, easy for us both to pretend that, and of course he let me go a matter of seconds later.

But what he'd released then, I couldn't put back.

CHAPTER 39

Paul

NOW

After two hours of driving, they are hopelessly lost. They must have taken a wrong turn somewhere, and who knows whether it was Julia's fault or his own – they were arguing too much to even realize. Now the sat nav tells them they have veered well off their route, but their efforts to right themselves have brought them round in circles. Paul wants to scream from the frustration of it all.

'We need to stop,' says Julia. 'We're going to have to ask for directions.'

Paul knows she is right but he doesn't want to listen. He wants to gun the engine, put his foot to the floor and get them wherever the hell they are supposed to be going. Grab Chrissie, kill Francis and run home.

'Here,' says Julia, leaning forwards in the passenger seat to peer through the runnels of rain on the windscreen. 'What's this place?'

Through the rain, he can just about make out the town sign as they pass: another place he's never heard of.

'Head for the high street,' Julia goes on, 'the main road or whatever. There must be someone around there we can ask.'

But the rain is still coming down, and barely anyone is out on the streets. They pass estate agents, hairdressers, a butcher's, each shopfront inserted into grey stone. He can see the shapes of people huddled inside shops and a group of bundled-up smokers crammed in a pub doorway, but none of them close enough to call out to. When Julia rolls down her window and leans out, letting the cold and wind and wet into the car, no one notices, and Paul wants to yell at these people for being so ignorant and useless.

'Park up,' says Julia. 'I'll get out.' She doesn't have a hood or an umbrella, but Paul does what she says, wrenching the unfamiliar hire car into a slanted parking space and watching as Julia clambers out. There's an elderly woman now, covered head to toe in a black cagoule, walking a small dog with a tartan jacket up the road. Julia stops her, in the downpour, and Paul sees her gesticulating. The woman shakes her head, frowns and then her face clears. She points ahead of her, back the way they've just come.

Julia returns to the car, head bowed under the rain. 'Get in,' she says. 'I've got it. They've dug up the roads here. The whole layout has changed.'

He does as she tells him. Of course the sat nav hasn't been updated. Ridiculous, for the price they've paid.

'Head back to the roundabout,' Julia says. 'This time, fourth exit.'

Wordlessly, he follows her directions, but even once they

finally find their route again, the sat nav happy, the anger washes over Paul relentlessly.

*

They reach Kilgarry at two in the afternoon, jittery and exhausted. Little spots dance at the corners of Paul's eyes. The rain has eased off now at least, and the sun is even trying to poke through the clouds, but everything is still sodden and it's bitterly cold.

Paul doesn't want to leave the stuffy heat of the car, but they have to stop here: the track to the camp isn't marked so they need directions. They can't just go driving off into the forest. He cannot imagine how the group is living out there, in this weather. From the pictures on the website, they seem to be set up with little more than tents. For the thousandth time, he wonders what on earth Chrissie and Francis are doing here.

'There's a newsagent's,' says Julia. 'We'll ask in there.' As they get out, a black dog comes running up to them, barking. Its owner doesn't seem to be with it, as far as they can see.

Paul follows Julia to the entrance of the shop, the bell dinging as she pushes through the door. Inside, the aisles are narrow; there's barely room for both of them. The lights are bright, the shop chilly. The milk cartons have Scottish flags on them. They don't belong here, and yet here they are.

The girl on the cash desk looks barely fifteen, with braces and a smattering of spots on her forehead. Julia goes straight up to her. 'Excuse me, we're wondering if you can help us? We're hoping to make our way to Camp Dìon.'

'Camp Dìon?' Paul realizes right away they've been saying

it wrong all this time – as though the word were French, not Gaelic. But the girl pronounces it something like *gee-on*. It's Gaelic for *protect*, according to the website they'd scoured.

'That's right. Can you point us in the right direction?'

'Have you been there before? It's a bit hard to get to.'

Julia smiles brightly. 'No. First time.'

'Oh. Okay. It's just that you have to go through the woods and everything. Hang on. I'll get my dad.' She leans backwards, calling over her shoulder, and a man appears from the back: big and burly, grey stubble on his chin.

'D'you think Ned's about?' the girl asks him. 'Or Barbara? This lady is trying to get to the camp.'

Paul can feel the man taking them both in: two middle-aged adults. He bets he and Julia don't look the right sort at all. Not by a long stretch. Maybe they should have mentioned Chrissie to explain it all. *Have you seen this girl? Have you seen this man?* But he doesn't want to tell their story to these strangers: *our daughter has run away from our beautiful home in Oxford, abandoned an opportunity I've worked my whole life for, and come here with a man who was having an affair with my wife.*

'You know some of the activists there, do you?' the man says. 'There was a new group of them arrived the other day. I thought you lot organized your own transport usually, though?'

'Well, no,' says Julia. 'We're not really with them. We're just doing a bit of … research. Trying to learn more of what they're all about.'

'Right, yeah. We've had a few journalists and what-not before. Well, there's probably about thirty of them camped out there now, all trying to prove you can live without heating and TV or a roof over your head. They're a bit' – the man twirls a finger at his temple – 'some of them. But they're harmless, really. Just passionate, I guess. Anyway, in terms of getting there, Ned across the way should help you.'

'Oh no, that's all right,' Paul says. 'We've got a car and everything. We just came to ask for directions.'

The man peers past them, out into the street, where they've parked. The bonnet of their car is glistening in the rain. 'Those are your wheels?'

'Yes,' says Paul. 'For now, anyway. We hired it.'

'You can't go in that,' the man says. 'You'll end up breaking an axle.'

'The road's really bad,' the daughter elaborates. 'You have to walk some of it. And after all the rain and everything ...'

Does she know the boys and girls from the camp, Paul wonders? Has she been there herself, or does her father insist that she steer well clear?

'Speak to Ned in the pub, like I said. Say I sent you, he'll sort something out.'

The man is already disappearing through into the back. His daughter leans her elbows on the counter, looking up at them with that bland curiosity teenagers have.

Paul smiles at her, still unsettled. 'Thank you.'

'No problem. Hope you get there all right.'

CHAPTER 40

Paul

NOW

They've bought a bag of crisps, two sandwiches and two bottles of water, and carried the haul back out to the car. This small, local pub, they've discovered, doesn't open until three, so what else can they do for now except wait? The rain has started up again and Paul thinks he can hear a faint rumble of thunder too. He wants to drop his head into his hands. He is exhausted, sleep deprived, starving.

'We aren't going to make it,' he says as Julia tears open the stale sandwiches.

'What?'

'We aren't going to get all the way to the camp, find Chrissie, and get all the way back to the Palace Hotel tonight. Not at this rate.'

'Don't say that. Of course we will.'

But Paul shakes his head.

He's right here in Kilgarry, so close now, but they are help-less – they can't walk to the camp alone in the rain; they don't know the way, or even how long it would take. He still can't understand what Chrissie – or Francis – is doing here. The more they learn about the camp, the less any of it makes sense. Outside, lightning flashes, then the inevitable roll of thunder comes. The car shakes, rocked by a gust of wind.

He watches the clock on the dashboard; the minutes tick past. There's no sign of movement from inside the pub.

The next thing he knows, his neck is hurting and Julia is there, shaking him awake.

'It's ten past three,' she is saying. 'Let's go in.'

Paul can see a light on inside now, through the gloom. It's still raining, he's still soaking, but at least the entrance door opens this time.

Inside, there's a bare wooden floor, and it's chilly, like the shop was. Don't people have central heating up here? There's a man behind the bar, polishing glasses, a football game already on the TV screen, a cluster of men on stools at the bar, watching. They look over their shoulders as Paul and Julia come in.

'Hi,' says Julia. 'We're looking for Ned?' Her voice is so much less confident than he's used to. Clearly they are both feeling out of their depth.

The bartender looks up from his polishing. 'That's me.'

Paul feels a wash of relief: small victories. He sees Julia's shoulders ease too.

'Oh. Hello then. I'm glad we found you. We're wondering if you can help us get to Camp Dìon.'

His eyebrows lift. 'In this?' He means the thunderstorm.

'It's a little urgent. The man in the newsagent's told us you could help with the transport to the camp.'

'Well, not me,' the man says. 'But my wife Barbara can. I'm afraid she isn't here right now, though.'

Paul feels another scream of frustration rising up in him. He has no idea how Julia is remaining so calm, but then she's good at that, isn't she? Not letting things show.

'Will she be back soon?'

The man checks his watch. 'Fifteen minutes? Twenty?'

'Maybe you could call her? To check?'

A murmur goes up from the men watching the football. One of them calls over, 'It'll cost ye.'

'That's fine,' says Paul. 'We can pay.'

We can pay. What a horrible phrase.

'I'll send her a text,' the man says. He sets down the glass and dishcloth and pulls his mobile from his pocket.

'Thank you,' says Julia. 'Honestly. Thanks.'

'Done,' the man says. 'Want a drink while you're waiting?'

'Can you do tea?' says Julia.

'Sure. Take a table. I'll bring it over in a sec.'

When they sit down, Paul says again, 'We won't make it.'

This time, Julia doesn't disagree.

'Did you see the sign?' says Paul. 'They have rooms here. We could change, dry off. Bring Chrissie back here.'

He is cold and damp; the chill is in his bones. He's desperate for a long hot shower, a soft towel.

Julia shakes her head, but she isn't contradicting him. 'Then you ask him.'

*

They are shown to the lodgings, up a narrow staircase. Unbidden, the memory comes to Paul all over again: the story of Julia's fall down the staircase at Bute Hall, the one that resulted in a patchwork of bruises, a broken arm and fractured ribs, and – worst of all – Chrissie's premature birth. That fall was only ever Julia's fault, not because – as the official story went – she had tried climbing a flight of stairs while *dizzy*, but because she'd allowed herself to *get high* while pregnant. Pregnant with Chrissie and she went and did that. The irresponsibility of it jams up Paul's throat, reigniting his anger all over again, because with everything he's discovered about his wife these last twenty-four hours, he wonders whether Julia ever really changed, or whether she's still that reckless, irresponsible person even now.

Ned shows them into a cramped bedroom; is this supposed to be the pub's best room or the worst? Paul's head almost touches the eaves. The space smells damp, but it's drier than they are, and there's a bed that he can lie down on at least.

'All right?' asks Ned.

'Yes,' Paul says. 'This is perfect.'

'Good. Well, make yourselves comfortable. I'll send Barbara up to you once she's back.'

Paul doesn't ask him how much longer that might be. They are already pushing their luck.

The owner pulls out his phone again. 'Give me your number. I'll give it to my wife.'

They've only met this man half an hour ago, but Julia reads out her number. A moment later and he is banging the door shut behind him, and they hear his feet clattering back down the stairs. They can hear the football match from up here and the voices and laughter of the men below.

Paul pulls off his jumper and jeans. Both are wet, sticking to his skin. His flesh underneath is goose-pimpled. He drapes his clothes on the radiator, even though it is barely giving out any heat.

'You should get out of your wet clothes as well.' But Julia just stands there. All her composure seems to have deserted her. She looks as though she's in shock or in pain.

'I found this,' she says. 'While you were speaking to Ned and arranging the room.'

She is holding her iPad out towards him. He doesn't know why she's brought it. There's nothing else of any use on there.

'How do you mean – found it?'

'A video. You said she used this to record her practices.'

'What?' he says. 'Yes.'

But there was nothing in the photo files when they'd looked before. She'd deleted them, hadn't she?

'You should look.'

Julia's arm is starting to quiver – she's still holding the tablet up for him. He takes it from her. It's small, but suddenly it feels so heavy in his hand.

'Where?' he asks.

She leans over and opens an app Paul barely recognizes. *Dropbox*.

'Chrissie saved it in here.'

Julia's voice is utterly hollow. He's never heard her speak like this before. He has been angry with her for five hours straight – with her and with his daughter. But he can't sustain that and the adrenaline is draining out of him now. In its place, a new emotion is forming. He thinks again of Julia's panic, her urgency to get here. The fear he read in her, and which he

265

assumed was only her desperation to hide her lies. But now he sees in it something else. Something worse.

She pushes the heather-coloured duvet on the bed to one side and sits down. Shaking, Paul sits down as well. Not right next to her – he can't bring himself to do that. But close enough. He is freezing, half naked in T-shirt and boxers. If there's a hot shower here, he's no idea where it is. He reaches behind them and pulls the thick duvet up over their shoulders. It sits there like a dense, heavy weight, though Julia makes no move to pull it around her.

He taps the screen. The video is clear as day. There is Chrissie, at home, in their bright, white kitchen. Rehearsing, eyes closed, sound filling the space. It's early evening – he can see the pink and orange of sunset through the French windows to her right.

Suddenly – Paul jolts – there is Francis. The back of him – torso, shoulders, but it's him all right. He must have walked straight in through the front door. Paul's heart pounds: *slam, slam, slam.* On screen, Chrissie stops playing and drops her violin from her chin, eyes wide open now. Francis says, *I've come to see Julia.* On the screen, their daughter is shaking her head. *Both my parents are out,* she says.

'I can't watch it again,' says Julia. But she watches anyway, as Francis steps closer. He's saying something, but even with the iPad volume right up, it's too low to hear.

On screen, Chrissie is so tiny. She's sixteen, she's truly only a child. Paul thinks of the messages he found on her phone, what he thought they were, and what they really meant.

Sexy girl …

Francis laughs, grabs her and pulls her towards him, fingers

266

tangling in her hair. Chrissie jerks herself away but Francis is tall, strong, and he's laughing. He plants a rough kiss on her cheek, right up against her mouth. She doesn't say a word, just strains away from him; he's still holding her and why doesn't she *say* something – anything to help Paul understand what this means? He can only watch until finally Francis releases her and disappears from shot, leaving Chrissie standing there, panting. Tinnily, through the tiny iPad speakers – Paul hears the slam of their front door.

On-screen, Chrissie lunges forwards and the video stops, black.

Dread horror sits like a ball of concrete in his stomach, fear finally breaking through after his shock and anger and disgust. *Sexy girl. Victim.* This isn't right, this is not what Paul imagined. Only now has he seen it: the violence in those moves. And yet, shouldn't alarm have been his very first reaction when the police shared their suspicions about his daughter and this man?

He reaches out for Julia. He wants to cry, scream. He can see where the rain has soaked through her shoes. She's frightened. Her fear was evident before, whereas he just felt furious and incredulous and humiliated. But now …

Paul thinks of the bruises he saw on her neck. He has to face this, even though it leaves him feeling so helpless. He is terrified to voice it, but he has to.

'Julia. I need you to tell me.'

She doesn't move. She's like a small creature, hoping to make herself invisible by staying still.

He goes on. 'Did you believe that Francis could … Is that what you were scared of? Did you know he could be like that? Is that what's made you so desperate to get here?'

Julia moves her head an inch, her short hair scratching the duvet, but she doesn't say anything and in the stuffy dampness of the room, Paul goes cold. A dread cold, this time. He fights to hold himself still. 'Answer me honestly, Julia. I have to know. *We* have to know. We have to be clear whether he's that sort of person.'

He desperately wants her to reassure him. To tell him that this man she's been having an affair with is good and kind and gentle and sweet. That he may have been impetuous and ridiculously misguided, but that he isn't cruel or dangerous or a true threat. He waits a long time with Julia hunched on the bed before he prompts her again.

'Julia. Say it. Do you think Francis could hurt her?'

'Maybe,' she whispers finally. 'Oh God.'

CHAPTER 41

Julia

THREE WEEKS BEFORE

I tried to climb out of it. I absolutely did. By now, I'd begun to see what I was doing, what was driving this, and how misguided and reckless I had been. I knew now that there was nothing good I would gain from this and that I had to get away, before things got worse.

I prayed to myself that it wasn't too late and that I could still recapture my healthy, wholesome life. Paul had already found the drugs, my stupid slip-up: that packet from my pocket that had seemed such a small detail that I'd forgotten it was there. There was no room left now for any more of my mistakes. Honestly, honestly, what had I been thinking? I had a daughter at home and a husband. I should have been fighting to drag myself closer to them. I should have been fighting to reclaim the ground that I'd relinquished right at the start. Instead I'd gone off digging in quicksand, and now I was in it right up to my neck.

The very next day, I sent him a text. It said, simply: *Francis, we need to talk.*

Francis had told me about his previous break-ups. He'd told me he was good at amicable endings, and of course, in this case, he knew from the start that I was married. He couldn't really have been expecting it to go anywhere. He was rich and young enough and handsome. He wouldn't have too much trouble moving on.

I've had a nice time with you. I really did have fun.

I really thought I could do it. I made a plan, rehearsed my lines. I was going to meet him somewhere neutral and public, not at one of our usual haunts. Somewhere ordinary and plain, with ordinary, boring people all around us. That was where I would do it. I'd wear something austere and formal. I'd order a soft drink – lemonade or plain tea – drink it quickly, say my piece and go. I would do my best to let him down gently. It wasn't his fault things turned into such a mess.

I hadn't thought about how he'd answer my initial text. In fact when I read his response, it was with surprise and even (I hated myself for it) a flicker of disappointment.

We need to talk, I'd written.

And he'd simply replied: *Sure.*

*

I'd arranged to meet him straight after work on Monday, but I never got that far. I came back from my lunch break and he was there in my office. Five punnets of strawberries were lined up on my desk, and immediately I had déjà vu about the time I found him in the lobby.

'What are you doing here?' I said, the same line as back then, the whole of my prepared script dissolving in my head.

'You said we needed to talk.' He was smiling.

I closed my office door behind me. I couldn't have anyone overhearing this. What was he doing here? What name and explanation had he given to Angela, our receptionist?

'We're meeting later,' I told him. 'At Carluccio's.'

'Oh my God, Julia. *Carluccio's*? Why would we go there – some yummy-mummy hangout?'

My jaw clenched. 'It's a restaurant.'

He was mocking me. 'I *know* that, but Julia – come on.'

I ignored the strawberries on the desk but their sickly sweet scent filled the room, turning my stomach.

'I'll meet you there later,' I said.

'To "talk"?'

'Yes. To talk.'

'You didn't seem interested in talking the other day. What do you want to talk about now?'

'You know what.'

'Do I?'

I made myself meet his eye. 'I can't have this conversation here, Francis. This is my workplace. Go to Carluccio's. In fact, go anywhere. Give me an hour and I'll come and meet you. But not here.'

Instead he sat down on my office sofa, the one people were always struggling to get up from. 'I brought you strawberries, Julia.'

'Yes. I see that.'

'"Strawberries in February". Wasn't that what you wanted?'

'Yes. Maybe. But ... now it's March.' I tried to smile. *Pacify him. Placate.* Skills I had practised with another man my whole life.

His facial expression didn't change, but his tone shifted. 'Julia.'

I bit my lip but kept my head up and tried to keep my breathing steady. This was not how I'd wanted to do it. There were windows in my office that looked out into the corridors. I had the blinds down, I always did, but it wasn't impossible for someone to see in. I had a meeting soon. Someone would come knocking for me any minute.

'Please, Francis. This has been something ... something amazing, but right now, I don't think ... I'm sorry, Francis. I can't keep doing this.'

This wasn't at all the way I'd wanted to say it.

'You don't mean that.'

'I do. I'm sorry.' I turned my head away. I couldn't look at him. I sensed him get up from the sofa – in a surprisingly easy move. Outside, I could hear people speaking in the corridor as they passed by my office. From the corner of my eye, I was sure I could see a shadow hovering at the window, listening, or even peeping through the blind.

Francis held out his arms. 'Julia. Come here.'

I stayed where I was, gripping the desk. 'I told you, I can't.' Who was out there? Who was looking in? A blur of pink, but I was too scared to turn my head.

He came towards me but he didn't hug me. Not this time. Instead, he brought his hand to my face and I startled as I felt his sudden grasp. His fingers were pushing into my flesh, my chin gripped almost brutally as he pressed his lips to mine. It was only a kiss; from the outside it might have looked like

272

passion, yet wasn't this exactly what I'd sensed was coming, wasn't this exactly why I'd tried to get away? This twisted knot of sex and violence; both parts converging in a moment like this. He covered my mouth with his own, held it there until I could hardly breathe, and all the while his grip was crushing my jaw, my neck, my throat—

Someone tapped on my door. I coughed, half choked as Francis let go of me.

I was weak with relief to hear Peter's voice. 'Julia, are you in there? Meeting's starting,' he said.

*

I never did meet Francis at Carluccio's. I went there at the time I had told him and waited half an hour but there was no sign of him. He didn't call or text me either. My phone was silent. When a kindly waiter approached and asked whether I wanted to order anything, I stuck to my plan, and ordered a lemonade.

When Francis didn't show, I put everything I'd wanted to say in a text instead. It took me very little time to type out the words that I had rehearsed so many times in my own head. In the end, it was a short message. Concise and to the point, leaving no room for misinterpretation.

I was breaking up with him. I was sorry if that hurt him. I wished him well, but I asked that he didn't contact me again.

Back in the office, I had already thrown all the strawberries into the bin, telling Angela they'd gone mouldy when she caught me in the act. Now I poured the remains of my drink into the glass and drank it down in one. I wanted to get out of there.

I re-read my message and finally pressed send. Then I deleted every single message that I'd ever sent to or received from him. I deleted his contact (filed under *IT Department*) from my address book.

I removed all trace of what we had done.

And that was when all Paul's calls and texts about Chrissie came flooding in.

CHAPTER 42

Julia

TWO WEEKS BEFORE

I think it was after that night when she ran off to the Botanical Gardens that I realized Chrissie's diary was a lie. There had been nothing in there beforehand to alert me and she didn't mention the incident in the days after it either. The whole thing was a red herring; she had always known that I read it, maybe she even wrote it *for* me, to keep everything sweet. But I pushed that knowledge aside and chose to utterly ignore it because this way I could continue sending my father my updates without lying. I could continue to keep him at bay, head off any questions, because by now there was far too much at stake.

After that night, I didn't hear from Francis for forty-eight hours. Enough time for the bruises his fingers had imprinted on my jaw to start to fade. Enough time for me to believe that he would simply leave me alone. Francis hadn't come to Carluccio's and he hadn't replied to my break-up text. At that point, I hadn't yet blocked his number or his WhatsApp or his email. He could still have got in contact with me if he wished. For closure, if he had needed that.

But he didn't, and gradually in the hours that followed, I felt the steel cage in my chest loosen. I wasn't underwater any more, I wasn't drowning. I could focus on my daughter and my husband and my work again, and I slept better that night than I had in months.

At three a.m., though, something woke me.

My phone was on silent, face down on my bedside table. It wouldn't have made a noise and in my sleep I wouldn't have seen it light up, but somehow I woke up and I knew.

For a moment I lay there, staring through the dark at the ceiling, hearing nothing but my own shallow breaths. Then I sat up and fumbled for my phone on the bedside table. I took it into the en suite bathroom, desperately not wanting to disturb Paul.

I unlocked the screen, my fingers shaking. There was no reason for anyone to be texting me at this time.

But I had been right. There were two new texts, both of them time-stamped just one minute before.

The sender's ID was just an 07 number, but of course I knew who it was.

At first, the initial message completely disorientated me, because the words that stared up at me were completely familiar. Then I realized: Francis had screenshotted and sent my whole break-up message back to me, setting it in quote marks, so that my own incriminating words filled up my screen again, even though I'd deleted them myself.

Below was his reply, a judgement and a ruling on everything I had said:

I know you, Julia. You want me. You need this. You cannot expect me to just let you go.

*

After that, he wouldn't stop. *See me again.* That was the theme of every single one of his messages, and they came at all hours of the day, and the night.

See me again, don't cut me off like that.

I replied, in as many ways that I could think of: *I can't, I can't, I can't.* But when had those words ever worked with him before?

It was the sheer relentlessness of his texts. I had to keep my phone permanently on silent, but at the same time I couldn't switch it off or stop checking it, because of course my work phone and my personal phone were one and the same, no separation between the office and home.

I deleted the messages as soon as I had read them, and I deleted my own replies too.

I tried to reason with him. I tried to be a broken record, reiterating everything I had said before, but nothing seemed to get through to him. I was somehow only making it worse.

I didn't have anyone to talk to about it. I imagined turning up on Sally Fairshaw's doorstep and bursting into tears in front of her, confessing everything. She would have had advice for me, but advice loaded with judgement and retrospective rulings on what I should have done differently up until now, how I should never have got involved with another man in the first place.

I thought about contacting Lynn, our couples therapist,

277

and paying for a secret, individual session, pouring it all out to her and asking her what to do. But whenever I thought of that option, all I could picture was her sitting there, looking at me, head tilted slightly to one side, saying the same things that my mother did, and my father. *For Christ's sake, Julia, what's wrong with you? We never taught you to behave like this. You should be ashamed – look at yourself. Look at yourself, Julia, what the bloody hell have you become?*

And I was. I *was* looking, but I had no words to properly explain what I had done. All I knew was that now I felt scared and ashamed and guilty. I wanted out; I just didn't know how. When Francis shifted his messaging, asking for a new thing, I told myself this would be the answer. I ignored the part that hated myself so badly that I would put myself right back in his hands.

I know we need to break up, Julia. Just see me once more so I can say goodbye.

It felt as if I would be walking right back into the lion's den, but what other choice did I have? In the end, I agreed. In the end, I did it.

I met him at an out-of-town hotel. I told myself that if we sat and had a drink, like old times, and saw each other face to face; if I even let him give me a goodbye kiss, then finally, finally, it would be over.

I was shaking as I drove there. I got lost on the way, taking the wrong exit from the motorway. I had told Paul I had an out-of-town conference, another fresh lie to add to all the rest. But I was doing this for him now. I did it while Paul and Chrissie went to her Category Finals audition.

It was raining so hard it was difficult to see out of the

windscreen. It was a shabby place that I pulled into, nothing like the places he had taken me to before. Was he trying to make some kind of point with that? I had no idea; I had long since stopped being able to read him.

I didn't have an umbrella with me so I got soaked running from the car to the reception. Inside, there was no sign of him, and I asked the receptionist, telling them I was here to meet Mr Maitland.

'Oh yes,' the young receptionist said. 'He's in room 201.'

I stared at her. 'Can you ring him, please, and ask him to come down? Tell him I'm waiting for him in the foyer.'

'Sure.' The receptionist lifted the phone and dialled. Her expression was smooth as glass as the phone rang.

And rang.

'I'm sorry, ma'am, but he isn't answering. Do you have his number to call him yourself?'

I fumbled in my wet bag for my phone. 'Yes, yes. I'll do that.'

I stepped as far away from the reception desk as I could before dialling. Francis had sent me so many texts that, even though I had deleted every one, I had his number imprinted on my brain. No answer again; just his impassive voicemail. I hung up and sent a text. *I'm here. Downstairs. Do you want to see me or not?*

It was half a minute before he sent his reply. When I saw it, my stomach clenched.

When I said see you, I meant *see* you, Julia.

I sank down into a chair, a thick padded armchair with plasticky seams. I pressed a palm to my heart as though to suppress the thudding in my chest.

'Everything okay, ma'am?' The receptionist was craning to look at me over her desk.

I nodded to her, almost cricking my neck to turn my head. 'Yes, thanks. Everything is fine.'

Well, what else had I thought he meant? That we would sit and have a civilized conversation, as though there were no thorns here, as though we were two pebbles, our soft sides smooth? Whatever we were doing here, it would be humiliating, brutal.

I stood up again and asked the receptionist, 'Where are the lifts?'

The receptionist pointed me down a corridor. 'Second floor.' She repeated: 'Room 201.'

The lift shuddered as it carried me upwards with its greasy mirrors and unforgiving overhead light. I had visions of its wire ropes snapping and me plummeting to my death. The whole thing felt like some kind of death-wish to me. On the second floor, the doors opened on a claustrophobic corridor. Someone's trainers stood outside their door, and down the end a housekeeping cart was piled with dirty crockery. I focused on the doors, searching for the right number.

205, 204, 202, 201.

Last chance to turn and walk back out of there, but I didn't. I so wanted to believe that after this, everything would stop.

The room was nauseating. Pink and brown. A crack in the cheap wood of the vanity, and a smell of bleach and peach air freshener in the air. It was as though he'd done his best to find the worst possible place for this. He lay on the bed, propped up on one elbow. I could tell right away that he'd done a line of coke; his eyes had that flickering look that I'd come to recognize. In fact, he'd clearly taken a lot of it, and maybe other stuff too.

'Julia,' he said charmingly. 'You came.'

I stood there. 'This is the last time. And then it's over.'

'Sure.' He sat up and smoothed out the ugly bedspread for me.

*

The sex was as ugly as the cheap hotel room. Cold, uncomfortable, like two plastic mannequins tangling together. With it, I felt something crumbling inside me, like a hope I'd held on to until these very last seconds, a belief that something good could have been born from this, that somewhere in this tormented mess, something broken could have healed. I almost cried as I forced myself to kiss him, and pretended to finish the moment that he did.

Afterwards, as I was pulling on my tights, he said to me, 'Thank you, Julia. That was everything I needed.'

I felt such a drenching of both relief and hopelessness, sitting on the edge of that grotty bed, untangling my bra straps. I really thought that he would abide by his promises, even if I was on my own now, with this weeping, ragged hole in my heart.

'You're welcome, Francis,' I heard myself saying. Like a mannequin, I smiled at him over my shoulder. 'I really do wish you well.'

Fool.

*

This time he left me alone for almost a week.

But then his texts started up again. If I said no or didn't reply, they escalated. He wanted us to go away together. He wanted me to tell Paul I didn't love him and was leaving. He wanted to be able to tell Paul that himself.

It felt as though I could never escape Francis without losing my whole life. I felt so stupid for ever thinking I could get out of this. I was a fool for trusting he'd ever let me walk away. Whatever absolution I'd been searching for through this love affair, it was crystal clear I hadn't found it, and now the realities of the mess I had made were rising up all around me, sharp shards of betrayal that could rip my whole life and family apart.

Day after day, the messages kept coming, and nothing I said seemed to make any difference.

The whole thing had become like a nightmare. Francis had the power to expose me and I was terrified of what he was capable of.

Then, two nights before Chrissie's semi-finals, for no good reason the messages just … stopped.

CHAPTER 43

Paul

NOW

Outside the damp walls and small bedroom window, the thunderstorm rages on. Paul sits on the bed, the duvet heavy on his shoulders. He can't bring himself to move. He is simply trying to take it all in.

He's just a few miles outside this place called Camp Dìon, a random activist camp where his daughter will be.

She is there with a man called Francis. A man Paul once met at a party, a man who kissed Julia – who did far more to her than that. A man who has run away with – *abducted?* – their child, and who is quite capable of hurting the person Paul most loves.

He feels so powerless, so desperate. He wants the thunder to tear everything away and deliver him straight to her, a bolt of lightning, *deus ex machina*, but there's nothing he can do. As a child, there was nothing he could do to stop his father's gambling. There was nothing he could do, either, to stop his mother's tears. It seems to be the way he's felt his whole life: dependent, helpless, the outcome always resting in other people's hands.

All the while, that alarm bell deep inside him is shrilling.

His heart leaps in his throat when the knock comes at the door.

CHAPTER 44

Julia

NOW

Someone is knocking on the door. At the same time, my phone is ringing beside me on the sagging mattress. I shuck off the duvet that Paul has put round my shoulders – to warm me, to comfort me; it has done neither – and reach for it. My heart is thumping. I fumble for my mobile and when I see the name on the screen – DS Brayford again – I immediately swipe to shut down the call.

I cannot speak to her right now.

The knock comes again, a little impatiently this time.

'One moment!' Paul is tugging his wet clothes from the radiator and hurriedly pulling them on.

I go to the door and open it just far enough to see the woman standing there, short blonde hair, a little overweight.

'Ned says you want a lift to the camp?'

'Yes, thank you. Sorry – my husband is just getting changed.'

'Well, listen, the best time to go is probably tomorrow

afternoon. The weather's supposed to have cleared up then. It'll be a lot less muddy, so there'll be less chance of getting stuck.'

'Sorry …' I stare at her. 'There must be some kind of mis-understanding. We want to go today. I mean, right now.'

Paul appears behind me in the doorway, dressed and pulling the door properly open. 'I'm Paul. This is my wife Julia.' I don't know if he's heard what Barbara just said.

'I thought you were staying the night here?'

I nod. 'Yes, yes, but we just need to go there and come straight back. We're … collecting someone.'

'You are?'

'Our daughter. She's expecting us.'

'Expecting you right now?'

'Yes. I'm sorry. But could you do it? Could we go now, can you take us? We've made it all this way and we don't want her to have to wait any longer.'

'Your daughter …' Barbara echoes my words as though finally digesting them. 'Right. We'd better go then.'

'Thank you. Really, we're so grateful. Thank you.'

She gives a tiny sigh. 'It's fine.' She glances down at our empty hands. 'Got what you need?'

'Yes. Just one sec.' I duck back into the room and grab Paul's rucksack, shoving the iPad in there along with our phones and our wallets. Then I join Paul and Barbara out on the landing, and close and lock the door behind us. 'Ready,' I say.

'Okay then. Ride's outside.'

She leads us back down the stairs, through the bar area and back outside, where a vehicle is waiting. The rain has cleared again, though the cloud cover is sullen. The vehicle is a huge thing, more like a truck than a car. Barbara tells us there's room for all three of us to sit in the front and I find myself squeezed in between her and Paul, having to twist awkwardly to stop my legs from blocking the gear stick. I hold the rucksack clutched on my knee. On his lap, Paul holds the bottles of water we bought from the store. The truck cabin smells of cigarette smoke and engine oil, despite the air freshener swinging from the rear-view mirror. Paul swings the passenger door shut, boxing us in.

'Ready?' Barbara smiles and I smile back, trying my best to be a good passenger. We're paying for this – Ned was clear about that – but I also want Barbara to be on our side.

As she releases the handbrake and drags the truck into gear, I steady myself as best as I can, bracing my feet against the gritty floor. She swings us round in a tight circle, and I glimpse the dog that ran up to us earlier. He lets out a series of barks then I lose sight of him as we lurch forwards and out along the street.

Barbara drives us right to the edge of the village, past three rows of houses, a tiny children's play area, a memorial stone. Then it's straight across a rugged field where there's nothing but churned tyre tracks to show you the way and we're shaken from side to side in the furrows.

'Don't worry,' says Barbara, 'there's a better track on the other side. This is probably the worst bit – except the part you have to walk.'

I try not to think about the fact that in a matter of hours, it'll be getting dark. It's past four o'clock now, and I know the sun sets earlier up here. For all I know, it could be pitch black by six.

Paul speaks above the engine noise, thanking Barbara all

over again. She smiles again and my mouth is stiff as I try to smile back. 'No problem. I actually needed to take a trip there anyway.' She jerks a thumb towards a load in the back. 'A sack of potatoes for the good citizens of Camp Dìon,' she tells us.

I can understand her perfectly, her accent isn't strong, but I have no idea what to make of this statement. It makes me picture Chrissie, starving. The truck jounces and lurches, throwing the three of us gracelessly from side to side. I long for fresh air inside this stuffy cabin, but it's far too cold to crack a window open.

We cross the far edge of the field, and Barbara's right, there's a rugged road in front of us. It's not exactly tarmacked, but at least it's mostly flat. As we turn onto it, something scrapes along the bottom of the truck, untangling itself at the end with a screech.

My phone shrills again in the rucksack. I hesitate.

'Go on. Answer it,' says Barbara. 'Don't mind me.'

I pull it out and look at the screen. That name. This time, there's no way I can hang up.

'Julia,' says the voice on the line. His voice is so loud that even with the engine noise, it bounces round the cabin. It's a shock to the system; it makes me want to burst into tears. I feel twenty years old again; I feel twelve.

'Daddy?'

'I've just read your email. Finally got Internet. What on earth is going on? What's all this about Chrissie going missing?'

I told him such bare bones in the email I finally sent to my parents. *Chrissie disappeared just after the concert. We're sure she's fine, but we've contacted the police.* A mixed message of alarm and reassurance.

'She's …' I break off. 'She's here. We've found her.'

'Found her? Where?' My father's voice is clipped and direct. I remind myself that this is how anxiety shows in him.

'Near Inverness.'

'*Inverness?*'

'Yes. She …'

Paul leans over and takes the phone out of my grasp. 'Duncan? It's fine. You don't need to worry. We know where she is now – she's at this place, this camp. We're on our way to collect her.'

'A camp?' my father says. 'What on earth is she doing at a *camp*?'

'She came here with a … a friend.'

'She did *what?*'

I wrench the phone back from Paul. 'Daddy, it's fine. Please don't worry.'

'But I *am* worried. Look, we're coming. We're already on our way back.'

'Daddy, no, you don't have to do that.' I don't want to tell him anything about Francis. I can't bear to say that Chrissie might be in danger from a man I knew, a man I slept with. Who I'm terrified has taken and might be harming my daughter, all because I refused to let him have me.

'It was your mother's decision. She'd already decided to cut our holiday short, even before you emailed.'

'Before? What do you mean?' I'm trying to keep the fear from my voice.

'She's got it in her head that I'm not well – not myself. It's nonsense, but she's managed to convince our tour guide …'

A wave of nausea rises up in me, hairs stiffen right across

my scalp. 'Listen, Daddy, it's all right, we're sorting it. We're driving there to fetch her right now. Just go home. If you're not well, you need to rest.'

'You're in Inverness, you say. In Scotland? Fine. *Fine*. Then we're flying straight out.'

'Daddy, no,' I repeat. 'You don't need to do that. Go home. We'll get her and be right with you. We can be back tomorrow. I'll come straight to you then.'

There's a silence, and then: 'You better bloody had.'

'Of course. Of course we will, Daddy.' I am cold. Shaky. It takes so much to stand up to him. My head is swimming. My words choke in my throat.

The line goes dead; I guess he hung up.

'What the hell?' Barbara says. 'Your daughter is *missing*? Why didn't you say so? Fuck.'

'It's fine,' I say, my voice weakened, whispery. 'She isn't missing. We've found her now. We know that she's here.'

'Yes. Yes – maybe you saw her.' Paul is pulling out his phone now from the rucksack I've got clutched on my lap.

He flicks through to find a picture of Chrissie and holds it up so Barbara can see.

She glances across. 'Oh yeah! That kid? She arrived here yesterday.'

I am awash with a rinsing wave of relief. 'She did? She *did*?' Until right now, I really didn't know for sure.

The truck lurches again as Barbara swerves round a pothole. 'Sure. Sweet kid.' She gestures. 'Long dark hair.'

'Yes,' I say, breathless. 'That's her. That's Chrissie.'

'We think she came with someone called Francis,' says Paul.

Barbara nods. 'Yes, that sounds about right. I gave them both a lift. Her and the guy, plus a couple of others.'

Oh my God. Oh my God. I choke out my next words. 'And she seemed okay? She wasn't hurt or anything?'

'What?' Ahead of us, the track is growing increasingly narrow and rough, but Barbara is driving faster than ever. There are more and more potholes, filled with water from the thunderstorm and rain. 'No. At least, I didn't see anything. But – you're saying she ran away? And the guy she's with – is he meant to be her boyfriend? Jesus, you guys must have been frantic. Bet you're fuming.'

I shake my head. It's so impossible to explain; I just want us to get there. We've been driving for ten minutes, fifteen, and every minute is too long. If we can just get to her, everything will be all right. This will go from being a nightmare to a dream, to something, to nothing. We'll take her back home and all will be well.

'She's a musician – a violinist. She was taking part in a big competition.' Paul fumbles the words. 'She's been under a lot of stress. A lot of pressure.'

Barbara shakes her head. 'You don't need to tell me. I've got three of my own. They're a nightmare – kids. But if it was my daughter, I'd give her a bloody good hiding.'

When she says those words, I want to be sick.

Suddenly Barbara brings the truck to a halt. The track is so stony now that it hardly looks like a road. More like a mountain path you'd have to scramble over. Initially, I assume that she's taken a wrong turn and ended up bringing us to a disused dead end. But I don't remember seeing any turn-offs, and anyway, now Barbara is opening her door and getting out.

'You have to walk the last bit,' she reminds me.

I turn to her. 'Won't you be coming with us?'

'I mean, I don't usually. But you said you're coming straight back, right? I'll wait here. Drive you back once you've got your daughter.'

Paul is already climbing out of the truck, stepping down onto the muddy, rocky road. I slide along the seat and climb out myself. My sense of dread is worse than ever. The pale sun is well behind the treetops now, and it's only going to sink lower. I'm still trying to calculate how long we've got.

'She's going to leave these supplies here,' Paul says, and I blink, trying to listen and focus on his words. 'Some of the group members will collect them later. The camp is only about a twenty-minute walk.'

I look down at my feet. I'm wearing running shoes that will quickly be soaked through. We should be wearing thick, waterproof hiking boots, Rohan walking trousers, cagoules, not jeans and our smart city jackets. This is ridiculous. Utterly ridiculous, but Chrissie doesn't own anything like that either and somehow she made it here. This camp, this whole environment, still seems so completely *not-Chrissie*. And yet, honestly, how much have I ever known about what goes on inside her beautiful head? The reality is, they are *actually both here*. Chrissie and Francis. And so I tell myself: if she made it to this place, then so will we.

I nod and manage to smile politely. 'Thank you again, Barbara, for all of your help.'

'No problem,' she repeats as she swings herself back up into the truck. 'Just – Jesus, you should hurry up and get her. In this weather, I bet she's fed up and miserable. Apparently it's not so bad in summer, but even then, I wouldn't want my daughter hanging about in that place.'

I shut the door of the jeep, and Paul and I stand in the middle of the forest on the rutted, narrow track. The foliage around us is dim and dense, but we only need to follow the path, and we'll get there.

'Be careful of the river,' Barbara shouts as she slams her own door closed. 'After the rain, it'll be running pretty deep.'

CHAPTER 45

Paul

Now that they are out of the truck and the engine is shut off, Paul can hear crows cawing all around them. It sounds as if there are hundreds of the things and their racket is like angry laughter. He thinks about taking Julia's hand to reassure her, but looking at how rocky the road is, how uneven, he imagines that will only make it harder to walk. 'Here,' he says instead, 'at least let me carry the rucksack.'

She hands it to him and he slings it over his shoulder, where the straps dig into his skin. 'All right then.'

They turn their backs on the jeep and set off along the track. There's a bend almost at once and so they lose sight of Barbara. Paul walks slowly so that Julia can keep pace with him, even though the impatience in him burns like acid. It makes sense to go slowly, he has to tell himself: it would be a nightmare to go twisting an ankle here. There are still puddles from the torrents of rain, the stones and rocks are loose, and in some places the mud is like a bog, ankle deep. Fifteen minutes, he reminds himself. Maximum twenty, and they'll be with her. One foot in front of the other, that's all it takes. He imagines the moment he sees her, grasping her, wrapping his arms round her. Deep in his heart and safe, safe, safe.

*

They hear the river well before they see it. Paul mistakes the noise for thunder at first, or an aeroplane crossing the expanse above them. He cranes up to scan the strip of grey sky before Julia says to him, 'It's water.'

And then it's obvious. That rushing roar, what else could it be? They walk-scramble along the remaining length of the track. It has smoothed out now – passable again for a vehicle, if a vehicle could be airlifted to here.

'Paul,' says Julia. 'Look.'

He follows the line of her finger to where she's pointing. A wooden sign for *Camp Dìon*, crudely painted with a white arrow, is nailed to a tree.

They round the final bend, and now the track fans out into a wide, gritty bankside, a semi-circular overhang, surrounded by trees. The earth slopes steeply down ahead of them, and four, five feet below them, there it is: the river.

Not blue and sparkling, but brown and writhing. Deep. Like Barbara said.

They slip-slide down to it. Their shoes are ruined anyway by now. There's a rope strung across it as a flimsy handrail. Paul's foot slips on the crumbly bank.

'We have to cross?' Julia says.

Paul scans upstream, downstream. 'I can't see another way.'

'I don't want to see him. I don't want to talk to him.'

He knows who she means. 'I know that. Neither do I.

295

But she's sixteen, Julia, and we are her *parents*. He can't do anything to us. In fact, what he's already done is probably illegal, leaving the country with a teenager. We won't let him do any talking. We're going to get our daughter and take her home.'

Of all the scenarios that have run through his head, he never imagined their reunion being like this. He never imagined that this was how they would find her. A nameless forest in the middle of nowhere? Rain, mud and crows, and only the kindness of strangers to rely on?

He almost jumps out of his skin when Julia's phone rings yet again, the noise totally incongruous in this setting. He's surprised she even has reception out here.

'Here. Please, Paul! Can you answer?' Julia is holding the buzzing phone out to him, as though it's a creature that is biting her hand. She's turning the responsibility over to him now, the way she's done with other things in their lives, asking him to deal with whatever she can't. Half dazed, he takes the mobile from her and hits the green answer icon. The line is poor, but he can just about make out the other person speaking.

'Hello? It's Ned. Yeah, Ned from the pub. Listen, I'm not sure what you two have got going on, but I've just had the police here.'

'The police?'

'Aye. And they're looking for you.'

Paul doesn't experience any shock or surprise, just a heavy sense of inevitability. Of course the police have traced them. DS Brayford and her colleagues aren't stupid. She must have known all along that they were lying. Finding them was only a matter of time.

'Ned,' he says. 'I'm sorry. For any trouble they've caused you.'

'It's fine, nae bother. But, mate, look. I can't be getting involved in anything ... dodgy. I've already texted Barbara and told her to come back.'

'No – wait. She said she would wait for us. Didn't she explain? Our daughter is missing but she's here – at the camp.'

'I dunno, mate. Seems there's more to it than that. Like I said, I don't want to get involved. The police are on their way, they're in a jeep coming after you, and look – if your daughter's missing, right, they're probably your best bet.'

When Paul hangs up, Julia's face is ashen. She has sunk to a crouch on the bank of the river, head between her knees. He crouches down beside her.

'You know what this is,' she says. 'You know what this means.'

Even if they reach Chrissie first, there are going to be some serious repercussions. It's so much to face; he can't think of how on earth they would explain all this. Instead, his attention shrinks down to practicalities. There is no way the police can drive all the way down here either. They will have to walk, like them, navigating the last stretch on foot. Even so, it's only a matter of time. He and Julia are on a track in the middle of a forest, the light is fading, and they have no transport back. But their daughter, Chrissie, is just a river-crossing away. They have to keep going. There is simply no way back.

'I'm going to go first, then,' Julia says. 'If I slip, I might need you to haul me back out.' She steps down into the water. It comes up to the middle of her shins.

'It's so cold.' She gasps. 'Why is everything so cold up here!'

She reaches down to grasp the rope that drapes across the river – a river that is clearly in flood – lifting it, dripping, up to waist height. Her hands are already red-raw with the cold, and the greenish cord looks ridiculously thin and flimsy. He can't even see whether it's properly tied.

'Shit. Julia. Shit. Be careful.' They shouldn't be doing this. Surely there has to be another way. Maybe they could try to get a message across to her. Why don't they just wait for one of the students to come out? For a moment, he even thinks crazily that they should just wait for the police. The police who are looking for them. Police who might arrest them – or who might help them. They could turn themselves in, explain everything. Offer money if needs be. Trust that – back home – DS Brayford is still on their side. Whatever has happened, Chrissie didn't mean it. He knows that now. She's just a child, a silly schoolgirl. Everything she's done, he's completely ready to forgive.

Julia steps forward. The water rushes up to her thighs and she staggers. She is so petite and you never think that water can be so strong. You never understand how people can be swept away in floodwater and die. You think of water the way it is in a bath or a swimming pool. Calm, placid; easy to sit and stand and swim in. Not like this. He can see Julia strain against the current. In his mind's eye, he can see her slipping, tumbling, falling, dragged away in that violent torrent … He can see himself losing her, irreparably, after everything. He can see himself never getting her back.

She is strong though, stronger than he might have expected, for all her delicacy, all her refinement.

His turn now; he steps into the water behind her. She's

right: the cold feels like a million needles piercing his legs. The sheer shock of it, even only up to his shins, steals his breath. He wades forwards, following Julia, the current constantly dragging at his feet, his legs. The two of them don't speak now. It would be hard to hear each other anyway over the tumult of the water. Julia wades on, close to reaching the halfway point. Surely it will grow shallower again after that. Leaves and twigs eddy all around them. The river, rain-swollen, is dragging pieces of the forest down with it. Upstream, a tangle of branches are jammed across the river, but the water pushes easily through and over. A force to be reckoned with.

But they are going to cross this river. Their family's whole future may depend on it.

Julia has reached the middle now, and Paul is only a few metres behind. She glances back at him and he takes in the grim determination on her face. They are going to make it. He lifts his voice above the roar and calls out to her: 'You're doing great. I love you.'

And then, over Julia's shoulder, he sees her, standing on the far bank, in wellington boots and with her familiar rucksack slung over her shoulder.

He almost collapses at the sight of her.

She seems thinner now, after only a few days. She looks childlike but also immeasurably older, dressed in clothes he doesn't recognize, her hair tied back in a way he's never seen.

It is her though.

Chrissie.

CHAPTER 46

Julia

Chrissie stands there, mouth open, a picture of complete shock.

I go stock-still as well, up to my knees in the icy water. My jeans and jacket are soaking; my legs, hands, lips are numb, but I don't care.

I've found my daughter.

I feel tears running down my cheeks, mixing with the freezing splashes of river water.

'Chrissie!' I shout. I drag myself forward on the rope, stumbling over rocks, my legs continually pushed away from under me. This is stupid. This is crazy. But I'm going to get to her. I'm going to bring her home.

Under my feet, the ground is sloping up on the other side now. I'm over the worst of it. All I have to do is get up the bank. My legs are streaked with mud and I have a thin, oozing gash on my forearm. I didn't feel it in the river but it's starting to burn now.

I reach out a hand. The bank is steep. 'Chrissie. Help me up. Chrissie.'

She doesn't move. It's as though she's frozen. There is no one else here. No sign of anyone else from the camp. Just the three of us and this huge, gushing river. No sign of *him*. We can get her away from here without having to confront that. Get her away from *him*. Bring her home.

I let go of the river rope and pull myself up the bank on my own, clawing at roots and mud with my hands. Paul is close behind me, scrambling his way up the bank too, frantically, clumsily.

I make it to the top. I'm drenched and my hands are covered in mud, but I grab her – so hard that I'm in danger of leaving bruises. Twigs and leaves tumble down the bank from under my feet. Immediately, the river snatches them away and they're gone.

'You found me,' she mumbles.

'Of course we did! Chrissie, what the hell are you doing here?'

'I didn't mean to. I honestly didn't mean it.' Her face looks bloodless. What is it – horror? Fear?

'We need to leave. Right now.'

'Yes. Okay. Please. I'm coming.'

I'm confused. I didn't expect her to be this compliant. We haven't even set eyes on the camp.

Paul steps forwards, gaining the top of the bank too. 'Is he here? Did he hurt you?'

She turns her gaze slowly towards him. 'Is who here?'

'*Francis.*'

There's noise behind us. When I turn, I see a flash of bright yellow at the end of the track. A police vest. They're here. I grab Chrissie's arms again. I want to shake her, but I'm on the back foot again, because now there's a figure coming up behind her. Brown hair, so familiar.

'Oh my God. *Reece.*' Chrissie's best friend.

There's a whole cluster of police on the opposite bank now; I see one of them set foot in the water. They are coming.

'But *Francis*, Chrissie. What about Francis?'

Her face drains even further of colour. 'No. Not really. He didn't,' she half whispers.

'Didn't what?'

Chrissie covers her face with her hands, her thin arms bending under my grasp. 'Hurt me.'

Now Reece speaks, his voice low. Serious. 'We just saw it on my phone. It's on the news. Didn't you see it too?'

'See what? Listen, Chrissie. Francis is *missing*.'

'He isn't.'

I try to pull her hands from her face. 'What are you talking about? Where is he?'

'In Oxford! Where else?'

'In Oxford? He never left?'

Reece repeats himself. 'It's on the news. They …'

His next words are lost on me: I simply can't process them.

'Hey!' The police officer is shouting, waving, splashing through the river towards us. He's a tall man, huge; the water barely comes up to his knees.

'They *what?*' Like me, Paul is staring at Reece.

DS Brayford's words hammer in my brain. *The last we know, he was seen with your daughter. Walking down towards one of the Cherwell towpaths. We picked them up on CCTV…*

'Don't you understand?' Chrissie says. She is crying now, tears flooding her cheeks.

'No,' I say. Because I don't want to. I'm trying to hold myself up; the cold, the shock – I'm in danger of collapsing.

Reece says it again. 'They pulled him out of the Cherwell river yesterday.'

I've never heard such misery in Chrissie's voice. 'Your boyfriend Francis isn't *missing*, Mum. He's dead.'

CHAPTER 47

Paul

'We have to go,' says Paul. 'We have to get out of here.' Although, this time, there's no way they can avoid the police. He's already pulling Chrissie back down the bank, tugging her by the sleeve of her unfamiliar clothes. He pulls at her, dragging her down the slope of the bank, even as she slithers and slips in his grasp.

'It's all right, Chrissie,' he tells her, like a good father, even in the worst of circumstances sheltering her in the reassurance that everything is okay. He helps her down the bank and into the water. Julia follows them; her arm is bleeding, a bright red gash, but they haven't time to stop. They have to get their daughter away from this place.

He steps back into the water and it feels almost colder than before. They meet the shouting police officer halfway across. The man grabs Chrissie, hustling her to the opposite bank. Paul glances behind; Reece is still standing on the far bank.

It's so obvious to him now. Reece with his *Save the Whales* T-shirt; it makes sense he'd come to somewhere like this. And of course Chrissie would run to him, wherever he was. He catches Reece's voice, shouting across to him. 'I'm sorry! I'm sorry, Mr Goodlight. She didn't mean to hurt anyone, she just wanted you to fix things! She ran away because she had to, but she always wanted to come back!'

*

Of course the police will need to ask a hundred questions. Paul has no idea how much they know. Are they under arrest? Is Chrissie?

'We need to take you back to Kilgarry,' the officers say. Paul nods, dumbly. He is soaked, frozen to the bone. Chrissie must be feeling the same. The police officers have silver foil blankets that they wrap round all three of them, and like that they have to walk back up the rutted track. It's a blur; time expands and contracts. Paul's mind feels frozen. He cannot seem to process what he's learned.

Round the last bend, there are two police jeeps waiting for them. Unbelievably, Barbara's sack of potatoes still sits slumped by the side of the road. A sense of horror begins to creep through him, a sense of reality cracking apart. It feels as though the last forty-eight hours is unravelling backwards, all the dot-to-dot connections coming apart. He thought he had this; he thought he knew what he was doing. He thought this was everything Celina had warned him about: Chrissie ending up in a sordid affair with some man. Now everything he's assumed has been flipped on its head.

Paul pictures them dragging a body from a river. *Francis's* body. Waterlogged. Cold. He thought he was rescuing Chrissie from this monster. But that was all wrong. That was never the story.

It can't have been.

Because Francis is dead.

*

An officer sits him on the tailgate of a jeep, the foil blanket still around his shoulders. In response to the initial questions he's asked, Paul tells this officer that he had no idea about Francis. Neither he nor Julia did. He explains about the Camp Dìon website they found on Julia's old iPad, and how from there they tracked Chrissie to this place. They had no idea about any of it, even though he always tried to keep such a close eye. All this time, they thought Francis was with her. They feared he would hurt her – if he hadn't already. They had no idea that he was dead.

They are interviewing Julia in a second vehicle. He can make out her head and shoulders in the back seat. Paul wonders whether she is telling them about her affair. She might as well. What's left to lose?

They are gathering Chrissie's initial statement too. She's sitting on a fallen tree branch a little distance away, wrapped in foil too. An officer crouches next to her; he can just make out Chrissie's voice.

'I only pushed him a little bit,' she says, 'just to make him go away.'

He closes his ears to the rest of it after that. He isn't sure he wants to know – not right now, maybe not ever.

*

After that they are driven back to Kilgarry. They brought nothing with them, so Paul and Julia have no clothes to change into, and Chrissie is empty-handed as well. Someone from the village brings some spare clothes for them: plain, worn, shabby items, and the police let the three of them change in the room above the pub. Chrissie's lips are blue with cold. She turns her back on him to step out of her soaked trousers and he turns away from her to pull on the donated too-big sweater and the bobbled grey jogging bottoms. Taking in the small, shabby room, Paul thinks back to another hotel room, the one in London before Chrissie's semi-finals, when they were on the brink of brilliance and it felt as if nothing could ever go wrong.

In the new outfit, he feels like a criminal, as though he's already wearing prison clothes.

'What now?' he manages to ask as they are ushered back downstairs.

They are to be driven back to Inverness, where there is a police station and proper interviews can be conducted, proper processes followed.

Paul still can't tell whether they are under arrest. There are no handcuffs and no one has cautioned them. He thinks vaguely that he should call a lawyer, but despite Julia's connections, he doesn't know who to call.

They should call the hire-car company at least, he thinks, and tell them a police officer will be bringing the useless vehicle back.

'This way.' Yet another officer directs them towards the police vehicles.

Back outside the pub, it's raining again and the wind is slicing. Julia and Chrissie are put in a police car together.

Paul is ushered into a second one, alone.

*

It's fully dark when they reach Inverness. The police station is uncannily like the one they visited in Oxford. Same colour scheme, same panelled ceilings, same stark lights. Paul feels as though they are circling back and starting all over again – except that this time, they have Chrissie with them, a dozen rugged stones have been turned over, and a man isn't missing, he's dead.

Paul is startled to see DS Brayford there, looking exactly the same as she did in Oxford. Same hair, same hands, same inscrutable expression. Even her outfit looks like the one she was wearing when he saw her last. She got up here on the first flight, she tells them, and has come to interview Chrissie.

She asks for one of them to come into the interview room with Chrissie, because their daughter is a minor and as such needs an *appropriate adult* present. Paul hesitates – which of them should it be? – but before he can answer, Chrissie speaks up.

'Or both of them?' she says. 'What about my mum and dad both?'

Now it's DS Brayford's turn to hesitate, but she seems to have read something in Chrissie's expression, and she nods. 'We wouldn't usually … but all right.'

So now all three of them are led to a room with a tape recorder. Are we 'appropriate'? Paul finds himself thinking, as both he and Julia sit across from the detective. What kind of parents have the two of them become? DS Brayford switches on the tape recorder and she has a pen and paper in front of her as well. She looks up at Chrissie, this girl she is meeting for the first time. *Christine Goodlight*. A missing child. A teenager, a musician. A star, his daughter. His hopes and dreams, an enigma to him. A *runaway*. And now – what else?

DS Brayford clears her throat, and states the date and all their names for the tape.

'Now then, Chrissie. Let's start from the beginning,' she says.

*

To begin with, though, Chrissie doesn't say anything about Francis. Instead, Paul is bewildered to hear her talking about *this*: the map of clues, signs and messages that she set out for them, each an accusation about their life, their family, their home.

'The prospectus,' Chrissie says. 'That was the first thing. Someone must have found it? I left it in my room.'

DS Brayford nods. 'My colleagues did the initial search. They found it in your wastepaper bin.'

'It was for the Royal Institute. I found it in my dad's ... stuff. I know I shouldn't have gone looking but ... It's nice, in a way. I know he thinks so much of me and my playing. He believes in me. He really does.'

'I understand you were taking part in a big competition. You had got through to the semi-finals?'

'Yes. That was all my dad's idea too. *Young Musician of the*

309

Year. It's … intense. I have to practise all the time; sometimes it's like there's no time to even breathe. Come the summer though, I knew that would be done. But the Royal Institute … I mean, that's residential. You're there twenty-four seven. Music's all there is.'

'That does sound intense.'

'Yes.'

'So … you didn't want to go?'

There is a silence. Paul is hardly breathing.

'I like music. I love it, sometimes. But … I didn't know why he was sending me there.'

DS Brayford doesn't look up; she just makes a note. 'Why did you think?'

'To help me, I suppose. But it never feels like help.'

'What does it feel like?'

'Like … like …' She hesitates, shakes her head.

DS Brayford turns a page in her notebook. 'So you threw the prospectus away.'

'I left it in the bin.'

'For him to find.'

'Yes.'

'Go on, then. What else?'

'There was the necklace, too.'

'A necklace?' DS Brayford checks her notes. 'I don't think I know about that.'

'It's my grandmother's. I found it a couple of weeks ago in our hallway. So I knew she had visited. She and my father are close.'

'You said your father and grandmother are close. In what way?'

'In a ... strange way.'

DS Brayford looks up. 'Meaning ...?'

'Meaning ... my dad always listens to her. He'll speak to her about me instead of speaking to my mum.'

Paul feels dizzy. It's as though an accusing finger – an accusing blade – hangs above his head and he has no way to scramble out from under it. He never knew that she understood so much.

'She and my dad,' Chrissie continues, 'there's something between them. I can't explain it. But I think it all comes from her.'

'All of what?'

'The pressure on me. The ... restrictions.'

'Why would that be?'

'I don't know. All I know is, sometimes I can't *breathe*. My dad, my grandmother – it feels like being crushed.'

Paul wants to kick himself, punch himself. Hasn't he always told himself this? *You have to push her, she needs to be pushed, but you must never, ever push her too much.*

'That's why you ran away?'

'Yes. Partly.'

'All right.' The detective doesn't chide her. 'Go on.'

'Okay. Well. I also left the glove.'

'The glove? Whose glove?'

'*His* glove. I left it on Mum's desk.'

Paul's dizziness intensifies. He tries to turn his head to look at Julia but his wife won't meet his eye; she is staring straight ahead. A glove? He didn't know about this. He knew about the prospectus, and the necklace – Julia showed him – but his wife never said anything about this.

'Francis came to the house one evening when both my

parents were out. You know about that, already. The video is on Mum's iPad.'

The images swarm through Paul's mind again. Francis grabbing and kissing Chrissie. All his supervision – what good did it do her?

'Yes,' says DS Brayford, 'I have. I'll come back to that, but thank you for showing me.' The detective hasn't flinched at the mention of Francis's name, or these details. Chrissie has already told police about the encounter, sitting in the jeep, foil blanket around her. And Julia handed the evidence over.

'He took his gloves off and left them on our kitchen table. This was after I learned about the affair.'

DS Brayford tilts her head. 'You knew about that?'

'I saw them together.' For the first time since she started speaking, Chrissie glances across at her mum, then looks away again, back at DS Brayford, her guide through all of this. 'Maybe my parents told you about me disappearing before?'

DS Brayford nods. 'Yes. My colleagues did.'

'That was because I saw them. I went to speak to Mum about the prospectus I'd found. I wanted her to … tell Dad not to send me away. I thought she wouldn't want me to go, I thought she would help me. Instead, I saw her and … Francis, kissing in her office. How could I tell her then? It felt like she didn't care about me one bit.' Chrissie draws a breath. Beneath the desk, one of her legs is jiggling. 'So instead I ran. I didn't even really know where I was going. I was always supposed to come straight home from school or rehearsals – Dad would always be waiting for me, with my snack. But how could I go home with what I knew he was planning, and what I had just found out about Mum? I couldn't.'

'All right. So, you went somewhere else?'

'Yes. To the Botanical Gardens. I just needed a few hours to … I don't know even what to call it. Be on my own. Make sense of things. Think.'

'I understand. You needed to process.'

Chrissie nods. 'Yes. That's it. Just for a few hours, that's all. But I was always going to come right back home.'

Paul wants to drop his head into his hands. He wants to cover up his face. How much of this has turned out to be his fault? His efforts to please Celina that have ultimately back-fired, because he was so willing, wasn't he, to go along with everything she said. He tried to curb everything in Chrissie's life except her music, until in the end she refused to take it any more. Because it served him well too, didn't it, to push Chrissie. To see her shine, to see her flourish: he liked being bathed in the reflected glory. He liked seeing her achieve the things he never did. It suited him to have such a tight hold on her. Always thinking she wouldn't mind it, always trusting she would never rebel.

'You know, initially,' Chrissie goes on, 'I thought maybe my dad already knew about my mum's affair. Afterwards, when he tried to talk to me, I realized he hadn't spotted anything – he hadn't even been *looking*. He was too preoccupied with keeping eyes on *me*.'

'But you wanted him to know?'

'I wanted …' Chrissie pauses, pressing the white tips of her fingers together. 'I wanted my parents to be honest with me.' Her breathing has risen up high in her chest. 'All these things they were doing – it was *me* who was getting hurt. But they weren't even being honest with themselves.'

'So, you planted these clues. The mess in your room – was that also part of it? What happened there?'

'I thought a lot about that. I didn't want Mum and Dad to be too frightened. This wasn't about scaring them. But it had to look bad enough that they would call you – the police.'

'I see ...' DS Brayford makes another note. 'Because the police would ask your parents questions.'

For the first time, Paul witnesses the smallest smile from Chrissie. He can almost feel her relief. *DS Brayford gets it.* His daughter nods. 'Yes.'

Paul has to tip his head back. His eyes are brimming. What a mess they have made of everything. He is ashamed of himself. He hates this. They have made a mess, and now Chrissie has made a terrible one of her own. It was a ploy, a game, but look where it's all ended. When really it was a simple cry for help.

'There was a lot you were trying to communicate, wasn't there,' DS Brayford is saying. 'You thought all this out very carefully indeed.'

Chrissie is quiet. 'I just didn't know what else to do.'

DS Brayford turns another page. 'So, you made your way to Camp Dìon.' Somehow she manages to pronounce it right. 'How did you get there? It's quite a long way.'

'I got an overnight coach from London Victoria. Reece met me at Inverness coach station, and then he had a friend who drove us on from there.'

'Ah. I wondered. We never checked those bus routes. Okay. All right then. Now ...' DS Brayford hesitates. 'I'm wondering about Francis. Would it be all right for us, now, to talk about him?'

Chrissie inhales through her nose, out through her mouth.

314

'He spoke to me when he came to Mum's party. But I didn't understand who he was until I saw him that day.'

'At the office?'

'Yes.'

'Then he came to your house another time, alone, afterwards.'

Chrissie nods. 'Yes. That was when … when he kissed me. Like you saw in the video.'

Paul thinks: *when he assaulted you.*

DS Brayford's voice is remarkably soothing. 'But you didn't talk to anyone about that?'

Chrissie shakes her head, 'No,' and again Paul hears the words she doesn't say: *How could I?*

'It's all right,' the detective says. 'You're doing very well, Chrissie. So if I can just be clear – you met him four times altogether?' DS Brayford lifts a hand to count on her fingers. 'The party, your mum's office, when he came to the house, the towpath.'

The towpath. The detective throws that one straight in there, like a dart.

'That last time, he followed me,' Chrissie says.

'Yes. I believe that.'

'He must have been waiting for me.'

She's just a girl, thinks Paul. *A sixteen-year-old girl.*

'And can you tell me what happened? Did he speak to you?'

'I didn't want to talk to him. I didn't want to see him.'

'But did he try?'

'Yes. He went on and on talking. Shouting a little bit. Telling me my mum was … in love with him.'

'And did you believe that?'

'I had no idea. I just knew that … I hated him. After what he had done to me.'

Jesus, don't say that, Paul almost blurts out. *What are you doing – trying to create a noose for your own neck?*

A lawyer, he realizes. Why don't they have a lawyer? Is he really just relying on Julia to speak up? He should stop this interview. He should reach out and stop the tape. But he doesn't move. They are too far gone by now.

'He kept saying I had to get my mum to see him. He was … all over the place. He kept grabbing at me.'

'And you?' DS Brayford's voice is so persuasively gentle. 'Can you tell me what you did?'

Paul shuts his eyes, braces himself. *Curtain up.*

'Just pushed him.'

DS Brayford echoes her. 'You pushed him.'

Paul tries to believe there's no accusation in her voice.

'Only to get away. I just pushed him, and ran.' Chrissie covers her face with her hands. 'I thought he was fine; I thought I heard him still shouting. But I pushed him and he must have fallen and now he's dead!'

There is stark silence in the room, even while the words pound in Paul's head. *Oh my God, Chrissie. That's murder, manslaughter; at best, self-defence.*

Chrissie's voice is choked. 'I didn't mean to. I'm sorry. I'm sorry!'

'No.' DS Brayford slides a piece of paper out of her folder. 'We got the autopsy results this afternoon. The estimated time of death, Chrissie – it doesn't match at all with when you were with him last.' She draws out a time-stamped picture from the towpath CCTV as well; there's a difference of many hours from what's written in the pathologist's report. 'What happened to Francis happened much later. He didn't drown either; no water in his lungs. Rather, there were extraordinary levels of drugs in his system. He had already stopped breathing when he fell into the river.'

Paul tries to grasp it. 'An overdose?'

DS Brayford nods. 'That's what this autopsy report points to.' She looks back to Chrissie. 'You've made plenty of bad decisions here, young lady. Made your parents very worried and wasted a good few of our resources. But if there's one thing I can assure you of, Chrissie Goodlight, it's that you had nothing at all to do with Francis Maitland's death.'

CHAPTER 48

Julia

There's a flight late tonight that we can get home on. On my phone, I book the tickets for all three of us, first class.

The interviews with DS Brayford are over. We just needed to fill out some forms and now we can finally return home. To our own city, our own house, our own rooms, our own beds. Chrissie has had to sign an official written statement. She isn't a missing person any more, but they needed to formalize the facts before they could close the case. Now it's all done, I text my parents to let them know we're coming home, and to reassure them again that Chrissie's safe and well.

I hope you are both well too, I write. *See you soon.*

At the Palace Hotel, we collect our belongings and settle the room bill. All the way in the taxi to Inverness Airport Paul, Chrissie and I hardly speak. There are no detectives around now to scrutinize us, and we desperately need to have a conversation, a hundred conversations, and yet it seems all words have shrivelled in my mouth. In the echoey airport, we sit in three chairs, resting our arms on the wide metal table. Not even looking at each other.

My daughter has been desperately trying to find answers. She has had so many questions clustered in that wise, sharp brain of hers, mysteries that hurt her and that she was longing to solve. She wanted to know why I had an affair. More specifically, she wanted to know why I chose a man like that. A man who would abuse and hurt me. Abuse and hurt my daughter too.

She wants to know what her father is afraid of. What her grandmother is afraid of, too. She wants to know why they clutch her so tightly, why she finds herself caged in by her music with no room to breathe. She wants to understand what's supposed to be wrong with her.

The way I've been asking what is wrong with me too.

All this time, the journey and questions have been leading towards Francis. Even with Paul. He told me about the investment, the tip he picked up on that night of our party, hovering on the edges of Francis's group. He's told me about the thousands of pounds of my money that he invested, as well as his precious inheritance, in a company that is now under formal investigation for fraud. I haven't the right to do anything but absolve him, but I wonder whether he's now shared all of his secrets with me. If he realizes just how many I still hold. We have found Chrissie; we have learned of Francis's death, but none of that, in the end, has provided any answers.

The police won't help us now; we have to go forwards on our own – but to what? The question circles my brain all through the flight from Inverness to Heathrow, and it goes on circling on the long drive home.

We have Chrissie with us now, and we're driving home from London, the way it should have been from the start. If I close my eyes tightly enough, I can pretend that the last three days have never even happened. I can pretend that we're simply driving back from Chrissie's concert, Paul and I delighted and proud, because Chrissie would have triumphed, of course. We'll go back to our house and carry on as normal. My affair will never have happened, and Paul won't have lied to me, and Chrissie will be happy and well-adjusted and free.

Instead, there's the three of us, the black-orange streetlights and so much between us that still needs to be addressed.

*

I am absolutely not expecting to see them. My father *never* comes to this house.

But when we let ourselves in through the familiar front door, clattering our way through the hallway, I discover them both standing there, under the bright spotlights in our kitchen.

Waiting for us.

I freeze in shock, and Chrissie bumps into me from behind.

Here we are – my whole family together. *Goodlight. Montrose.*

'Celina! Duncan!' Paul has somehow managed to step around me and is holding out his arms to welcome them both.

My mother's posture is stiff and upright. Her skin looks sallow, yellowish under these lights. I find myself wondering if her shoulder has healed by now or whether it's still hurting her, and I take in her outfit, her clothes: the high-necked blouse, the stiff, tight cuffs. It's the way I always think of her. And at her side, head and shoulders above her, is my father. Head of the household, patriarch of our clan.

My mother is the first to call out and step forwards. 'Chrissie, darling! Thank goodness you're home!' There is genuine concern in her voice – how could I ever have doubted that? Of course they want to see her. That's why they've come here, they want to be completely sure she's all right.

My father has the bones of the story now: he called again as we alighted at Heathrow. I told him that Chrissie had taken herself off to Scotland, but that we'd found her up there with a friend, a boy called Reece. I didn't mention a thing about Francis. There was *no way* I could let him know about the affair. I didn't go into any of the rest of it either: none of Chrissie's clues or accusations. My father only needed to know that his granddaughter was safe.

Now I try to smile, move, make my parents welcome, but my whole body seems to have gone stiff. Needles of anxiety are rushing through me, and yet my parents seem smaller than they appeared in my imagination. In the flesh, or in the wide space of our own kitchen, their figures seem to have shrunk. I just can't get over the fact that they are here, in our house.

My daughter, though, drops her bag as soon as she realizes who's here. Duncan steps forwards and opens his arms.

'Come here,' he says to Chrissie.

His voice was always so authoritative. It can make almost anyone acquiesce.

Naturally, then, Chrissie goes straight to him, slipping round our big kitchen island, almost running straight into his arms. There shouldn't be any reason for me to be frightened, but somehow I'm just standing stock-still in the doorway. They say that, though, don't they? About trauma. That it is so easy for the same old responses to be triggered again. Paralysis. Helplessness. The *just submit and get out of here alive.*

He hugs her first. That's an unexpected move.

'What is this, Chrissie? What did you think you were doing?' His voice is gruff.

Chrissie shakes her head. 'I'm so sorry, Grandpa.'

He pushes her backwards, holding her at arm's length. Nobody stops him. 'What did you think you were doing?' he asks again.

'Tea? Coffee, anyone?' Paul is asking. 'Celina, do you want some water, perhaps?'

My mother doesn't answer.

'You've been travelling for hours,' Paul chivvies her. 'Here. Look. Why don't you sit down at least.' He pulls a chair out for her, but my mother doesn't take it. She is rigid and on edge, just like me.

My father is still standing there, framed by the French windows, still holding Chrissie by the arms. Suddenly everything I told him replays through my head and a wave of dread courses head to foot: *we found her at the camp, with a friend, a boy called Reece.*

In any normal family, he would give her a good talking-to. Firm but fair, brooking no excuse. *Upsetting your parents, causing such a fuss. It's not acceptable, you know that.* Chrissie would be grounded for a week, no phone for a month, apology letters written to everyone involved. But I know in my bones that's not what's going to happen. So why am I still just standing here like this?

The big French windows show the dark night around us. I imagine someone seeing this tableau from outside. I imagine myself out there, banging on the glass from the wrong side, completely unable to make myself heard.

We found her there with a boy called Reece.

'Perhaps something to eat?' Paul is saying to my mother. 'I'm sure I can make you a sandwich at least.'

I want him to shut up and stop distracting her. I want him to stop talking and stop distracting *me*. He thinks things are fine now, he just doesn't *get it*.

'Paul,' I find myself saying, '*stop fussing*. You're not helping, you're only making things worse.' I don't look to check my husband's reaction. I cannot take my eyes off the two of them: the bulk of my father; the slip of my daughter. My mother hasn't moved either and I want to slap her, but then I think again of those trauma responses. I know the ways she has tried to survive.

Again and again my words replay, crystallizing: *we found her with a friend, a boy.*

Julia, Julia, what have you said? It's like watching the whole thing in slow motion. I'm telling myself again and again, like a mantra: *he wouldn't do that, he won't*. But I already know it's here: the re-enactment. It's as if I see it happening before it even starts.

I wonder if my father always knew what he was going to do before he did it. *I* knew; I just couldn't seem to do anything about it. Even now, to my horror, when it's happening all over again, I feel as though I'm chained to the floor. I scream at myself, to move, keep moving, but already I can tell I'm going to be too late. *We found her—*

My own smart advice rings in my ears: Don't contribute to it. *You mustn't provoke him.* Against the bright panes of glass I see my father lift his arm. *He's ill. Irritable, impulsive. He doesn't know what he's doing.*

My limbs strain, like in a dream of running through treacle. At last, I push myself forwards, away from the doorframe, rounding the solid marble block of the island, bashing my hip on a bright metal stool as I pass. But it feels as if I'm floating, still in slow motion.

'Disgraceful!' my father explodes. 'Debasing yourself! I should have known what you were like! He wasn't just a friend, was he, that boy? No one runs away with a *friend* in secret. Do you think I'm blind? Do you think I'm that stupid? I know exactly how girls like you behave – like all the women in this family. I know exactly what you were doing with him up in Scotland – you were *fucking*! My God, I can't believe you're such a disgrace!'

I don't get there in time to prevent the first blow. Or the second. Chrissie throws her arms up to protect herself, but her limbs are so thin and she is so tiny compared to the massive bulk of my father that it offers almost no protection at all.

I crush myself between the two of them, Chrissie and my father, using my body to protect my daughter, the way I would protect her from the blast of a bomb. My father's fists rain down on me instead, head, neck, back, finding those long-hidden places where they fell once before, when Chrissie wasn't in my arms but in my belly.

The whole damn thing comes into excruciating focus.

There was never a staircase, drugs in my system or a fall. Only this violence. Only this man. I see the whole thing, only this time it is *Chrissie, Chrissie, Chrissie*. She is tiny, contrite and helpless, and it's truly *wrong wrong wrong*. How can I ever have thought anything else? How could I ever have blamed myself like that?

'Stop it!' I finally yell at my father. I say it. 'Daddy, stop hitting my child. She's done nothing wrong. You're monstrous – how dare you do this to her!'

At last, time moves again, returning to normal. Paul is beside me, pulling my father away. My mother watches from the doorway, clutching the collar of her blouse, a wail emanating from her throat. My father is strong, but my husband is stronger. He pins my father against the far wall, immobilizing him, disabling him.

Well, he has seen everything now, my husband. Here is my family, finally revealed.

Here is what everything has always been about.

CHAPTER 49

Julia

My father was always this person. Terrifying, abusive. Even if it only showed once a year, or once every two.

So infrequently that you could just shut it away behind a door in your mind, convincing yourself it would never happen again or even forget it ever happened in the first place. Because the rest of the time he was such a generous and loving man.

Part of me even believed he loved me when he hit me. It was less painful to accept that he was right, that I was bad, that broken bones, fractured ribs and an emergency Caesarean to save Chrissie were no more than I deserved.

When I was a child, he directed his violence towards my mother. I was eleven before I ever found out, and even when I suspected it, we never talked about it.

Those instances were so rare, and my mother was so proud.

It was tiny things that would set him off, but it always had something to do with sex. Sexuality, to be more specific. A woman's sexuality, to be exact.

My father wasn't particularly religious. Not beyond the

usual adherence to Church of England rituals typical for people of our class. Where did it come from then? I have never been able to ask my mother – not then, still not now, so it's a piece I still struggle with. I still don't fully know.

What I do know is that he would claim that she had provoked him. Deliberately. Yes. Exactly. That old trope. My mother tried not to. She was careful in her choices of what clothes to wear, the make-up she applied, how she held herself in public; she was careful not to catch the eyes of other men when the two of them went out. She was careful with the books she read, the TV programmes she preferred. She was very, very careful about how to be his wife.

There were very clear lines, and she took care to never cross them. She was a quick learner. Well, we tend to learn quickly when it's a matter of survival. Every so often though, she would slip, breaking one of his impossible rules. After all, it's very difficult not to, over the course of a marriage of thirty-six years.

It must have been suffocating to live like that. Not least since, no matter how hard she tried, he always seemed to find fault with something. The drinking probably didn't help – the alcoholism she ended up developing as a way to cope. He always assumed the worst of her if she had been drinking. Sometimes he just assumed the worst of her anyway, even when she didn't put a single foot wrong. That was the thing. That made him so dangerous. It was hard to know exactly what the trigger was.

I was no use to my mother back then. I stuffed my ears: quite literally, on at least one occasion that I can recall.

As a teenager, it was easier to blame her rather than him. *Bitch, cow, fool.*

If she didn't provoke him, he wouldn't be like this.

That's a security mechanism, you know: victim blaming. A way to give a sense of control. You can say: *I* would never do that, *I* would never say that, so no one is ever going to abuse me. If it's the victim's fault, then the victim can stop it.

If it's not the victim's fault, well then – you're fucked.

I blamed my mother, and otherwise, I ignored it. On the outside – and for the vast majority of the time – we were a perfectly loving, successful family. Well, aren't they all?

And then I got pregnant. I tried to assure myself it wouldn't be a problem, even though it was *out of wedlock* and I was only twenty-one. It wasn't the same as whatever my mother did to rile him.

What a fool. I should have known.

Deep down, I think I did know. The whole time that Chrissie was growing inside me, I was terrified of my father finding out. And yet, somehow, on the surface, I convinced myself that he wouldn't act like that. I wasn't like my mother. Whatever *she* did was utterly unacceptable. But I was his daughter. I knew he loved *me*.

It's still so hard to describe how it feels when your own parent hits you. Beats you. There is shock, of course, and the fear, the disbelief.

But there is such shame too. I was so ashamed of myself, knowing what was happening to me, that my own father was assaulting me with his fists and feet. Because my father was supposed to love me, but instead he was hurting me, and how disgusting a creature must I be for that to be the case?

I remember saying over and over: I'm sorry, I'm sorry! I was curled up in a foetal position by then, cradling my swollen belly. I wasn't sure how else to make him stop except by blaming myself, going along with his view that I was wrong, and this was the exact punishment I deserved.

He didn't stop, though, not for a very long time. He went on so long that my mother called an ambulance.

She called a *fucking ambulance*, something she had never, ever done before.

And never mind the tipped-over furniture and smashed glass cabinet in the drawing room; she told the paramedics that I fell down the stairs.

*

Due to the trauma of it, Chrissie was born prematurely. She was fine, thank God, but I was in tatters – physically and mentally. Two broken ribs, a fractured elbow, extensive bruising and a weeping Caesarean scar. And inside me was screaming, terrified shock. Then in the weeks afterwards, once I was discharged from hospital back to the care of my parents, I fell into a sort of numbed depression, punctuated by little else but searing fragments of what had happened, and nightmares that made me scared to fall asleep. I was in pain, I was in shame; I didn't know how to deal with what had happened. Never mind dealing with the new baby I had.

My crowd had all used drugs at university: the expensive, clean kind only, of course. Back then, it had been all about fun: feeling good and getting higher. But when I took cocaine after my *accident*, it was different. Desperate. This was me trying to climb out of a pit. This was me skidding right off the rails.

My honourable parents stepped in for Chrissie, and I stepped out. I lost myself.

Until I found Paul. Poor Paul. He only ever knew half the story. He's only ever known half of any story to do with my family.

My family never, ever talked about it. My parents – my mother, especially – simply painted different stories on the top. About a fall, about my drug use.

And because we never acknowledged or addressed it, the whole legacy of it landed on Chrissie. She found herself at the crux of it all.

*

It wasn't until the day that Francis wrenched me by the hair that I slowly began to piece all of this together. That afternoon, I think I identified the first piece at least: I realized what I'd been looking for in Francis. When I did, I felt such a fool, the answer was so obvious. And it was so obvious then, too, that I was only about to make everything much worse.

I can put it more clearly into words now than when I was still entangled in it, but I grasped the basics of it that day at least. I was trying to shake off my father's devastating view of me: I was trying to prove that being sexual as a woman wasn't shameful, but good.

That afternoon, Francis and I had sex in an ornate hotel bed and – for a fleeting moment – I felt liberated, unconstricted and free. But that moment was followed by a sense of uncertainty: a chilling, shivery sense of unease. I couldn't ignore the fact that this man was not my husband. Instead, I had chosen to have an affair, something that dragged intrinsic disgrace with it.

Then came the violence. Then came the punishment, the stinging pain of his hands in my hair.

Apparently, it's very hard to change our belief systems. More often than not, we just reinforce them instead. I often think back to the first time I saw Francis, walking into the opulent bar of Duchelle's. Something in me must have spotted it immediately: the sex, disgrace and violence that were already nestled there within him. All perfect reflections of my trauma, just waiting for me to clutch at them, just waiting for me to fall.

All I did with Francis was unleash a gross re-enactment on myself, in a way that gave me no resolution. Worse than that, I ended up hurting Chrissie, my own daughter, my actions devastating her and becoming part of why she ran.

God knows how much more damage this legacy of unspoken rottenness might have done. But finally my father showed his true colours to all of us – and most of all, to Chrissie – and I did what I should have done years ago. Finally, I stood up to him.

And we're all in a whole new story now.

CHAPTER 50

Julia

FOUR DAYS AFTER

I stand in the cool of our bright, white kitchen in my bare feet, shoes kicked off, just allowing myself to feel present in the space. Sunlight bounces off the water in Jackson's steel bowl. The French windows are open. The smell of hot petrol floats in the air.

On the gleaming counter top sits a letter. It's the confirmation that Chrissie is through to the finals of *Young Musician of the Year*. In the end she was only missing for a few days, even if it felt like a lifetime for us. The question of whether she'll go ahead with a final performance hangs in the balance. But we all know better now than to pressure her on that.

Since we came home, Paul and Chrissie have had many conversations. I've been part of a number of them too. They have drawn up new agreements, loosened old boundaries. Paul understands all the ways in which he was getting it wrong: he handed himself too far over to my mother, letting the warped narratives in our family affect him too, seeping into his own precious role as a parent. Now he's discovering how to be Chrissie's father in a new way; how to trust her. Chrissie is learning to trust herself too. It's time for her to blossom properly, into whatever shape she wants.

A gentle breeze filters in through the open French windows, ruffling the competition letter a little, nudging it across the smooth surface. I pick it up and fold it carefully, propping it up against a little vase of daffodils, where it will be safe.

It feels as disorientating to be back here as it was initially to land in Scotland. Uncanny valley. Something that looks like a known thing – but not quite. So much has changed. Last night, I only got about four hours of sleep. Chrissie woke me up early, appearing in the gloom at the side of our bed, the clock on my phone registering not even five a.m.

'Are you awake, Mum?' she whispered.

Beside me, Paul lay deep asleep and there was no need to wake him. Instead, I held back the covers so that Chrissie could clamber in beside me, her body warm and soft against mine, and unbelievably familiar. I drew up my knees and put my arms round her, and the three of us slept on through the early hours like that.

I step forwards into the frame of the French windows. It's hot and sunny outside: an early salvo of summer, an unexpected April heat. Chrissie and Paul are out in the garden. Paul is cutting the grass and the buzz of the mower fills the air; Chrissie is half sitting, half lying on our white-painted garden bench.

Paul turns at the end of a track. Now he sees me, and immediately reaches down to turn the lawnmower off.

'Everything okay?' he calls to me.

I think of the conversation we had two nights ago. When

we told each other, *I love you*, and the words felt true in a way they hadn't done in years. Maybe, in a way, we both used each other at the start: Paul to get a leg up in the world, and me to gain some sanity in my life. But we stayed together for years after that, didn't we? We raised Chrissie together – for better or worse. Over these last few days, we have each forgiven the other for such a multitude of sins. What is that, if not love? So – I love him. I know now that is true.

'Where's Jackson?' I ask, and just as I do, he comes lolloping round the corner of the house and right up to me, pushing his wet nose into my palm. His stay with the Fairshaws has done him no harm; he is as happy and content to be with us as ever. I reach down and ruffle his ears, then let him go to lope across the lawn to where Chrissie is sitting – and my mother too.

My mother's skin is quite tanned now, soaking up the sun's rays in our back garden far better than she was able to out in Kenya. She has pushed the sleeves of her blouse up – a blouse she has borrowed from me, something cool to wear in this heat – and I can see the fine wrinkles that bracelet her forearms. Small signs of age that I was never privy to before. Small signs that she is flesh and blood after all.

My mother has come to live with us for the time being. After what happened that night we returned home, she needed a place to stay. My father remains alone in the big house, my childhood home, Bute Hall, a court case pending against him after Paul took it upon himself to press charges.

When, after all these years, someone finally did.

It is unspoken, but I know that this means my parents have separated. My mother, in her own way, has made it clear that she will not go back. There's a tiny part of me that wonders whether she would still return to live with him, if it had been someone other than Chrissie that my father attacked.

After all, my mother stayed with him after every time he took his wrath out on her, his wife.

She never left, even when he did what he did to me.

But then, I never left him either, did I? I still visited him; I let him buy me a house; I emailed him updates on his granddaughter all the time. So how can I judge my mother differently? I have to give her credit for leaving in the end.

She sits beside Chrissie now, with something quite new opened up in their dynamic. They relate in a way I would never have imagined before. I saw it in the moment when Chrissie handed my mother's stolen necklace back to her. An understanding passed between them. I wonder where both of those necklaces are now: the silver and the gold, scored with symbols of chastity. Part of me thinks they should just go in the bin.

'Are you joining us, Julia?' asks my mother. She is already making room for me on the bench. Paul is emptying the grass from the mower. He's finished now and the lawn looks lovely. The four of us can sit outside, in the stillness, and soak up the heat.

'Yes,' I tell them. 'Just give me a sec. I've got a hat somewhere; just let me fetch it.'

I retreat back inside, back into the shady coolness. I will join them – in a second, a minute. For now though, I make my way upstairs, through our master bedroom and into the bathroom attached. In the bright en suite, I sit on the closed toilet seat, a handful of toilet tissue pressed into my mouth. The sobs that come feel like strange contractions; I'm grieving, I suppose, for all the losses that have come from this. The loss of the idealized image of my parents; the loss of any last trust in their respectable, loving marriage; the loss of the pretend perfection of my own. Everything is so much more honest now, more authentic, but it doesn't mean I'm not mourning for what I fought so hard to make true.

Eventually, my sobs calm and I feel all right again. Steadier, maybe even a little cleansed. I rinse my hands in the sink and splash water on my face, before digging out an old straw hat from the back of my wardrobe. I hold it up to my mouth, my cheek; it smells of summer, sun cream and warm straw. *Strawberries in February?* No. No more of that.

Back out on the landing, I stop in the doorway of Chrissie's bedroom. We have sorted everything now; put everything back in its place: the chair, a new phone, the duvet. Her window is open to let in fresh air. Paul has fetched her violin from the studio and placed it upright in the far corner of her room. Quiet. Unobtrusive. Days have passed without her even touching it. Paul has left it there, not asking for anything, simply allowing Chrissie her own space to decide.

There's room for us to decide all kinds of things now. Chrissie's disappearance broke things, but those things needed smashing. Now we can put the pieces back together the right way.

I head back down the stairs and back through the kitchen. At the threshold of the garden I pause to set the broad-brimmed hat on my head, where it sits lightly, snugly. We made it through. We survived; we are healing.

Shoulders back, chin up, I step outside to join my family, entering the warmth and the sun's bright embrace.

Acknowledgements

Completing this third book has felt like a huge milestone for me, not least since I had a pretty bad failed attempt at it first time round! Thank you to the wonderful team of people who got me to the finish line at last.

A huge thank-you to my writing friends in the D20 Authors group, who were invaluable in helping me keep my faith when everything seemed to be going wrong with my writing. Laure Van Rensburg too was essential in getting this story out of me in the end.

To my wonderful agent Sarah Hornsley and my brilliant editor Cicely Aspinall: thank you for being so patient with me when I totally crashed and burned! I am so happy to have finally created another book that I am so proud to publish with you: *I'll Never Tell* owes a huge amount to you both.

To all the wonderful team at HQ/HarperCollins who have always been so hardworking and supportive of me and my books, including Penny Isaac for her astute copy-edits and Izzy Smith for her great publicity work.

Thank you as well to all the fantastic booksellers, journalists, podcasters, fellow authors and event organisers who have spread the word of my books far and wide. You are legion, but I would like to especially mention: Nick Quantrill, Mick Finlay, Sally Rear, Nick and Mel of the Rabbit Hole Bookshop in Brigg, Gill Hart, Jill Hughes, Sue Morrison, Jackie Russell, Bianca Marais, Beki Dover, Katie Havelaar Cook, Sara Cox, Nell Arthur, Sara Bullimore, Brad King, Dan Simpson, Amy and Kate of Waterstones Lincoln, Chris McDonald, Sean Coleman, Rob Parker, Lesley Kara, Lauren North, Jack Smellie, Audrey Keown, Andi Osho, Cameron Ross Ritchie, Sarah Buckenham, Stu Cummins, Tim Rideout and Anna Burt.

As ever, Stuart Gibbon helped me with the police-y bits of this book; as ever, all the dodgy bits are mine. I also want to give a big shout-out to fellow author Lucy Martin who devised the name of my fictional Montrose home: Bute Hall. Also to Donald Murray, @koolard and Anstey Harris who helped me with my Gaelic pronunciations.

Of course, I would be nowhere without all of you brilliant readers, who buy or borrow (or burn – Rob Parker) my books, and make it all worthwhile. Thank you to every one of you who have taken the time to turn the pages of my novels, and especial thanks to those of you who have gone the extra mile to write reviews – or even whole articles – in support! It will never stop being amazing to think of you all reading the words I wrote.

To all my remaining friends and family who continue to support and delight in my writing career: it makes a world of difference to have you on my side.

Finally, to the most special person in my life, who remains by my side even after the craziest ride of the last couple of years. Elliot, thank you. Here's to you.

Discover more gripping psychological suspense from Philippa East...

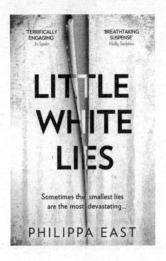

She only looked away for a second...

Anne White only looked away for a second, but that's all it took to lose sight of her young daughter.

But seven years later, Abigail is found.

And as Anne struggles to connect with her teenage daughter, she begins to question how much Abigail remembers about the day she disappeared...

Out now in paperback, ebook and audio.

Home can be the most dangerous place...

In a small London bedsit, a radio is playing. A small dining table is set for three, and curled up on the sofa is a body...

Jenn is the one who discovers the woman, along with the bailiffs. All indications suggest that the tenant – Sarah Jones – was pretty, charismatic and full of life.

So how is it possible that her body has lain undiscovered for *ten whole months*?

Out now in paperback, ebook and audio.

ONE PLACE. MANY STORIES

Bold, innovative and
empowering publishing.

FOLLOW US ON:

@HQStories